Praise for Helen Chandler

'Well written, believable characters and a good plot. I am a big fan of this writer!' - *Katie Fforde*

'A second novel from an author whom I believe is a star of the future . . . a most satisfying read' - *Lovereading.co.uk*

'A page-turner that keeps you gripped until the end' - *Daily Mail*

'An enjoyable romantic comedy with some entertaining twists' - *Sunday Mirror*

'Charming . . . warm, confidently written, very addictive . . . I thoroughly enjoyed it' - *Bookseller*

'A really impressive debut. The writing keeps you on edge and has you wanting to read more and more and more! Helen is definitely an author to watch out for' - *chicklitclub.com*

'A wonderfully written debut... Written in a lovely laid-back style that quickly absorbs the reader's attention and provides witty, warm-hearted reading with regular giggles and loads of fun' – *Handwrittengirl.com*

Also by Helen Chandler

Two for Joy

To Have and To Hold

On the Third Day of Christmas

About the author

Helen Chandler was born and brought up in Liverpool and read English at Oxford University before working as a manager in various NHS organisations.

She now lives in East London with her husband, two daughters and very needy cat.

Helen recently trained as a doula, and she loves her family and friends, reading, baking and being by the sea.

She wrote her first novel *Two for Joy* in any spare moments she could get while her first baby was asleep (rare) or could be palmed off onto one of her grandparents for a little while.

You can visit Helen's website at www.helenchandler.co.uk to find out more about her or follow her on Instagram at @helenchandlerwrites or on Twitter at @helenlchandler

HELEN CHANDLER

A
Thoroughly
Modern Marriage

First published 2021

Copyright © Helen Chandler 2021

The right of Helen Chandler to be identified as the Author of the Work has been asserted by her in accordance with the Copyright, Designs and Patents Act 1988.

All rights reserved. No part of this publication may be reproduced, stored or transmitted in any form without prior permission of the author.

All characters in this publication are fictitious and any resemblance to real persons, living or dead, is purely coincidental

ISBN: 9798531991119

For my darling daughters – Anna Victoria and Sophia Rose.
You inspire and fulfil me every single day.

1

A sunny winter Sunday in the suburbs. The enticing smell of a proper traditional roast; beef and Yorkshire pudding, gravy and roast potatoes, honied parsnips and braised red cabbage. A family sitting round the table; middle-aged parents, content and prosperous, and their trio of handsome young adult children. Wine glasses clinking and mingling with the light-hearted chatter.

As so often, Lydia Manders felt that she was taking a bird's eye view of the family that was meant to be hers but to which she didn't truly belong. So much of that normal, happy scene wasn't quite what it seemed, and she wondered to herself, whilst aloud commenting favourably on the pink juiciness of the roast beef, if every family had these multi-layers of meaning and double meaning, secrets and half-truths, or if it was just this one. Or maybe just her twisted perception as the changeling, the problem child. The rest of them looked straightforward enough.

Henry, grey-haired, bespectacled and suave. Not quite a silver fox, but a still attractive man in his sixties. Smiling benignly and circulating the wine he bought by the crate from the independent merchant down the road. Delia, immaculately dressed and made-up, slightly flushed either from slaving over the proverbial hot stove, or from pleasure at feeding up her beloved boys. Heaping the goose fat roast potatoes onto their plates while internally calculating the dietary macros of her own.

Then the twins, the golden boys literally and metaphorically. Strikingly similar, very tall, broad-shouldered, handsome, though so very different to her. Dominic, feeling her eyes on him, met her gaze and gave a tiny wink and her mouth quirked upwards despite herself. Delia, intercepting their glance, narrowed her own at Lydia and asked acidly

"So, Lydia dear, are you any closer to getting a *proper* job? You can't cramp Dominic's style living in his spare room forever, can you?"

Her tinkling laugh indicated she was joking; her frosty gaze belied this.

Lydia sighed. If Daniel and Dominic could do no wrong, *she* could do no right. Never had been able to. Of course, Delia wasn't *her* mother. Presumably that was the difference.

The twins both leapt in to defend her, leaving her free to pursue her own thoughts.

Lydia's parents had died when she was three years old, and Henry Nicholls, apparently a close friend of her parents, had been named as her legal guardian. She had only the haziest memories of her life with her parents, snapshot memories to go with the snapshot photographs which she still kept in pride of place on her dressing table. Her subsequent childhood hadn't really been unhappy. She had quickly forged an unbreakable friendship and alliance with the then-four-year-old twins, which had now lasted a quarter of a century. Henry had always been kind, if a little distant. She had always had plenty of material comforts. And, really, if the woman who was meant to have replaced your mother hated you, was that really so big a deal?

The twins' private nickname for her was Cuckoo. It dated from many years earlier when they had still been small children, playing hide and seek in the garden with friends one summer's day while Delia drank tea and chatted with the friends' parents on the patio. Lydia could still remember it in vivid detail.

One of the adults had made a laughing remark contrasting Lydia's dark colouring to the twins' fairness, and Delia's faux-lighthearted response, accompanied by the same tinkling laugh she had just heard was seared on Lydia's memory.

"Oh yes, there could be no mistaking Lydia for mine and Henry's child, could there? She's our little cuckoo in the nest."

She and Dominic, hiding behind a large shrub on the patio, had looked at each other in puzzlement. There was a cuckoo clock in the hall which they all loved, but what had that got to do with Lydia? There was a cold sinking sensation in her stomach that she couldn't explain, but which became clearer later that evening when, at dinner, Dominic asked

"Mummy, what's a cuckoo in the nest?"

Delia had stiffened and snapped

"What do you mean? Why are you asking that?"

Henry had launched into a calm explanation.

"Ah, well, it's an expression for someone who is taking something that isn't really theirs. Apparently mother cuckoos lay their eggs in anther bird's nest so that they don't have the bother of feeding or taking care of them, and the other mother bird looks after them along with her own babies, sometimes even looking after the cuckoos so well that her own chicks starve. Does that make sense?"

Dominic and Lydia had already filled Daniel in on what they had heard, and they all exchanged glances and nodded solemnly. Yes. Even at 7 or 8 years old it had made sense.

"So, that's why your mother hates me." she had said to the twins later. "She thinks I'm stealing things from you two."

"She doesn't *hate* you." Daniel had protested, but his words lacked conviction.

"You eat loads less than us, anyway." Dom had added.

"Anyway" Dan giggled "We love having a cuckoo in our nest, don't we, Dom?"

Dom nodded gleefully

"That's what I'm going to call you! I'm sick of explaining to everyone at school that you aren't my sister, even though you live with us, I'm going to tell them you're our Cuckoo."

It was, she reflected now, a classic case of owning

an insulting term. Black rappers could use the 'N' word. The LGBTQ community had reclaimed the word queer. She was happy to be called Cuckoo by the twins because it came from a place of true affection, and somehow made her feel she was getting one over on Delia. She dragged her thoughts back to the present. It was a long time now since Dominic had called her Cuckoo, although Daniel always did.

They were still debating her career, or lack of it. Of course, in typical golden boy fashion, Daniel and Dominic had first class degrees from first class universities, and were a paediatric doctor and secondary school teacher respectively. It was a good thing she loved them, or she would hate them for always effortlessly doing the right thing and making her look worse by comparison.

"Lydia is welcome to live with me for as long as she wants, Mum." Dom was saying. "She earns enough to pay half of the mortgage anyway, and I'd struggle without her contribution."

As he had hoped, this deflected Delia.

"Oh I know, darling. It's ridiculous how little you get paid. When you went to Oxford as well! And all you have to put up with all those horrible children. I wish you'd get a job at a *nice* school."

'Nice', to Delia, could only mean private, or perhaps an Oxbridge feeder grammar school like the one the twins had gone to themselves. Lydia, thanks to the money her parents had left in trust for her education, had gone to an exclusive all-girls school as a weekly boarder from the age of 10. She had hated it, and seen it as one more example of Delia's loathing of her that she was forced to live at school during the week while the twins got to go home every night.

Daniel, listening with half an ear to his brother's impassioned defence of the comprehensive system, looked thoughtfully at Lydia. She was miles away. The dreamy expression in her dark eyes reminded him of the photo secreted in his wallet, and his stomach churned with hideous familiarity as he tried to decide what best to do. His hands balled themselves into fists, and he swallowed hard. Why did life permanently feel like a series of impossible decisions accompanied by a sickening sense of responsibility? Of course, he knew what he had to do really, he just wished he didn't. Suddenly unable to sit still any longer, he pushed back his chair, and started to stack the empty plates.

His parents favoured a traditional separate dining room rather than the modern kitchen-diner, and as he took the plates through to the kitchen and started stacking the dishwasher, he was joined by Lydia.

'Y'ok, Cuckoo?' his warm smile was a little strained, and Lydia put her hand on his arm.

"I'm ok, are you?"

He shrugged.

"I'm fine. Finding things a bit tough at work. Couple of difficult cases at the moment, and I made a bit of a boob last week. It was alright, someone else spotted it, but it could have been awful, and I feel sick every time I think about it."

Lydia made sympathetic noises, but he could tell she didn't really get it. How could she? Most people didn't work in an environment where a second's lapse in concentration could kill a child.

"Do you and Dom want to come to the pub after we get away from here? I wanted to talk to you about something."

Lydia nodded.

"Yeah, I think Dom was going to suggest the same thing, actually. We can have the proper unvarnished catch up without your mother butting in with her two ha'porth every few minutes."

Right on cue, Delia bustled into the kitchen.

"Daniel, darling, you go through to the living room and make yourself comfortable. You're looking tired. Dad is lighting the fire – it's a lovely bright day, but bitterly cold."

As she spoke she was simultaneously loading dirty dishes into the dishwasher, putting the kettle on and setting a tray with delicate floral china and cake forks. As always, her effortless competence which she managed literally without turning one strand of perfectly coiffed ash blonde hair, made Lydia feel lumpen, dishevelled and cack-handed.

"I haven't made a proper pudding, just some scones and a Victoria sandwich, and some of those Viennese biscuits you like so much, Danny. And tea or coffee, obviously. But I just thought it would be nice to all go through and be cosy in front of the fire. I've got some crumpets if we're hungry again later, or I could do cheese on toast...Lydia, could you go and finish clearing the table...do go and sit down Daniel."

"Umm, actually Mum, I think we all need to head off quite soon. Work tomorrow, you know, and..."

He broke off at the sight of Delia's crestfallen face.

"But I've baked all your favourites! And I haven't seen my boys for weeks, surely you don't have to dash off just yet?"

Tender-hearted Daniel prevaricated

"Well, maybe we've got time for a quick slice of cake."

Less naturally tender-hearted, and with less reason to be so in this instance, Lydia held the line.

"Thanks, Delia, it's very kind, but I'm stuffed after that delicious roast. The boys and I were thinking we needed to go for a brisk walk, and then head home."

Delia let her eyes slide down Lydia's curvaceous figure.

"Yes, I can understand why you need to watch what you eat, dear, but Daniel and Dominic need feeding up. I'm sure Daniel doesn't eat properly with all his shift work, and you were never much of a cook to take care of Dominic, were you?"

Wondering for the thousandth time how Delia's values and outlook had been perfectly preserved in 1958, Lydia gritted her teeth.

"Let's see what Dom thinks, shall we?"

She pushed past Delia, calling through to the living room as she did so

"Dom! Your mum has made cake, but we need to head off, don't we? Dan's going now too."

Dominic emerged from the living room, and gave his mum a bear hug. His gaze flitted between his mum's somewhat pleading countenance, and the steely determination on Lydia's face. He sighed inwardly, always hating to have to make a contentious decision or to upset anyone.

Lydia, seeing his lack of resolve, leapt in.

"We'd better get going now." she repeated in slightly steely tones.

"Yeah, you're right, I've got loads to do this evening. Another time, Mum. Sorry."

Daniel hesitated, torn between the need to act on that photo in his wallet, loyalty to Lydia, and loyalty to his mum. As so often since Lydia had moved in with Dominic and his workload had increased to ridiculous levels he felt slightly left out. Whereas the three of them had always formed an alliance, if ever they split into a two and a one for any reason then naturally it had been he and his twin brother together, and Lydia slightly separate. Blood was thicker than water, so they said. Now it was suddenly the other way about, and he didn't much like it. Suddenly the thought of a cosy evening eating cake, basking in his mother's uncritical adoration and postponing all the difficult decisions that faced him was much more appealing than a potentially awkward conversation in the pub.

"I think I'll stay for a bit, guys. Can't resist Mum's cake!"

His hesitation was all the time Lydia had needed to propel Dominic into the hall, and they had left on a cloud of thank you and goodbyes, before Henry Nicholls had fully realised what had happened. Half an hour later, sitting opposite his wife and eldest son, contemplating a coffee table laden with two dozen scones, a 3 tier Victoria sponge and a plate of elaborately iced biscuits he asked in some confusion

"I thought you said the kids were all staying for tea?"

Stirring her coffee slowly, and staring out of the window, Delia's tone was as bleak and dark as the rapidly advancing January evening as she replied

"That's what I'd thought too."

2

"What do you mean, you're leaving?" Claudia Holmes heard her voice rising shrilly, and made a concerted effort to calm down, slow her breathing modulate her tones.

"I mean, we're married! And we have Juliet! And...all this!" She waved an arm around to encompass the huge perfectly appointed kitchen, complete with Aga, and French windows opening onto the 50 foot garden, decked patio, and summer house.

Ethan's face was stony. She was so unused to seeing it set in those lines that she felt wrong-footed and disconcerted. Ethan could be a bit grumpy and irritable at times, especially recently, but deep down she had always been sure he was one of the good guys. This man with set lips and flinty eyes seemed a stranger.

"I'm glad you remembered we're meant to be married, Claudia. Because to be honest, recently – in fact pretty much since Juliet was born – I've been feeling like the unpaid nanny and housekeeper!"

Claudia felt her own anger rise. They had discussed this, ad nauseum. After 6 months maternity leave it was sheer common sense that she should be the one to go back to work fulltime whilst

Ethan took on the bulk of the childcare duties. She earned a six-figure salary, and usually the same again in bonuses, as a lawyer in a top City firm. Ethan was a journalist. His earnings simply couldn't compete with hers, and he was able to work freelance and from home. The idea had been that he could dash off an article during nap-time, or a feature after Juliet was tucked up in bed. It wasn't like Claudia ever made it home before about 9pm anyway. Of course, it hadn't quite worked out like that. She wasn't exactly sure why, but now Juliet had started school he'd have loads of time to write. Or whatever he wanted really. She worked her butt off to give him that freedom, and to provide security and a comfortable lifestyle for all of them. His contribution was meant to be to look after the domestic stuff, and give their daughter the stable, loving home they both believed she needed. Had believed, anyway.

"And what about Juliet? Have you considered her at all in all this?"

His face softened as he considered their beloved daughter.

"Yes. Of course I've considered her. But I don't believe that her interests are best served by me being so stifled and unhappy. I can't take her to America with me, obviously, but Antonia's placement there is only for two years. When I'm back we can discuss where it's best for Juliet to live. And, in the meantime, I think you'll both benefit from a bit of quality mother-daughter time!"

Flinching at the bitter, patronising sarcasm in his voice, not to mention the implicit threat that he might one day take her daughter away from her, Claudia fought down waves of rising panic. What the bloody hell was she going to do?

"So, you're leaving now! Just like that. When do you and 'Antonia' –" she almost spat the word out "- leave for the US?"

He was still irritatingly calm.

"Tuesday morning."

It was Saturday evening.

"I'm all packed, and obviously I'll spend the next few nights at Antonia's flat. The details are on the fridge, if there's any crisis. And I'll email you my American address and phone number once they're confirmed."

Claudia unleashed her own sarcasm.

"Crisis? What crisis could there possibly be? You don't mean a crisis like my husband of ten years abandoning my daughter and me to run off abroad with his mistress, do you? God, Ethan! You are unbelievable! What am I meant to tell Juliet? What do I do about childcare at this notice?"

He shrugged.

"You can explain to Juliet that I have gone to America for work. I have been preparing the ground a bit over the last few weeks, mentioning that I might have to."

"And while you were 'preparing the ground' did

you happen to make any arrangements for wraparound childcare? Because it might have escaped your notice that I work more than six hours a day!"

Ethan smirked.

"It had hardly escaped my notice. Perhaps if you had worked a bit less, been a bit more present for me and Juliet, actually talked to me and listened to the answers then I wouldn't have got so close to Antonia."

Claudia felt red-hot rage bubbling up. At that moment it was so potent that it left no room for the other layers of emotion that might be lingering underneath – jealousy, sadness, betrayal.

"So it's somehow *my* fault that you have been cheating on me with another woman? That you are abandoning our family and your responsibilities? And what did I do to deserve that? Oh, that's right, I worked hard to provide a stable income and home for us. How dreadful of me. No wonder you couldn't help but find solace in the arms of another woman when I am such a bitch."

Ethan was still maddeningly calm. Of course, he had been preparing for this scene, learning his lines for heaven knows how long while she had gone from contented security to betrayed wife in a split second. "I told Juliet that if I did have to go to America for a while that Mummy would be here, and Mummy would look after her, so she had nothing to worry about."

Claudia ground her teeth in frustration.

"I can't believe you manipulated our daughter like that. You are so low. What am I meant to do? Mummy might be here, but Mummy also has a job to do, and it's a job which doesn't fit in 9am-3pm! I can't get a nanny at less than 48 hours notice!"

He smiled. It was not a particularly kind smile.

"I know it's not your branch of law, but it can't have escaped your notice that you are entitled to parental leave in a family emergency. To request flexible working. And…"

He raised his voice as Claudia tried to interrupt
"AND, it is illegal to discriminate against you because of your family responsibilities."
There was a ghost of the old Ethan as he smiled faintly.

"You're the most determined and resourceful woman I've ever met, Claudia. I have no doubt you'll manage. Now, I must collect my things from upstairs and book an Uber. I did the weekly food shop this morning, so there's plenty to keep you going. Don't forget that Juliet has Arabella's 5th birthday party tomorrow afternoon. The present is over there, wrapped, but you'll have to get Juliet to write her name in the card. She needs to practise her handwriting."

His voice softened.

"Look, I know this isn't ideal. It hasn't been an easy decision for me, honestly. But Antonia has no choice about moving to America now, and that has precipitated things for me too. I was worried that if I stayed I would just end up resenting you, and even Juliet too, and I couldn't bear that. And I know this is sudden, but a clean, sharp break seemed easier than weeks wrangling about it all. I know it will be a shock for Juliet, but that seems healthier than her listening to weeks or months of us bickering about it all."

Claudia sighed. His calmness seemed to have affected her, diffusing her anger into an overwhelming tiredness. She just wanted him gone now so she could stop talking and try to think.

She went over to the huge American-style fridge and started to assemble the ingredients for a G&T.

"Go on then. I'll see you when you get back. Do be in touch with those details."

"Right."

Now it was his turn to be disconcerted by her.

"Oh, one other thing, Ethan?"

"Yes?"

"You told Juliet you might have to go to America for work. Is that a total fabrication?"

He smirked guiltily.

"Erm, no, not exactly. I've got a commission for *The Guardian's* Family supplement on a Saturday. It's a weekly column called 'Starting Over'. The first column will be in next week's paper. You see, Claudia, this isn't just about my personal life. This is the professional opportunity of a decade. It will really get my name out there again. I can't turn it down. Not even for Juliet."

With that he was gone. She heard his footsteps on the stairs up from the basement kitchen to the first floor, and then, distantly, on the stairs to the bedroom floor. A few minutes later and they came down again, slower, and with a clunk of suitcases being dragged. She sank back on the kitchen sofa with her ice-cold gin, and closed her eyes.

She heard his footsteps hesitate at the stairs down to the kitchen, and then move on down the hall, the wheels of the suitcases making an inordinate din on the ornate original Victorian tiles. Then the slam of the front door. She hoped vaguely that Juliet wouldn't wake up, but no other thoughts emerged from her mental stupor.

***

Lois Harper opened her front door and in an instant was being smothered by a bundle of soft tabby fur. She stroked the bits she could reach, and murmured soothingly whilst trying to remove her coat and shoes and put her bag down. The cat, Horatio, missed Janey as much as she did. They had always joked, the two of them, that he was the neediest cat in the world, that he had been absent from cat-school they day they were taught that cats are independent creatures. He thought he was a dog, and craved human company. Janey's job as a cookery writer had meant she worked from home, so she was around all the time, although she had often had to resort to locking herself in the study to enable her to actually do any writing as, given the chance, Horatio would insinuate himself continually between Janey and her keyboard.

She had wondered whether she ought to re-home Horatio – find somewhere he would have the company he craved – but she couldn't bring herself too. Perhaps it was selfish, but he was the last link to Janey, and their idyllic life, and she felt that losing him would break her heart entirely. She consoled herself by reflecting that he was a creature of routine and habit, and might well prefer his own familiar home, and her company albeit sporadically, than a complete change.

In the old days she would come home to delicious cooking smells. Often the same cooking smells for several nights in a row as Janey tweaked a recipe to get it just right, but that had never bothered her. She definitely didn't have the energy to cook for herself tonight, it would be a posh ready meal again. She popped it in the microwave. Although she was almost shaking with fatigue after a thirteen hour shift, she knew she was too strung up to sleep just yet. Tempting though the bottle of chilled Sauvignon Blanc was, she resisted it. It would be hard to stop at one glass, and she had to be back at the hospital in just over nine hours time – there was no way she could risk a hangover. Instead she put the kettle on for a cup of herbal tea. Five minutes later, eating at the kitchen table with Horatio draped over her lap, she reflected on her life.

Daniel, bless him, had been so grateful when she

had offered to work this weekend and give him some proper time off. Heaven knows he looked like he needed it. He was a fantastic doctor – intelligent, kind, sensitive, and a fabulous communicator with the patients, their parents and his colleagues. If he had one flaw it was an inability to switch off and that, combined with the hours he'd been forced to work recently, meant that he was looking dangerously close to burn-out.

And the sad thing was, it was no real sacrifice to her to lose out on her weekend. Her life had been in limbo for the last couple of years. She had friends, of course, and they had been marvellously supportive. But the harsh truth was they all had their own lives. Partners, careers, children, travel, and she was only ever peripheral to that. She and Janey had been the centre of each other's lives, and now that the intensity of her initial grief was starting to wane slightly, she was starting to think about what her new centre could possibly be.

She couldn't really imagine a new romantic relationship. Meeting your soul-mate once was staggeringly fortunate, twice seemed vanishingly unlikely. She had been on a few dates set up by well-meaning friends in the last few months but although they had been perfectly nice women there had been no spark, no—one she could really even picture becoming a close friend, let alone falling in love with.

There was work, of course, and she loved her job, but for her it wasn't enough on its own. Travel by herself didn't particularly appeal. What remained was to continue the project which she and Janey had been discussing before the diagnosis. Their dearest dream. Could she, should she, try and make it a reality on her own?

3

Lydia surveyed herself in the bedroom mirror. She had always had an equivocal relationship with her looks. On one hand she had always known that people – men – found her sexy, and she had tended to dress in a way that played up to that and made the most of her curvy boobs and bum, and wearing lots of make-up to emphasise her big brown eyes and full lips. It was useful not necessarily to sleep your way to a job, but certainly to look as though you *might*.

But despite her clothes and make up outwardly indicating confidence, inside Lydia had always been deeply insecure. A lot of that came from Delia's jellyfish stings about her weight, and the fact that growing up her female role model had been a woman who was a carefully and constantly maintained size 8 and had indoctrinated her with the conviction that this was the ideal of feminine beauty. Knowing that she was never going to be a cool, slender icy blonde, Lydia had taken things to the opposite extreme and rejected all Delia's maxims about grooming and personal appearance. There was a perverse satisfaction in winning her disapproval through a new nose-piercing or a pair of ripped fishnets with micro-shorts and Doc Martens for church.

Recently, though, now she was finally with

someone who truly loved her, she didn't feel the need either to validate her existence through overt sexiness or treat her personal appearance as an act of oppositional defiance, and she could relax in simple jeans and t-shirt, expressing her personality with some cool shoes or jewellery like the flamboyant flamingo ear-rings she had chosen tonight.

She applied a final coat of flamingo-coloured lipstick, spritzed some perfume, and called Dominic.

"Hey, Dom! Are you ready? We're meant to be meeting Daniel in the pub in less than ten minutes."

Dominic strolled out of the living room, cool and laid-back as ever.

"I've been ready for ages! Come on."

They set off the short walk to the pub – their local.

Lydia tucked her arm through Dominic's.

"Do you reckon Dan's ok?"

He looked down at her.

"Dunno. Why?"

She shrugged.

"It's hard to put my finger on. I just felt like I was getting a slightly strange vibe from him that Sunday at your parents'. And then he suggested this drink, and you know it's not like him to have finished work at 7.30pm, is it?"

Dominic chuckled. His brother's workaholic tendencies were the family joke, although the laughter could get a little forced when he stood you up for the fifth time in a row due to a work crisis. But then what kind of bastard did you have to be to suggest that a casual drink or Sunday morning run with your brother was more important than a ward full of sick children?

"I wonder what he's going to make of what we've got to tell him! Do you think we're definitely doing the right thing?"

Lydia nodded emphatically.

"Yes! We have to start somewhere, and Daniel deserves to be the first to know anyway."

As they entered the pub they spotted Daniel at the bar, and gave their orders before finding a quiet and cosy corner. When he came over, Dominic and Lydia were sitting in the corner of the banquette, his arm draped around her shoulder.

Daniel did a double-take. There was something in their body language subtly suggesting that they were more than close friends. Dominic was watching his brother's face closely, and as he saw his raised eyebrows his face broke into an enormous grin. He pulled Lydia closer.

"Yes! You are thinking exactly right! Lyddy and I are…well…we've fallen in love."

Daniel sat down rather suddenly, and took a gulp of his pint. He was totally lost for words. Lydia was surveying his face anxiously, and Dominic began talking again, somewhat fast and nervously to fill what was threatening to become an awkward silence.

"It happened a couple of months ago. We haven't told anyone, because we wanted to make sure it was the real deal – given what close friends we are we didn't want any awkwardness if it didn't work out. But it really is the real thing. I mean, we are just so bloody happy. I can't believe my luck."

His voice tailed off, as Daniel still hadn't spoken.

Lydia reached out her hand and covered Dan's where it lay on the table.

"Dan? You are pleased for us, aren't you? We're relying on *you* at least to be pleased, because God only knows how your parents are going to react!"

Daniel shook himself slightly.

"Oh God, you guys. I don't know what to say. I hope I'm pleased for you. I want to be pleased for you. But…I just don't know."

He took in the surprise and consternation on their faces, wiping out the happy excitement of a few moments earlier, and felt like a complete bastard. Was he doing the right thing? Should he let sleeping dogs lie? But then could he live with himself if this relationship carried on and went further and his suspicions were correct? And surely it was better for him to break the news than leaving it to his parents?

He reached into his pocket, and pulled out an envelope.

"Look, you two. I had something I wanted to talk to you both this evening, and I certainly wasn't expecting your announcement first. A few weeks ago I was looking through some old photo albums that Mum gave me when she cleared out the loft – you know I'm quite interested in family history, and I found this photo."

He took it out of its envelope, and pushed it over the table. It was a black and white photo of a beautiful, dark-haired, curvy woman in 1940s style clothes.

Dominic looked at it in confusion.

"I don't understand? Who is that? It looks like Lyddy...but obviously it isn't. Is it her grandmother? What was that photo doing in our family albums?"

Dominic nodded grimly.

"It's *our* grandmother. Granny Nicholls when she was a young woman."

Lydia had turned pale.

"But why would I look like Granny Nicholls? I don't understand."

She moved her hand from Daniel's, and nestled closer to Dominic.

"What does this mean?"

Daniel shrugged.

'I don't know. Maybe nothing – it could just be one of those freakish coincidences. But there is another possibility which occurred to me, and that's why I wanted to talk to you both.

He paused, breathed deeply and then plunged on.

"You know how resentful my mum has always been of you, Lydia?"

She nodded ruefully.

"Well, what if it's because you are my dad's love-child? That would explain everything. Why you look so like Granny Nicholls – and it's not just in that photo, there are others too – why mum has always had such a problem with you, why my parents had you to live with us when your parents died. Maybe it was just your mum who died, and then dad was your only other relative."

Lydia's head was reeling. When she was growing up her own parents had never really been spoken of by the Nicholls family, and any questions she or the twins had tried to ask were usually shut down by Henry and Delia. She had put that down to their habitual reserve. Since reaching adulthood she had sometimes contemplated trying to find out more about her family, but there had always been something more pressing – the business of earning a living for a start – and she was a fairly pragmatic person and couldn't really see the point of delving too far into the past when it was the present and future that really mattered. And since getting together with Dominic it had all seemed even less important – he was her emotional centre of gravity now. Then it struck her.

"Oh my God! If you're right…that would make you and Dominic my half brothers!"

She felt violently sick, and Dom loosened his hold on her and shifted away slightly.

She gazed at Daniel, horror-struck.

He looked sheepish.

"I know. You see obviously I realised that as soon as I had the idea, but at that point I basically thought it would be a good thing. I mean, I knew that finding out our dad was also your dad would be really disconcerting for you, but I was quite pleased that we would be your brothers...you'd be a proper part of our family. But when you and Dom told me what was going on...:

His voice trailed off and he averted his gaze from the stricken faces opposite him. Lydia started to cry. Dominic suddenly leapt up, and without speaking to either of them, stormed out of the warm sanctuary of the pub into the chilly darkness.

Lydia glared through her tears at the man who might be her brother.

"Brilliant, Dan. Just brilliant. This is the happiest I have ever been in my whole life. The only time I have truly felt that I belong, that I am truly loved. Couldn't you just have kept your crazy half-baked ideas to yourself?"

Daniel shook his head slowly.

"You wouldn't want to hide from the truth, Cuckoo. Not really. Especially not in the circumstances."

She flinched at the once-beloved nickname.

"*Don't* call me that. I'm sick of being the Cuckoo. And do you know what, there are some truths it is better not to know. I just want Dominic, and I want to be happy, and I DO NOT want to know about anything that might get in the way of that."

With those words it was her turn to stalk angrily out, leaving Daniel to stare into his pint, and curse the impulse that had led him to browse through those old photo albums.

4

"Mummy! Mummee! MUMMEEE!"

Claudia jabbed her mascara wand into her eye and cursed softly. It was already 8am. She was going to be late for work for the third morning in a row. The culture of presenteeism in her office meant that most of the team were already at their desks by 8am, but not making it by 9am was unheard of.

"What is it, Juliet?" she snapped, hating the shrewish tone in her voice, but unable to change it.

"Where is my homework folder? I need to hand it in today?"

Claudia sighed. How the hell was she meant to know where her homework folder was. She hadn't fully realised Juliet got homework. Wasn't five a little young?

"Umm. I'm not sure. Hang on, let me finish my make-up, and I'll come and have a look."

She swung round, and noticed to her horror that her daughter was still in vest and knickers, one leg in a pair of red tights with the other leg of the tights flapping round her feet.

"Juliet! I thought I told you to get dressed! We need to leave to go to Samara's now. We're going to be late."

Juliet pouted.

"I don't want to go to Samara's again. Why can't you take me to school?"

Claudia's heart contracted with pity and guilt at the same moment as the iron band of stress headache round her temples tightened another notch.

"I'm sorry, sweetheart. I can't, I have to go to work. I'll take you in on Friday, I promise."

The little girl's blue eyes filled with tears.

"But it's only Wednesday, Mummy. It won't be Friday for ages yet."

Claudia gave her a brief hug.

"It'll be Friday before you know it, poppet. I promise. Now, why aren't you dressed?"

Juliet sighed.

"I spilt smoothie on my shirt yesterday, and I can't find a clean one. And, to be honest with you, Mummy, I always find tights a bit tricky."

Hiding a smile at her daughter's grown-up manner, Claudia sped down the landing to the airing cupboard, and pulled out one of Juliet's white cotton school shirts. Un-ironed, but that would have to do. She slipped it round her daughter's narrow shoulders, and pushed her arms through before buttoning it quickly. Crouching down she pulled Juliet half onto her lap and sorted her tights.

"Right, we're getting there! Now, where are your skirt and cardi?"

The answer, of course, turned out to be on her

bedroom floor. Claudia pulled them on, grimacing. They were also decidedly crumpled, and there was a sticky patch on the arm of the cardi which she suspected might be further evidence of the smoothie spillage, but she didn't have time to let that bother her. She tugged a brush through Juliet's curly blonde hair, dropping a kiss on it as she did so. Juliet turned and buried her face in her mother's chest.

A kaleidoscope of conflicting emotions spun round Claudia's head. Disbelief that her tiny baby was now a school-girl. Panic that traces of school-girl stickiness were going to distribute themselves on her cream silk blouse. Regret that she couldn't just sink into the luxury of a cuddle with her precious girl, but instead had to carry on pushing them both down the morning conveyor belt. She hugged her tightly, and then released her.

"Great, all dressed! Now, you run downstairs and put your shoes on, and I'll find that homework folder."

Halfway down the road Juliet suddenly stopped

"Mummy! Where's my packed lunch?"

Claudia's heart sank. She hadn't made a packed lunch.

"School dinners today, sweetheart." She chirruped faux-cheerfully.

Juliet burst into tears.

"NO! I NEVER have school dinners on a Wednesday! It's yukky cottage pie on Wednesdays, and I HATE it, so Daddy always makes me a packed lunch."

For the umpteenth time in that interminable week Claudia cursed her husband.

"Well, I'm sorry darling, but Mummy didn't know that. And I haven't made you a packed lunch, and we don't have time to go back and do one now. Maybe you could try the cottage pie again? It might be yummier this week?"

Juliet redoubled her sobs, and began beating at Claudia's legs with her small fists in the kind of tantrum Claudia hadn't seen since she was a toddler.

"I want Daddy to come back! *Why* has he gone to 'Merica for work? He's meant to be here looking after me because you're too busy to."

Claudia strove to keep calm, even though she could feel tears gathering in her own throat.

"Look sweetheart, Daddy had the chance of a really fun job doing writing in America, and he wanted to do it, because he hasn't had a chance to do much writing while you were little and he was looking after you. But now you're a big girl at school he's got more time. And Mummy is here. I'm sorry I didn't know about packed lunches on a Wednesday. I'll remember next week."

Juliet's sobs started to subside, and Claudia scooped her up and staggered along the street, wincing slightly at the weight of a 5 year old on her front when she already had a laptop, charger and several files in a rucksack on her back.

It was 8.30am by the time they arrived at her friend

Hasina's house, and Claudia's mind raced with calculations - drop Juliet, ten minutes to the station, 20 minute train journey if she was lucky – if the gods were with her, she would be at her desk by just after 9am. Which was hardly ideal, but probably liveable with in the short-term. She couldn't really think beyond short-term at the moment.

Hasina opened the door with her youngest daughter, Jasmine, balanced on her hip.
"Hi, Claudia, hi, Juliet. Sorry, it's all a bit at sixes and sevens here at the moment. I've been up all night with Jasmine. *Samara*! Come on down, Juliet's here!"
She smiled tiredly. Claudia felt herself tense. As a good friend she ought to check her friend and her baby were okay, and offer some sympathy. As a good mother she ought to take a couple of minutes to settle Juliet and give her a last cuddle after the upsetting morning. As a good employee she needed to turn tail abruptly and sprint to the station.
"Oh no, Hasina! Poor you. What happened?"
Her friend shrugged.
"Who knows? Babies are a law unto themselves, aren't they? But I'm a bit worried about her, she seems to be running a temperature now, and she's so clingy which just isn't like her. I've managed to get her an appointment at the doctors for 5.45pm this evening. Do you think you could manage to pick Juliet up at 5.30pm? I know I said I'd have her until 7pm again, but I didn't know Jasmine would be

poorly…"

Her voice tailed off as she clocked the expression on Claudia's face.

"No, don't worry about it. I'll manage. I just thought it wouldn't be much fun for Juliet to have to hang round the doctors' surgery with us for goodness knows how long."

Claudia sighed. Of course it wouldn't be fun for Juliet, but, more importantly, it would be horrific for Hasina to have to entertain two tired five year-olds and a poorly baby in the shabby germ pit that was the local surgery's waiting room. It simply wasn't fair to ask her to.

"No, don't worry about it, Hasina. I'll collect Juliet at 5.30pm. Don't worry about feeding her, I'll take her out for a pizza for a treat."

She saw Hasina relax.

"Oh, thank you. If you really don't mind? You see then I can ask my mother-in-law to pop round and give Samara her tea while I'm at the doctors, but I wouldn't like to leave her with two of them. Are you sure you can manage?"

Actually, Claudia was perfectly sure she *couldn't* manage, but that wasn't Hasina's problem. She plastered a smile on her face.

"It'll be great – we'll have fun, won't we, Popsicle?" Juliet nodded, tears now forgotten, and jumping up and down in excitement at the prospect of tea out with her mummy.

Claudia gave her a quick kiss.

"Right. I must dash now. Thanks so much, Hasina. I'll see you at half five. Love you, Juliet."

***

Lois opened the file marked 'Baby' on her computer. Now she felt she had reached her decision, she was investigating the options in her usual calm and organised way.

Obviously she and Janey had already done a lot of research, but things were different now. Their original plan had been to use Lois' eggs, because she was younger, but for Janey to carry the baby. Sperm would have come from a donor. At some point after Janey's cancer diagnosis, and the realisation that she would need a hysterectomy, she had smiled ruefully at her wife.

"Looks like you're going to have to provide the eggs *and* the womb now, darling."

Lois hadn't cared. At that point the idea of a baby, previously her most heartfelt desire, had receded to the very back of her brain, all she really cared about was Janey's recovery. Unfortunately that never came. Despite all the treatment modern medicine could throw at the cancer it had spread inexorably. One of the last things Janey had done was to implore her to have a baby with someone else.

"You're still young, Lois. And lovely. You'll meet someone else. You can still have a baby. I know how much that means to you."

Tears streaming down her face, Lois had shaken her head. She would never, ever meet anyone she could love like she'd loved Janey, and for a while it had seemed like that also meant she never could have a baby. Over the years following Janey's death, grief that she would never be a mother, would never feel what she had seen from her work to be the strongest of all human bonds, became almost as strong as the grief at her bereavement. It seemed irrational that the loss of something she had never had could be as tangible as the loss of the woman who'd shared her life for over a decade, but that seemed to be how it was.

Then, recently, it had occurred to her that she didn't necessarily need to meet another woman in order to have a baby. She and Janey would have needed to use donor sperm in any case. She was healthy. There was no reason why she couldn't have a successful pregnancy. The only problem was age. At thirty-eight Lois knew that her egg quality was declining almost by the day. By forty the chances of a successful IVF pregnancy fell dramatically. If she was going to embark on this project, which seemed so crazy she had yet to discuss it with anyone except Horatio, she was going to have to act quickly.

She wondered, endlessly, if she was being selfish, having a baby solely to gratify her own thwarted desires, and to try and create some meaning in her life. But then, what was an *un*selfish desire to have a baby? Lois was absolutely sure that many, if not most, women conceived a child to satisfy some need in themselves, rather than a purely altruistic desire to create new life. What would an altruistic reason be, anyway? The world certainly didn't need more babies. But when a heterosexual couple decided to have a child, no-one questioned their motives. It was as simple as flushing the contraceptive pills away or not using a condom. It wouldn't be so straightforward for her, and so somehow she felt compelled to build her own moral case to present to an imaginary jury. She thought of a parent she had met at work recently.

This woman was twenty-three, and heavily pregnant with her third child. Scans during pregnancy had shown that the baby had problems with the way its heart was developing, and would need surgery shortly after birth. The birth would have to be by caesarean section to avoid putting any unnecessary strain on the baby during birth. Lois had to meet the mother to explain what was going to happen.

"Is the baby's father joining us?" she had enquired at the start of the meeting.

The woman had rolled her eyes

"No, I shouldn't think so. I did tell him, but he probably won't remember." She looked desperately tired. "We're not together any more." she added.

"Oh. I'm sorry to hear that."

The woman, Ellie, had snorted.

"I'm not sure I am. He's not much use."

Lois hoped that she hadn't looked judgmental – she didn't particularly feel it, and even when she occasionally did, she was used to maintaining a professional exterior – but Ellie still seemed to feel that some explanation was required.

"I got pregnant in my last year at uni. That's where Pete and I met. It wasn't planned, of course, but we decided to keep it. Then we discovered 'it' was twins." She grimaced.

"Everyone seemed to think it was a bit of a joke, lots of cracks about me having my hands full and so on. But it wasn't remotely funny to me. It seemed like a waking nightmare. We had nowhere to live, Pete got a job but it was a graduate scheme that paid peanuts. I couldn't get a job because I had no experience, and it was impossible to earn enough to pay for two sets of childcare. We ended up moving in with Pete's parents – luckily they've got quite a big house."

She paused to draw breath, and Lois smiled sympathetically and waited. She had been planning to talk to the mother about the procedure which would be carried out on her baby, the risks and the benefits, but she sensed that Ellie needed to get all this off her chest before she would be in any state to take the information in.

"Pete was pretty good really. I mean, he loved the girls, and they love him. And he was sweet to me. But it was SO hard. They never seemed to sleep at the same time. And Pete's mum kept saying it was important he got a good night's sleep because *he* had to go to work. So he moved into another room, and I had to manage all night long by myself. And then all day long. All the other mums I met were loads older than me, and only had one baby, and a lot more money. So they'd all go off for coffee together, and all these baby sensory and baby massage classes, and all I did was push the bloody double buggy round the park for hours on end."

Ellie's eyes filled with tears, and Lois placed her hand briefly over the other woman's, noting the painfully bitten nails.

"So are you still living with Pete's parents now?"

Ellie shuddered.

"No, thank God! Pete completed the scheme, and got a job that paid better. And once the girls turned two we got some free childcare hours, so I could get a part-time job, and so we managed to get a flat. It's only small, but it's *ours*."

She sighed.

"*Was* ours. Pete has moved back in with mummy dearest now."

Lois was dying to ask why, after her first experience, and with life just starting to get back on track, Ellie had let herself get pregnant again. Of course she couldn't, but Ellie herself supplied the answer.

"I was stupid, I suppose. But I got pregnant with this baby because I wanted a chance to do it properly. Like real grown-ups. Not students living in someone else's house, but proper adults with jobs and our own flat. It was all such a blur when Bella and Florence were little, I just wanted a chance to do it all again. Properly. But it didn't work. I was really sick, and everyone in Pete's new job was going out drinking all the time, and he got pissed off because he couldn't afford to, and anyway, I was always nagging him to come home and help with the girls. We were rowing all the time. And then when the scan showed that this little one had the heart problem, he said we should have an abortion. Can you imagine?"

Her eyes were wide with horror at the idea.

Lois considered. This girl seemed so young, and desperately naïve. She was now a single mother, living in a two-bedroom flat with three-year old twins, and a baby on the way who would require possibly many years of hospital treatment and special care. The chances of his mother being able to continue working seemed remote, which would make finances even tighter. Pragmatically, it seemed like an abortion might have been quite a good idea.

"Did you never consider that option?" she asked gently.

The girl shook her head adamantly.

"No! Never. I didn't like the idea the first time round, but *now*...now I've held my babies, now I know just how much I love them...I absolutely couldn't."

She looked defiant.

"I know this baby is going to be poorly. I know it's

going to be hard. But I love him. I love him so much already. I can't wait to meet him, and look after him. And be his mummy. And you're going to make sure he's alright, aren't you?"

It was a child's plea, but there was nothing childlike in the determined love that blazed from Ellie's eyes. Suddenly Lois had felt like the naïve one. This girl had carried, given birth to, and raised twins, practically single-handedly, when she was barely out of her teens. And she had been propelled by the force of a maternal devotion which Lois had never experienced, but was now desperate to.

Ellie's story kept coming back to her. Firstly because it illustrated the point about selfish and unselfish reasons for having a child – Ellie had got pregnant to make up for what she'd missed out on with her twins, which was basically entirely selfish. But secondly because, even in what Lois considered to be horrendous circumstances, her overwhelming emotion was still happy excitement at the prospect of meeting her baby, and unwavering determination to get him well. Her strength was awe-inspiring, and it renewed Lois' determination to have a child herself.

Now only one niggle remained. Even if she could do it all by herself, should she? Ellie might be a single mother, but the children at least *had* another parent who loved them. Maybe a single woman and a cat wasn't enough of a family. Maybe she didn't need a sperm donor for her baby, maybe she actually needed a father.

5

It was lunchtime at Dominic's school, and for once he wasn't on playground duty. He sank into a chair in the quietest, darkest corner of the staffroom. There was a tacit understanding that sitting there meant you wanted to be left alone. In pre-smoking ban days it had been the smokers' corner, and the faded 1970s chairs still gave out an aroma of stale nicotine. But it was calm enough for Dominic to nurse his headache in peace, and try to compose himself sufficiently for a double lesson with the notoriously difficult 9B after lunch.

He downed a couple of Nurofen with a few gulps of tapwater. Hungover. Again. He fancied a drink now, just a steadier, a stiffener, but retained sufficient self-control to avoid drinking during the school day, even though he had spent all his time out of school during the past ten days drinking vast quantities of alcohol in a vain attempt to numb the excruciating tangle of all-consuming, overwhelming love, lust, guilt and crippling anxiety about the future.

Lydia just didn't seem to see it. It was the only thing they had ever disagreed on, and the most crucial. She maintained that love as strong as theirs couldn't possibly be a bad thing, couldn't be wrong, that Dan must have made a mistake, and that they should just forget all about it and carry on as they were. And when they were together, when they could talk and laugh and confide in each other as they always had, and when he was lying in her arms, breathing in the maddening scent of her skin and hair, then he agreed with her. This felt so good that it *couldn't* be bad. But when they weren't together the guilt and the doubt and the crushing sense of uncertainty, of letting everyone down, came flooding back. He would resolve to tell her that they couldn't carry on like this, that he was finishing it. To this end, he would have a couple of stiff drinks for Dutch courage. And he would say his piece.

Then she would cry inconsolably, and he would be unable to resist taking her in his arms to comfort her. Promising himself it was purely platonic. Fraternal, even. But then the feel of her body pressed yearningly against him was irresistible. Before he knew what he was doing he would be kissing her, and then they'd be back in bed together.

And alcohol was the only thing which seemed to ease the crushing guilt these encounters now engendered, the only thing which enabled him to quiet the relentless anxiety about what the future held for both of them. He envied her her quiet conviction that it must surely be alright somehow, because for the life of him he couldn't see a way out of this mess which wouldn't either break both their hearts, or destroy the lives of those around them.

He was meeting Daniel for a drink that night.

Blaming Dan was undoubtedly part of the problem. Previously he and his twin had shared everything, and he had gone through his thirty years a living embodiment of the saying that a problem shared was a problem halved. Until now. This was too much of a problem, and ironically his twin was the one who had caused it. He couldn't stand the thought of seeing Daniel and watching the expression on his face turn from brotherly concern to hatred or disgust or revulsion if he admitted that he and Lydia had continued sleeping together and that he didn't know for the life of him how he was going to find the strength to stop.

***

Daniel arrived at the pub where he and Dominic had agreed to meet out of breath and over half an hour late. He'd promised some parents he'd see them to discuss their child's test results before he left, and of course the results had been late coming back from the lab. It wasn't the kind of discussion you could rush, and so he had left far later than he intended, and had sprinted to and from stations, up and down escalators like a madman to try and make up time. As happened more and more frequently these days he found himself questioning whether always putting his patients first was necessarily the right thing to do. It seemed like the unselfish thing – certainly he would have felt selfish leaving tonight before he had fulfilled his promise, but then his family and friends were normally the ones who bore the brunt of his 'unselfishness'.

He spotted Dominic at once, sitting rather morosely in the corner, empty glass in front of him. He slipped past him, unnoticed, to the bar, and bought two pints of their favourite draught beer.

Two minutes later he slid onto the banquette next to his brother, clinking the lint glasses down on the table.

"Hey. Sorry I'm late. How are you?"

Dominic turned to face him, and Daniel noted two things. Firstly, Dom was already significantly drunk. And secondly he looked utterly heart-rendingly miserable.

"Dominic! God, what on earth is the matter?"

There was a heavy silence. Then Dominic shook his head wonderingly.

"You know what the bloody matter is!"

Daniel felt a sinking sensation in his stomach. He had been plagued by guilty thoughts about Dom and Lydia since their evening of revelations, but had managed to convince himself that it wasn't really a significant problem. That Dominic and Lydia couldn't possibly be *that* serious about one another. That they had mistaken close friendship for something more, but that now that there was a concrete reason to keep things platonic it wouldn't be such a big issue. But the naked misery on Dom's face was telling a different story.

"You and Lydia?"

His brother nodded mutely.

"You dropped a right fucking bombshell, Daniel! I just don't know what we're going to do. Lydia is just adamant that you have made a mistake, that there is no evidence we are related, and we can just carry on as we are."

"But you're not convinced?"

Dom shrugged.

"I don't know. I certainly don't *feel* like she's my sister! But obviously if she is…then we can't carry on like this. And that photo was an uncanny likeness. Are you *sure* it was Granny Nicholls?"

Daniel nodded, sombrely.

"Yep, certain. And, like I said, it *could* just be a freakish coincidence, but the more I think about it the more likely it seems that there is something odd going on. I mean, thinking about it rationally, don't you think mum and dad were always weirdly secretive about Lydia's family? And, given mum's not Lyddy's biggest fan, why do you think she would have agreed to look after her if she *wasn't* dad's biological daughter?"

Dominic struck the table with his hand.

"I don't damn well know! They don't exactly do emotion, do they? Lydia always thought they suppressed discussion about her parents because they didn't want her getting upset and tearful. Which kind of makes sense, doesn't it?"

His tone was more pleading than confident.

"Look, Dom. The only way around this is to ask Mum and Dad. Do you want me to talk to them? Or will you? Or does Lydia want to do it by herself?"

Dominic looked despairing.

"Lydia is flatly refusing to have any conversation about it at all. She says it's all nonsense, there is no evidence we're related, and she won't discuss it at all – let alone with mum and dad. Not least because we just weren't ready to tell them about our relationship yet in any case."

"But you don't have to! I mean, Lydia is entitled to ask them for her birth certificate, and for more information about her parents just because she wants to know! She's being really silly. And you can't *be* in a relationship in the romantic or sexual sense until all this is cleared up anyway, so…"

He broke off as he clocked the look on Dom's face.

"Dom! You aren't still sleeping together when you know there's a chance she might be our sister, are you?"

Dominic looked agonised, embarrassed and furious all at the same time.

"There's no evidence that she's our sister! And you don't fall out of love with someone because of an unfounded rumour. When Lyddy and I fell in love there was no suggestion she could possibly be related to me – she had been brought up as, well, the classic 'friend of the family' I suppose. It felt like falling for my best friend, definitely *not* my sister! What's that Shakespeare quote – "love is not love which alters when it alteration finds"'.

"Oh come on! You can't start using Shakespearean

sonnets to justify anything you like! You both need to get a grip, stop being ostriches, find out what is going on, and above all stop bloody shagging while you do all that."

Dominic exploded at that point.

"And you just need to mind your own bloody business! Who asked you your opinion? It's nothing to do with you! What Lydia and I do is up to us and only us! We're only in this mess because you had to start interfering and looking up photos and weaving erroneous stories around them! You know nothing about love! You're so wedded to the bloody hospital that you never let a woman get close to you. Probably because it's easier to prance around being 'Dr Dan' the hero, with all the nurses fawning over you, and never having to take responsibility for anything in your personal life because you can always justify not by being too busy at work."

Daniel felt his own anger rising. Alongside his hurt that his brother could speak to him like that, and his outrage at the unjustified accusations, there was also just enough truth in the jibes about him being wedded to the job to really rankle. All the more because his devotion to work wasn't really paying off right now. The harder he worked, the harder it seemed to get. He had made more 'almost' mistakes than he cared to think about, and he was spending drained, exhausted evenings sitting alone in a sterile flat having flashbacks of the things which had gone wrong, the patients he hadn't been able to help, the heartbroken parents. He could see that Dom was lashing out in hurt, though, so he managed with a supreme effort to keep his own temper.

"Look, I don't pretend to understand what it must be like. I'm sorry I was the unwitting cause of this upset, but I couldn't unsee that photo. I need to go now, because I'm on an early tomorrow, but I'll be in touch. And you know where I am."

With that he walked out of the pub, feeling strangely empty at leaving a conversation with his brother like this. And after watching him leave, Dominic walked over to the bar and ordered a double vodka.

6

Daniel could see from the blue glow of his phone screen that it was 2.40am. That same alarm would be chivvying him to wakefulness in just four hours' time. Assuming, that is, that he had managed to go to sleep in the first place. He had never suffered from insomnia before – the opposite - junior doctors learnt to snatch sleep in any odd moments they could, never knowing where the next nap would come from. On the other hand, this was the first time in his life he'd received what was effectively a formal warning from his boss just a few days after something that felt uncomfortably like an estrangement from his twin and one of his best friends.

He sat up and turned on his bedside light. Lying here wasn't doing any good, so he might as well get up and make a drink. He pulled on his dressing gown, wandered through to the kitchen, and started rummaging around in the cupboard. Strong black coffee, his hot beverage of choice, didn't seem like a great choice for lulling him to sleep, but he wasn't sure he could stomach warm milk. Or even that he had any milk. He found an ancient packet of camomile tea-bags, presumably bought at the start of some long-forgotten healthy-living kick and promptly discarded. Waiting for the kettle to boil, he looked round his flat with some distaste. It was tiny; the kitchen area where he now stood was separated from the living area by a piece of plywood masquerading in the estate agent's description as a breakfast bar. A door led out onto the entrance hall, which was about the size of the average cardboard box, and contained the front door and the door through to the bedroom and tiny en-suite shower room.

In defiance of the bachelor cliché the whole place was scrupulously clean and meticulously neat. Partly because Daniel was tidy by nature, partly because he employed a weekly cleaner, and mainly because he was never here to make a mess or accumulate clutter. His life revolved around the hospital. This wasn't his home, it was simply somewhere he re-charged his batteries with food and as much sleep as possible before the next shift.

He knew, of course he knew, that his work-life balance was way out of kilter. But the satisfaction and fulfilment he found in his work, the fact that he knew day in, day out he really was making a difference, had always seemed to justify that. But now, sipping tasteless yet strangely unpleasant hot water at 3am, he forced himself into a little more honesty.

At its best he did love his work. He had always seen medicine as a vocation rather than a job, and his natural rapport with children made paediatrics the perfect choice of specialty. But it was gruelling, and he knew he was getting far more exhausted than he used to, and far more exhausted than his colleagues seemed to. Lois had been concerned for a few months; had spoken to him several times about needing to take a step back, to cut down his emotional involvement. And it was true that the bad cases, the children who couldn't be helped, who were going to die tragically young or endure hideously painful treatment with only limited chances of success, bothered him more and more. Some of it was sheer physical tiredness. Cut-backs and staff shortages meant that punishingly long shifts and few days off were very much the norm rather than the exception.

Some of it was his increasing feelings of loneliness and isolation. The hard-drinking, hard-partying culture of many junior doctors had never held much appeal, but as he progressed in his profession it was increasingly hard to maintain friendships with non-medics because time didn't really allow it, and the demands of his job made him a fairly unreliable and therefore unappealing friend.

The same was true, only more so, for relationships. He had never had a girlfriend of more than a few weeks. He felt that was because girlfriends were even less tolerant than mates at being stood up at a moment's notice, and the endless weekends and evenings worked, but he did wonder uncomfortably if there was any truth in Dominic's assertion that he used his work as an excuse for not putting enough effort in to his relationships. Whatever the reason, he had certainly never imagined being single at 30. Not necessarily married with 2.4 kids, or anything like that, but certainly on a trajectory that would take him there before his 40th birthday, but he was a million miles away from that.

Then there had been that hideous mistake a few weeks ago, just before all the Dominic and Lydia stuff blew up. Thankfully one of the SHOs had spotted it and had his back, and there was no harm done, but fretting about the might-have-beens made him sick to his stomach. And now this. The conversation he had had with Lois a few days ago. She said that concerns had been raised about him from nursing staff and medical colleagues. Concerns that he had made some little mistakes, that he looked exhausted, that he seemed over-emotional.

Unfortunately for his chances of rebutting these accusations, this conversation had come the very night after his row with Dom, and after a difficult conversation with a child who needed to be admitted for yet more treatment with very uncertain chances of success. He had started crying. His toes scrunched in embarrassment. A thirty-year old man, an experienced doctor, sobbing in a meeting with his boss. Not good.

"Look, Daniel." Lois had said. "You have the potential to be an exceptional doctor. You are intelligent, thoughtful, perceptive, caring...but at the moment you don't have sufficient detachment. You are burnt out, and letting emotion affect your judgement. We need to deal with this before something goes badly wrong.

You could probably go to your own GP and get signed off with stress, but I know you will worry about having that on your record, and I think you would end up coming back sooner than you should. I suggest you take a sabbatical for 6-12 months, and use the time to chill out, reconsider your priorities, reconnect with friends and family, maybe travel…"

He had smiled wryly at her.

"Are you giving me a choice?"

She had grinned back.

"Not really, no. I would be failing in my duty of care, to you and our patients, if I didn't do something. If you would prefer to see your own doctor and treat this as a medical issue that is absolutely your prerogative, and I will totally support you. But, I have to say, that it might be better for you in lots of ways if you made it less formal and just took a bit of a break. Work out how to get your balance back."

"There is the little matter of managing without a salary for best part of a year! If I was off sick I'd get paid at least!"

"Yes, that's true. But you are very unlikely to get the length of time I think you probably need on full sick pay without the powers that be deciding they need to look at issues of capability. I don't want to seem like I am threatening you, Dan, but you can't carry on like this. If you take some time off you can earn money doing a few shifts as a barista or a bartender! Could you give notice on your flat and move back in with your parents? You just need to have a proper break from the intensity of this place, and see if it is definitely what you want to be doing with your life."

Daniel had promised to go away and think about it, and meet Lois again to discuss the outcome of his thinking. And now he *was* thinking.

Suddenly he could barely keep his eyelids open, and he headed back to bed to fall asleep almost instantly. Perhaps the healing and relaxing properties of camomile tea were more potent than he had expected, or perhaps the it was the result of his sudden decision. A decision which seemed so blindingly obvious that the second it was made he couldn't understand what the difficulty had been.

He did need to stop. Take a break from the hospital, from being a doctor. To find our who Daniel Nicholls was when he wasn't hiding behind the Dr Dan persona. To try and reconnect with Dominic and Lydia, and see if he could make some amends for his tactlessness, and maybe help them through the current situation. To get some proper sleep. He would need to get some sort of part-time job to pay the rent, of course, because he really didn't fancy moving back in with his parents, but that was surely possible. He had earnt his way through university and kept student debt to a minimum by putting his natural rapport with children to good use in various childcare roles, and that might be something he could do again. Maybe if he saved up some money he could then do some travelling. The prospect of time and space and freedom made him feel lighter hearted than he had done for months, if not years.

***

Claudia smiled tiredly at her friend.

"I know it's only lunchtime, but it is Friday – and after the couple of weeks I've had I reckon I deserve a drink. Share a bottle of Chablis with me?"

Lois nodded. What the hell. If her plans went ahead successfully then it wouldn't be long before she couldn't drink at all for nine months. And it wasn't like she had to work that afternoon – this was a proper, long, girly lunch. Although in the nearly twenty years since she and Claudia first started having girly lunches together, the conversations had moved on from who they fancied, what they would wear to go out that night or the latest designer to bring out a line for Topshop, to cancer, bereavement, work pressure and motherhood – and today it seemed as though adultery, divorce and fertility treatment were going to be added to the agenda. Wine probably was a good idea.

Lois had been the first person Claudia had told after Ethan left. In fact, she and Hasina were the only two people who knew at all. Lois was her oldest friend. They had met right back at the beginning of university as they had rooms on the same corridor, and had somehow clicked straight away and their friendship had never wavered. They were more similar than the hospital doctor and city lawyer might seem at first glance. Both intelligent and career focussed, determined to succeed in professions which could still be deeply sexist. They had both been in stable, happy marriages, and now it looked as though Claudia was joining Lois in being involuntarily single.

"So, you had no idea at all this was coming?" Lois was asking now.

Claudia shrugged.

"No. Not really. Not this. I mean, I knew things hadn't been great between us recently. We hardly saw each other for one thing, and I felt like he was constantly resentful of my working hours. And sex is a bit of a distant memory. But, according to my other friends who work full-time and have young children, that's just the way it goes. I certainly had no clue he was planning on leaving me for another woman and moving to America, and writing a column in a national newspaper about the breakdown of his marriage and what it is like to start life over aged 40!"

Lois' mouth twitched.

"Well, you can't accuse him of doing things half-heartedly!"

Claudia met her friend's eyes, and suddenly the stress of the last couple of weeks caught up with her, and she broke into slightly hysterical laughter. Lois joined her, and the two women laughed until tears filled their eyes.

Finally Claudia pulled herself together, took a deep gulp of her wine, and turned her attention to the waiter who had been hovering nervously.

"Two grilled sea-bass with salad, please."

"And two side-orders of chips with the home-made alioli as well, if you don't mind."

Claudia looked at her friend in surprise. Lois grinned.

"You think we need Chablis? I don't disagree. But we also need carbs and saturated fats!"

"Well, you're the doctor, who am I to argue?"

Claudia took another swig of wine, and then began to vocalise the thoughts which had been bubbling away in her mind since that fateful Saturday night.

"I hate him for dumping me in it like this. He's done it to make a point – childcare is hard work. And I do know it is. But childcare plus a full-time job, on your own, isn't just hard, it's bloody impossible."

Lois winced. She hadn't shared anything about her baby plan with Claudia, so her friend had no idea the extent to which she was twisting the knife by confirming Lois' own niggling suspicions. And Juliet was at school for six hours a day – it would be years before her potential baby was that independent.

Claudia was staring into her wine glass and so missed Lois' disconcertion.

"Juliet is coping quite well, I guess. All things considered. But it is massively destabilising for her, and I need to get some proper childcare sorted out asap. In fact, it is worrying about Juliet, and how I manage the practicalities that is bothering me almost more than Ethan actually leaving!"

Lois' eyes widened.

"Really?"

"Yes, I think so. I mean, of course I am bloody furious with him for leaving like that. And it feels so out of character. Which is why I think he is deliberately making a point, trying to make sure I appreciate everything he did to make our lives run smoothly by leaving me totally in the lurch. But he's got it wrong. I always *did* appreciate what he did, but I think he failed to appreciate what *I* did. That I didn't always want to be at the late meetings, or the breakfast ones, or doing the business trips. That sometimes I didn't want to be off to the office in heels and a suit, I wanted to be heading to playgroup in jeans like a 'proper' mummy. I missed out on a lot, but I didn't mind too much, because I do love my job, and I knew Juliet was totally happy with him. But we weren't really happy as a couple, even though we'd taken a joint decision – in the days where we actually talked instead of bickered – that I should be the breadwinner and he should be the homemaker. But then I feel like he spent the whole time resenting that."

"It just seems so out of character for Ethan! I would never have predicted him doing something like this. And moving so far away from Juliet! It doesn't make any sense.

Claudia shrugged.

"Early mid-life crisis, I guess. And clearly falling in love with this Antonia woman has had a lot to do with it." Her mouth twisted bitterly. However sincere she was in her declaration that her marriage hadn't been particularly happy for years, it wasn't easy to think of Ethan being with someone else. Someone with whom he was sufficiently infatuated to leave her and Juliet for. Someone, reading between the lines, who was at least 10 years younger than her.

"You're being amazingly calm and brave about it."

"Well, I don't always feel calm and brave! And when Juliet is screaming blue murder at 3am because she is thirsty but I gave her a drink in the wrong coloured cup, and she wants Daddy back, then I feel hysterical and murderous! And that's why I really need to sort something proper out for her. This is such a massive disruption for her, she needs some proper consistency, and so do I if I'm going to keep my job and sanity!"

Lois reflected for a moment. She had expected a lot more mopping of tears than this.

Perhaps Claudia was still in shock.

"What about your friend Hasina? Can't she carry on helping out?"

Claudia shook her head.

"No, not really. She was a lifesaver for a couple of days, but it's not a long-term solution. I want Juliet to have some proper stability. Plus Juliet really needs to be in bed at 7.30pm, and I'm barely home from work then. I did think Hasina would be able to help for a few weeks while I got something else sorted, but now her baby is poorly, and she's not getting any sleep, and I just don't think it's fair to ask her to cope with Juliet too."

Lois pursed her lips.

"Hmm, tricky. Can you take some compassionate leave while you get sorted?"

Claudia laughed wryly.

"Well, legally I *could* of course. But it would probably set my career back about ten years." She sighed. "I guess that's what I'll have to do, because Juliet is more important, but it's galling. Especially galling that it's Ethan who has deliberately forced me into this position to make some kind of ego-salvaging point!"

She sighed.

"I guess I will have to talk to my parents, tell them about Ethan leaving, put up with all the questions I can't answer and bewildered sympathy, and then beg them to come and look after Juliet for a little while until I can sort out a more permanent solution."

Lois frowned slightly.

"So, let me get this straight. The problem is that you want…what, a nanny?"

Claudia nodded

"Yep, I think that's the only feasible option, given the hours I work."

"But the difficulty is recruiting someone suitable when you need them now?"

Her friend nodded again.

"Yes. There are agencies who provide temps, but I don't want Juliet to get used to someone for a couple of weeks and then have it all change again."

Lois smiled.

"I actually think I might have a solution for you! Are you planning for them to be live-in?"

"I don't mind. It might be easier for the hours I'll need. We've got an en-suite spare room, as you know."

She was interrupted by her phone ringing.

"Oops, sorry, I'll just turn that off, it'll be bloody work...oh, no, hang on, it's Juliet's school, I'd better take it."

Lois watched first absent-mindedly, and then with anxiety, her friend's side of the conversation.

"What?! Oh my god...Yes, of course. No, I'm on my way...which hospital? Ok, I'll be there as quick as I can. Tell Juliet I'm coming."

Lois had already motioned the waiter over and was paying the bill.

"What's happened?"

Claudia was white.

"It was Juliet's school. She's ill. They're on a school trip today, and she complained of not feeling well. Blinding headache, and they realised she had a temperature. Then someone noticed she had a funny rash, so they decided to get an ambulance 'to be on the safe side'. She didn't spell it out, but it's obvious they think it's meningitis."

Lois had been fiddling with her phone.

"OK. There'll be an Uber outside in 2 minutes. Keep calm. Where are they taking her?"

"Your hospital!"

Lois smiled.

"Well, you know she's in good hands then! Come on, get your coat on."

She helped her friend pull on her coat as she could see her hands were shaking.

"Will you come with me, Lois?"

"Oh for heaven's sake! Of course I will."

The taxi ride felt endless to both women, although in reality it was less than half an hour.

As well as terror of what might be wrong with Juliet, and what might happen, Claudia also felt racked with agony at the thought of Juliet ill and in pain without her there. There was the guilt as well. Had she missed something crucial? Her daughter had seemed a little bit quiet that morning, hadn't eaten as much breakfast as usual, but surely there hadn't been anything to indicate she was really ill?

Lois kept up a flow of comforting inconsequential chatter. Claudia let it wash over her, breaking in at one point to ask, almost in a whisper

"If it *is* meningitis...what...what" she couldn't quite formulate the question.

"If they think it is likely to be meningitis they will start her on a high dose of antibiotics immediately, and they will do a lumbar puncture to get a proper diagnosis. But don't panic. Chances are, it isn't. And if it is, they'll whack the antibiotics into her and she'll be fine."

Claudia nodded, mutely. When they arrived at the hospital she was beyond thankful that Lois had been with her when she took the call. Layers of bureaucracy melted away in seconds, and Claudia found herself in a small cubicle where Juliet lay on the bed, eyes half closed, cheeks hectically flushed. She crouched down so that she was level with her, and kissed the hot little cheek.

Juliet's eyes flickered open.

"Mama." She murmured, and her eyes closed again.

Claudia felt hot tears well up behind her eyelids and fought them. She needed to keep calm, for Juliet. The first thing to do was to find out what was happening. She psyched herself up to go into professional lawyer mode, calm, confident and assertive – knowing she would get far more information this way than in her current 'hysterical mum' setting. Then she realised Lois was already talking to a young doctor in a white coat.

She heard snatches of the conversation:

"My goddaughter…rash…blood test…lumbar puncture" and decided to leave Lois to it for now, and concentrate on Juliet.

She pulled a chair to the side of the bed and sat down, taking Juliet's hot little hand in her icy cold one. She had been relieved when Juliet spoke, and recognised her – all the way in the taxi she had been imagining her to be unconscious or totally delirious. But she looked so poorly, and so heartrendingly tiny and vulnerable. She concentrated every atom of her consciousness on willing her daughter to get well, fancying sheer determination and the strength of her love could vanquish the disease.

She wasn't sure how long she'd been there, but her muscles were beginning to stiffen, when Lois tapped her softly on the shoulder.

"Right. The first thing is, the rash Juliet has definitely isn't the type associated with septicaemia, which is a good thing. It's probably some kind of viral rash, or a heat rash caused by her high temperature. But because she seems quite poorly and does have a very high temperature they have done some blood tests, and are going to do a lumbar puncture test, to rule out meningitis. I've arranged for her to be admitted to the paediatric ward – to a private room in case she is infectious. She'll be more comfortable there."

Claudia nodded, still clutching Juliet's hand. Within moments a porter was there, and the trolley Juliet was on was being manoeuvred. Lois bent down to speak to Juliet.

"Hey you!"

The eyes flickered open again.

"Auntie Lo!"

"What have you been up to, Missy?"

"My head hurts, Auntie Lo. So much. And I feel funny."

"Don't worry, sweetheart. You're in my hospital,

and we're going to look after you. You're going to have a ride up to a special little room, and then my friend Dr Dan is going to work out what's making you poorly so we can give you the right medicine to make you better."

"Can Mummy come?"

"Yes, of course she can."

So Claudia found herself jogging along next to the trolley, feeling like an extra in Holby City, until they got to a cheerfully decorated paediatric side room.

The lumbar puncture was hideous. Juliet had local anaesthetic cream rubbed on her back, and a young nurse held her in position while the doctor stuck an unfeasibly large needle into her back. Claudia clutched her hand, feeling desperately nauseous, but forcing herself to murmur comforting phrases and not black out.

Then it was over, and Lois was introducing her to the doctor. Incredibly tall, with thick blond hair, blue eyes and the shoulders of a prop-forward, at any normal time Claudia would have been extremely appreciative of his physique – now she was more interested in his clinical skills, and more appreciative of the kindness in his eyes and the warmth of his smile.

He somehow created an instant rapport with Juliet; nauseous, feverish and drugged as she now was, he still managed to raise a watery smile as he joked with her about the bizarre ingredients he claimed went into hospital food.

Then he turned to Claudia

"OK, Claudia – we've done the blood tests, we've done the lumbar puncture, and now it's just a waiting game until we get the results back from the lab. Juliet has had a shot of very strong antibiotics in case we are dealing with meningitis, and we've given her something to bring her temperature down and make her a little more comfortable. I'm also going to get the nurse to put a drip in so that we can get some fluids into her – she was quite sick earlier I believe, and I suspect she's a little dehydrated, which won't help anything. Otherwise, she'll probably be quite drowsy, so it's best to let her sleep – that will do her most good, whatever turns out to be wrong with her. Do you have any questions?"

Claudia shook her head. The only questions which sprang to mind – will she be ok? can you make her better? will she die? – she knew only too well weren't answerable.

Then he was gone, and Lois also vanished to get coffees for them both, and Claudia was alone with her little girl. She was sleeping peacefully now, and looked a little less flushed. Claudia sat, stroking her hand, crying, and making bargains with God.

If you let Juliet be ok I will never shout at her again. I'll reduce my hours so I can take her to school more, like she always wants me to. I'll sort proper childcare with someone she really likes. I'll take her to the hideous leisure pool with waves that she loves so much but that stinks of stale pee and worse. I won't complain when she watches *Frozen II* for the 1001st time, and joins in tunelessly and slightly out of time with every song.

In this situation everything which had seemed so complicated was suddenly simple. Juliet was the most important thing in her life, and everything else had to fit round that. Work was the next in line – it defined who she was, it set her daughter an example of what women could achieve, and it provided them with the financial security she craved. Ethan, actually, wasn't important. She was only missing him functionally, not as a person, so probably he had been right to leave. Life was too short to spend with someone you didn't really care about, and at least he had been brave enough to admit that. And although she still deplored the way he had chosen to do it, it no longer seemed worthy of so much of her emotional energy to stay angry with him.

Of course, she would have to tell him Juliet was in hospital. But there didn't seem much point until the test results were through, and she knew what she was telling him. And, anyway, there was no way she was leaving Juliet's bedside right now.

She didn't know quite how much time passed, but after the peaceful stillness of the room with just her and Juliet, suddenly it was full of people again. Lois was back, there was a nurse checking Juliet's temperature and pulse, which of course woke her up.

"Hi Mummy! Ouch, why have I got this thing in my hand? It hurts!"

She tugged at the canula which had the drip attached to it. Claudia moved to stop her, but then Dr Dan materialised from nowhere.

"Does it hurt, Juliet? Poor you. We can take it out soon. Do you know what it's there for?"

Juliet shook her head.

"Well, you see that bag up there? That's got special water in it. And instead of you drinking the water, it's going into your body through your veins – they're the tubes that normally carry your blood round your body for you."

"But why?" Juliet was all wide-eyed fascination now, and had stopped clawing at her hand.

"Because your tummy was a bit poorly earlier. Do you remember you were sick? Well, we wanted to give your tummy a rest, but we didn't want you to feel thirsty, so we're giving you a special drink through this tube so your tummy doesn't have to do any work. Now, as soon as all that water has gone out of the bag, Nurse Kaya can take the tube out for you. So, can you watch it for me, and let me know as soon as it's all gone? Auntie Lois will stay with you, and I'm just going to take Mummy and have a quick chat with her, ok?" Juliet nodded happily, her gaze fixed on the drip-stand.

Lois took Claudia's seat, and Claudia followed Daniel out of the room bathed in icy sweat with churning stomach and thumping heart.

He smiled down at her.

"It's OK! Don't look so nervous! Juliet is going to be

fine! It isn't meningitis. All her results were completely clear. And you can see for yourself, she's looking better already."

Claudia felt light-headed with relief, and swayed slightly. Daniel, at least a foot taller than her, put steadying hands on her shoulders.

"Hey, careful! Don't want you in hospital as Juliet comes out!"

Claudia smiled faintly.

"Can I take her home, then? And what *is* wrong with her?"

He shrugged.

"This doesn't do my professional reputation much good to admit, but I honestly don't know. It's that glorious catch-all term 'a virus'. Has she been around anyone who's been unwell recently?"

Illumination struck Claudia. Of course.

"Yes! My friend Hasina has been looking after her this week, and her baby Jasmine has been sick. And Juliet loves Jasmine, she's always cuddling her and playing with her. I think Hasina said that was a virus."

Daniel nodded.

"There you go then. Some children, especially little ones like Juliet still is, can have a really nasty reaction to viruses. Her temperature shot up as her body tried to fight it, and that made her sick, and gave her the heat rash which worried her teachers. They did the right thing, by the way. It's much better safe than sorry, and it is hard to rule meningitis out without the tests we've done. But the good thing about small children is that they're incredibly resilient. They go off quickly, but bounce back too. Juliet is going to be fine. She needs a restful weekend, lots of fluids – don't worry too much about food if she doesn't want it. Calpol for achiness and to keep her temperature down. And probably a few days off school next week because she'll feel fairly washed out, I should think. But we don't need to keep her in hospital, she'll be far happier in her own bed."

Impulsively Claudia reached up and hugged him.

"Thank you! Thank you *so* much. You've been amazing."

He smiled back at her.

"All part of the job! And Juliet is delightful. Right, that drip should have finished by now, so let's get that sorted, and then you can take her home."

7

Dominic and Lydia didn't really go out much together. In fact, since their relationship had shifted from friends to couple, they didn't go out much at all. Going out meant you might see other people, and that instantly complicated things, because they had both known that they weren't ready to share this relationship anyone else just yet. It was too new, too important, and the way in which their lives were already so interwoven meant that there was no room for mistakes. So they had become more insular, wrapped up in each other, and their own little world which was entirely magical, partly because it was totally private.

Normally this meant Friday nights at home together with a box-set on Netflix. Sometimes Lydia would cook for them, or they might get a takeaway. They would snuggle up on the sofa together, share a bottle or two of wine, chat about what they were watching, and then eventually go to bed together, content in the knowledge they had two blissfully uninterrupted days to look forward to.

This Friday was different. It was only a couple of weeks since they had told Daniel their delightful secret and he had dropped his bombshell, and that intrusion of the outside world they had both been trying to avoid had already caused seismic shocks.

Lydia was been worried. Dominic had been behaving so oddly– drinking heavily, and seeming quiet and withdrawn. Sometimes he seemed to be keeping her at a distance physically and emotionally, but then at other times had clung to her with almost feverish intensity.

Lydia didn't work Friday afternoons, and so had spent the time acting the ideal housewife – a role which still felt so much like playing house had done when she was younger that she quite relished it.

She had tidied the flat, put clean sheets on their bed, made a complicated Moroccan style lamb and apricot tagine, which was all ready to warm through, and had taken a long luxurious bath, smoothing scented body lotion all over, before pulling on yoga pants and a hoodie. Then she had lit a delicious Lime, Basil and Mandarin scented candle, a birthday present from her best friend, and settled down with a book to wait for Dominic's arrival home, determined that this would be the evening she got things back on an even keel for them both.

Only it didn't quite work out like that.

Dominic had been an hour later than she expected him, and arrived stinking of alcohol with a face like thunder.

Determined not to nag, Lydia kissed him and massaged his shoulders.

"Tough day, sweetheart?"

He moved so that her kiss landed on his cheek not his lips, and as she pressed herself close to him, burrowing her hands up under his shirt to run them over his strongly muscled back, he pulled away.

"No, Lyddy. We need to talk. I've got something I need to tell you."

He glanced in the direction of the fridge.

"Do you want a glass of wine?"

Lydia nodded. She didn't want to encourage him to drink even more, but she had a feeling she might need a glass herself this evening.

He poured them both a large glass of white wine, and then sat down on the sofa, opposite Lydia who had curled up in the battered leather arm chair, pulling one of their many crocheted blankets over her knees as the serious expression on Dominic's face made her feel suddenly shivery.

Dominic took a gulp of wine, and then blurted out.

"I had a drink with Daniel last night."

Whatever Lydia had expected, it certainly hadn't been that. She thought there had been an unspoken agreement between them that they would give Daniel a wide berth for a while. Lydia had emphatically not wanted Daniel nagging on about the ridiculous photo, and despite herself she was more than a little worried about the influence Daniel might have over Dominic. Although she told herself one hundred times a day that one old snapshot was no kind of evidence, she was also entertaining fantasies of how they could escape and leave behind them any chance that something – or someone – was going to try and split them up.

Lydia had spent a few years in Sydney, Australia when she was younger, and had loved it. The culture, the food, the people, the chilled pace of life, the beaches, sunshine and al fresco lifestyle all seemed to suit her in a way that rainy, uptight, frenetic London never had, and the thought of vanishing off there now, far away from Daniel and Dominic's parents, and anyone else who was going to try and make life difficult was very seductive.

"Oh? How's Daniel?"

She fought to keep he tone cool and neutral.

"Not great. We had a row."

"Oh?"

"Yes. About us. You and me."

Lydia flushed angrily.

"I knew it! I knew we should avoid him for a while! Why has he got such a problem with us being together? I think he's just jealous that he's not the person you're closest too any more."

Dom shook his head.

"No, it's not that, Lyds. Daniel isn't like that, you know he isn't. He's really upset that he's thrown a cat among the pigeons for us, but he's too bloody ethical to keep quiet if he really thinks there's a problem."

Lydia harrumphed irritably.

"We argued because he was horrified that I am still sleeping with you. And I was so angry. But do you know what? I was angry because deep down I know he's right. I haven't been happy the last couple of weeks – not because I don't love you, because I really, really do – but because I just don't feel comfortable with this situation."

"What situation? We have no evidence there is any 'situation' except in Daniel's over-active imagination! There has never been the smallest hint from your parents that you and I are siblings! It's ridiculous."

"Look, Lyddy. Hopefully it is nonsense. God knows, I don't in any way feel like you are my sister! But I think Dan's right. Until we have confirmed that there isn't a problem, we should put our physical relationship on temporary hold. And once, hopefully, we have cleared it all up, then we can start afresh."

He gestured round their cosy little room, their cosy little world.

"When I'm here with you, it's all I want. All I can ever imagine wanting. You are incredible, and I love you *so* much. But at the moment, when we're not together, I panic, because I know – and you know deep down – that it's not enough. We're not kids, and we're not extras in *Wuthering Heights*. We can't really exist in a bubble apart from the whole world trying to pretend we didn't see that photo, and that we're not worried about it. That's why I've been drinking so much. To try and stop my constant obsessing on that dilemma. And I just need us to have a break, and find out what the hell is going on."

Lydia let out a long breath she hadn't been aware

she'd been holding.

She knew, obviously, that Dominic wasn't truly happy this last couple of weeks, that he was drinking far too much. But she had worried it was because he didn't love her as much as she loved him, that he was going off her and she had been desperately scared to really confront him in case he broke things off between them. And now he had. It was different for her. Although she knew the circumstances weren't ideal, she had never felt happier or more secure than she did in Dominic's arms, and she was more than prepared to turn a blind eye to what Dan's suggestion might mean, because knowing the truth might mean losing Dominic. But now he was saying that *not* knowing the truth would mean losing him too.

Her thoughts returned once again to her childhood. She always joked that the boys were the favourites, literally the golden boys who could do no wrong, they laughed over her Cuckoo nickname, but the jokes hid a sadness, and an anger, that she'd never really expressed even to the twins.

She remembered Sunday afternoons when she would beg Henry and Delia not to send her back to school, to let her go to day school with the twins. It wasn't that she hated school particularly; living with her friends was actually quite fun. It was just that constant feeling of not belonging. She couldn't belong with her own family, because they were dead, and it felt as though everything Henry and Delia did was designed to underline that she didn't belong in their family either.

"You are incredibly lucky to have this opportunity!" Delia had shouted at her. "Glenton Hall is a top-rated school, and you get to go there because your parents left money for you to get a decent education. You should pay them back by working hard and making the most of it, not crying like a baby to not go."

"I don't want them to have left me money to go to private school! I just want them not to be dead. I want a family of my own!"

Delia's face had softened a bit, and she had held out her arms in a reconciliatory gesture which Lydia had stubbornly ignored.

"I know that Lydia, and obviously I wish they hadn't died too. But you are still very lucky to be able to go to Glenton Hall, and you should make the most of it, and be grateful. And of course you have a home with us in the holidays."

Somehow Delia's reassurances had always left her feeling more unwanted and out of place than ever.

Travelling had been an attempt to find her own place in the world, independent of Nicholls charity, and in Australia she thought for a while maybe she had found it. But underneath she had still felt rootless, and had missed Daniel and Dominic and her other friends in the UK.

When had she realised she felt differently about the two Nicholls boys? On some level it seemed like she always had, but it was only two years ago, when she returned to England permanently after her travels, that she had acknowledged to herself that the jolt of pure lust which shot through her when Dominic kissed her cheek, the feverish excitement which consumed her before she saw him, the desperation to be first in his attention and esteem was not remotely friendly or platonic. When Dom had bought his flat, at roughly the same time that the landlord of the flat she shared with a couple of friends had served them with an eviction notice she had been possessed of a frenzied hope that he would ask her to live with him, and when he did she had been thrilled and terrified in equal measure. She knew it was insanity – tortured herself by imagining how awful it would be to hear him in bed with a girlfriend, to be so close to him yet unable to be as close as she wanted, but she still couldn't resist.

And it hadn't turned out like that. She'd only been living there a few days when she realised that the air between them was crackling with sexual tension, and it wasn't all coming from her. She had had enough men fancy her to be able to spot the signs, and they were all there. A few days later they had slept together for the first time, and it was everything the tension had promised and more besides. Sex had never really worked for her before, she had never been able to lose herself in the moment, always anxious about how she looked or smelt or felt, whether she was doing it right. With Dominic, in and out of bed, she was utterly unselfconscious and able to live totally in the moment. This was what convinced her that, whatever law and moral code might say, their relationship was not wrong, but it didn't look like she was going to be able to convince Dominic of that.

She gazed lovingly at his anxious face. She was angry that, after all that he'd said, he had talked to Daniel and listened to him rather than her. And she was desperately worried what the outcome of all this was going to be. But she was relieved that he had at least got it off his chest, and been honest with her.

"So what do you want me to do, then? Move out?"

He shook his head, vehemently.

"No! Of course not. I'll move into the spare room tonight, and then you just have to talk to my parents and hopefully we'll figure out what's going on. It will be fine."

"If you really think that, then why do you want us to break up until we find out? It doesn't make sense."

"No, I know. But I just feel so uncomfortable with even the vaguest possibility that I'm having sex with my sister. I just think it's best that we go back to being friends until we know for sure."

She glared at him.

"You mean *Daniel* thinks that! Because if I recall, that was not what you were saying or doing or thinking on Wednesday night before Dan went and stuck his oar in – again! I don't seem to get any say in this at all, just have to be a good little girl and do what

I'm told! You and Dan may or may not be related to me, but you're certainly acting like a pair of big brothers! Fine. Move into the spare room if you like. Your loss! But don't expect that the prospect of having sex with you again is so enticing that I'm prepared to go and have a hideously humiliating conversation with your parents to find out if I'm, what, 'suitable' for you. There's food in the fridge you can heat up. I seem to have lost my appetite. The spare room is made up. I'm going to bed."

8

Lois opened Claudia's huge fridge, and started to sift through for ingredients. Eggs, cheese, mushrooms. A bag of salad leaves. Excellent; her cooking skills were limited, but she could manage an omelette and tipping some salad into a bowl. It was turned 9pm, and so neither of them wanted a heavy meal anyway, but it was a long time since their largely uneaten sea bass at lunchtime, and she knew she was hungry, and felt that Claudia could do with something to eat after her horrific afternoon. Poor Claudia. What a time she was having– her husband walking out, a full-time job, a small daughter and no childcare, and then her child being taken frighteningly ill.

Lois hoped she had thought of a solution to at least some of Claudia's problems, but seeing first hand what her friend was going through had also helped her make a decision about her own life. She still wanted a child as desperately as ever, but could equally see that single parenthood was a challenge she wasn't sure she could cope with. Perhaps she was crazy, but she was going to opt for Plan B.

Claudia came into the kitchen as Lois was whisking eggs. She carefully set a baby monitor down on the table, and then flopped onto the sofa.

"She's fast asleep! It was such a good idea of yours to root out the old baby monitor so I know I'll definitely hear her if she wakes up. And I've made the sofa-bed in her room up so I can keep an eye on her tonight as well. Thank you so much again for offering to stay over. To be honest, I do feel like a bit of limp rag now, and it makes me feel so much better that I'm going to have a paediatrician in the house – just in case!"

Lois smiled at her friend.

"I'm not surprised you're exhausted. What an afternoon, hey? But she's going to be fine now, Claudia. She really is."

Claudia nodded.

"I know. She was so much better already. She drank all that diluted apple juice, and she was quite chatty for a bit."

"She'll be up and down for a few days, maybe. I don't think school next week is probably a good idea."

Claudia shook her head.

"No, I know. I've already phoned work and told them what happened. They were actually really supportive, and I've arranged to have next week off. I can look after Juliet, and try and get some proper childcare sorted out too. Although goodness knows what I'll be able to manage at a week's notice! I'll have to phone my parents tomorrow and hope that they will be able to provide some back up for a little while. The problem is, they'd have to move in here – they'd have to get up at the crack of dawn to be here in time to do the school run, and they have such a busy social life! I just don't know if they'll be willing to put French class, and bridge club, and yoga, and the allotment and all the rest of it on hold to come and bail me out."

Lois carefully lowered a perfect golden omelette onto a plate, halved it and transferred one half to another plate, before topping it with sautéed mushrooms. She placed the plates on the table.

"Come and have something to eat, and I'll tell you my idea. Do you remember, a million years ago, at lunchtime, I told you I thought I might have a solution?"

Claudia dragged her aching bones across to the table.

"To be honest, no. This afternoon has wiped everything out. God, Lois, I don't know how parents of children who are really sick cope, I really don't."

Lois nodded sombrely.

"I know. It's heartbreaking to watch. Most of them are unbelievably strong, but looking after that child becomes their world – relationships, jobs, even other children go to the wall sometimes. Anyway. Let's not talk about that now. Juliet is fine, and that's all you need to think about today."

"Hmm, yes. That, and who the hell is going to look after her. When I thought she had meningitis I promised myself that if she was ok I would sort something out properly – reduce my hours, get a proper nanny, make her life work properly. And I will, but it's a challenge!"

Lois nodded.

"It is, but as I keep saying, I do have an idea. Shall I tell you now, or are you too tired?"

"God, no, tell me!"

"Well, you know Dr Dan, who you met today?"

Claudia nodded enthusiastically.

"He's lovely! And totally lush too. I bet the nurses can't keep their hands off him!"

Lois' eyes twinkled

"And some of the mums too! He certainly has a following. But anyway. I have been trying to persuade him to take a sabbatical. He is a lovely man, and a brilliant doctor, but the recent cuts and so on mean that he has been working ridiculous hours, and he isn't great at emotional detachment, so I think he is perilously close to total burn-out. But, of course, if he has a break from doctoring, he'll still need an income and a place to live…"

Claudia's eyes widened.

'You don't mean…"

Lois nodded.

"Yes. I think it could be perfect. His brother lives locally to you I think, so he'd be able to see more of his family. You've seen for yourself how lovely he is with children. And he used to work as an au pair during the university holidays to earn some money, so he's got lots of childcare experience. And obviously has had all the police checks and everything because he works as a doctor! And I would personally vouch for him anyway – he's one of the nicest, most genuine, most caring people I have ever come across."

Claudia's eyes were shining.

"Wow! Lois! That would be so perfect. I mean, a bloody paediatric doctor looking after Juliet! You can't get safer hands than that! And she really took to him, I could tell. But does he truly want to work as an au pair when he's a qualified doctor?"

Lois shrugged.

"Well, I can't promise anything without talking to him, obviously. But from our conversation yesterday, I think this might be exactly what he wants. It might only be for a few months, because as you say, he most likely won't want to be a nanny forever, but it would give you a workable solution right now, and the chance to investigate other options in a relaxed way. And your parents can continue their pilates uninterrupted! Now I know that you're up for it I'll have another chat with him and let you know as soon as I can."

***

For pretty much the first time since Janey's death, Lois opened her front door and survived Horatio's welcoming assault feeling positive and optimistic. Everything about her home had caused her pain for the last couple of years because it was so deeply imbued with memories of Janey, and their shared life, and because they had served as bitter reminders that she could never be that happy again. If she was 'lucky' she had at least as long to live again as she had already had, and that seemed like four decades to endure rather than enjoy.

Today a slow smile spread across her face as Horatio writhed ecstatically round her legs and she bent to caress his soft head. She searched for a metaphor to express her feelings. Was it as though she'd been living in black and white and the colour had returned? Maybe a little. No, it was more as though she had been looking at life through a very dirty double-glazed window. Everything had been dreary and muted, but now she had cleaned the window and thrown it open, and was amazed at the difference it made to see the sparkling sunshine and hear the birdsong.

Hmm. Looking round, Lois began to wonder if her analogy was so metaphorical after all. She employed a cleaner for a few hours a week, but since Janey became ill, nearly four years ago, she had done nothing else with the house, and it was starting to look distinctly shabby and uncared for. Flooded with sudden energy Lois decided that it was time for a spring-clean.

Humming to herself, she continued to make a fuss of Horatio with one hand, and jot down a task list with the other.

- Clean windows
- Clean rugs

- Plant window-boxes
- New bed-linen?
- Paint bedroom?

She hadn't really been able to listen to music since Lois' death, finding it just too evocative and poignant, but she down-loaded a selection of that week's Woman's Hours to her phone, and started to hunt out cleaning products. Horatio glared at her. This activity, he recognised, meant that Lois was not going to light the fire, settle herself on the sofa and put her lap at his disposal, which was how he had planned to spend the afternoon. Lois caught sight of his face as she looked up from the cupboard under the sink and laughed out loud at his obvious disgust.

"I'm sorry, Horatio! But I don't feel like sitting still today. For once I'm not exhausted, and I want to make the most of it. I'm tired of being unhappy, and I'm going to change things."

He miaowed loudly and disapprovingly. She gave his ears a consolatory tickle, and then tipped some of his favourite Whiskas prawn chunks in jelly into his bowl. He glared again, recognising a bribe when he saw one, but was unable to resist the fishy lure. Lois laughed again, grabbed her car-keys from the dresser, and headed off to Homebase.

A couple of hours later, flushed with the triumph of successful retail therapy, and with cramming several hundred pounds worth of purchases into her little car, she reflected on the day's achievements so far.

After checking that Juliet was continuing to make a good recovery, she had popped into the hospital first thing, knowing that Daniel was working an early shift, and wanting to catch him as soon as possible to talk about Claudia and Juliet.

"Wow! God, Lois, thank you so much!" he'd hugged her briefly. "You are such a star, and I'm incredibly grateful."

She smiled.

"So, I can tell Claudia it's a yes, then?"

Daniel nodded vigorously.

"Damn right! You're a bloody genius! It's just what I need. And she lives in Walthamstow as well, which is where my brother lives, and one of the things I have been thinking is that I need to spend some more time with him. I think I do need a change for a bit."

"I know that! That's what I have been trying to tell you. You are a very, very good doctor, but you need to cultivate a little bit more professional detachment. You get so involved, every time, and it is draining you."

Daniel looked down.

"I know. But it's so hard. Some of the people we come across are so desperate, and it just makes me want to do anything I can to help. And if I can't..."

His voice trailed off, miserably.

Lois patted his shoulder.

"It's not easy. I don't always manage it myself. And you shouldn't stop caring - when you stop caring, that's the time to end your career in medicine. But you have to set boundaries. You *are* responsible for doing your job as well as you can, and you do that. You're *not* responsible for other people's happiness."

So that was the first achievement of the day - she had solved Claudia's childcare problem, and given the space for Daniel to sort himself out. She'd fired off a few emails to the powers that be regarding Daniel's sabbatical, and no doubt there would be a few repercussions to deal with over the next week or two, but nothing she wouldn't be able to handle.

After leaving the hospital she had decided to go to a cafe before going home as she felt her next job might be better carried out in a neutral environment. Having come straight from Claudia's she didn't have her laptop with her, but after a few false starts she had scribbled out what she wanted in her little notebook, and would type it up later. She was pleased with what she had eventually written:

WANTED: Male partner for a thoroughly modern marriage. Single woman (38) wants a baby, and a father for that baby. No romance, and the only passion will be in your commitment to joint parenting. If you are male, single, solvent, caring and want to be part of a non-traditional but loving family, please get in touch.

Later, after some window-cleaning and a little light gardening, she would post this advert on Fertility Friends, the main website for people who, for whatever reason, were looking to conceive a baby through IVF using donor eggs and/or sperm. She knew that most of her friends would think she was totally mad - after all, she could easily obtain anonymous donor sperm and do the whole thing by herself, but every instinct told her that this was the right way forward for her, and the surge of energy and optimism she had experienced since making the decision seemed to confirm it. She wanted a baby, very much, but she wanted that baby to have more family than she alone could provide it with. She didn't want a new relationship, couldn't ever imagine wanting one, but she did want a partner for this big adventure on which she was about to embark.

9

Daniel put his suitcase down on the floor, and his big hold-all on the end of the bed, and looked round his new room appreciatively. It was a loft-conversion - a large, modern-feeling room, flooded with light from the Velux windows. The floor-boards were blond wood, the paint-work gleaming white, and the walls as soft grey. A colourful rug with a vibrant geometric pattern, and a turquoise blanket thrown over the end of the bed with its crisp white linen, saved the room from sterility. There was a small desk on which he could set up his laptop, one wall was discreet fitted wardrobes, whilst the space under the windows had been filled with fitted bookshelves. Tucked into opposite corner was a comfortable looking arm chair. Next door was a small en-suite with a luxurious power-shower.

Claudia looked anxiously up at him, reminding herself what a great idea this was. It had all seemed so simple in principle, but now push had come to shove and she was helping a handsome young man she barely knew move into her spare room, she was assailed by qualms of doubt. He was so big, for a start! One of the things she had loved about the loft conversion was that it didn't feel as poky as some she had seen, and the ceilings felt a respectable height.

But what seemed a respectable height to her at 5 foot 3, or even Ethan at 5 foot 9, didn't seem quite so generous when Daniel's fair hair was pretty much skimming the ceiling. And she had found herself wondering if his shoulders would actually fit though the door. Was this going to work? Would she be constantly nervous and at edge in her own home, unable to fully relax, continually worried about his comfort and what he was thinking of her? Then he turned to her, and her anxieties seemed to melt away in the warmth of his smile.

"Wow, Claudia! What a lovely room. Absolutely perfect. Thank you so much."

She let out a deep breath and returned his smile.

"I'm so glad you like it! I hope you don't feel too cramped. Let me know if you need any more space. Or any more furniture. I wasn't sure what you'd want, so I kept it simple. I did clear those bookcases so you've got some room. But it's not huge, obviously. But you haven't brought much stuff..." her glance fell on the two pieces of luggage.

Just stop babbling, Claudia, she admonished herself.

Daniel laughed easily, seeming totally relaxed and at home already.

"No, I've got my clothes and bits here, and then a few books and my computer and so on in these two boxes downstairs. I've put a couple of boxes into storage, but really I haven't got much. I've always lived in furnished flats, and I've never seemed to accumulate much stuff."

"That's probably a good thing. I seem to have masses of crap. I should probably sort it out, but there never seems to be time."

Shut up, shut up, shut up, repeated her internal voice. She was deeply relieved when Juliet shot like a whirlwind into the room. She was perhaps a little paler than usual, and had lost a couple of pounds, but her energy levels were totally back to normal, and there was no real sign that it was only a week since Claudia had feared she was fighting for her life.

She had none of her mother's reservations, and had been talking nonstop about 'Dr Dan' coming to live with them. Given that she'd only met him on one occasion, for no more than a few hours, and had been barely conscious at the time, he seemed to have made a very big impression.

"Hi Juliet. How are you feeling now?"

She flashed him her mega-watt smile.

"I'm fine! I didn't go to school all last week, and Mummy was at home *every day*! And at first I was really tired and we just cuddled on the sofa and had stories and watched Cbeebies, but then I felt better, but Mummy said I didn't have to go back to school 'til Monday, and we went to the Science Museum and the Museum of Childhood and I had ice-cream in the park."

She paused for breath, then demanded.

"Have you been to the Science Museum?"

"Yes, I have, but not for years. I used go with my

brother and sister when I was at school."

Juliet nodded in satisfaction.

"I thought you must have done, cos you're a doctor, and Mummy said doctors know all about science. Can we go again, together?"

Daniel nodded gravely.

"I should think so, yes. Do you do science in school, Juliet?"

She nodded

"Yes! We put white flowers in jam jars, and made the water different colours with special colour stuff, and then the flowers changed colour too cos they drank the water!"

She frowned.

"But I still don't really understand it, because I don't change colour when I drink different coloured things."

Claudia had been shifting from one foot to the other, on one hand delighted that Juliet seemed to have taken to Daniel so strongly, and he seemed so relaxed with her, but also feeling a little out of place, and almost jealous of her daughter's unselfconsciousness. Daniel was delightful - polite, friendly, charming - but for some reason she couldn't fathom he made her feel slightly on edge.

"Come on, Juliet. We need to leave Dr Dan to sort himself out and unpack. You come with mummy."

Her lip came out in an ominous pout, and Claudia braced herself for a strop, but Daniel stepped in.

"Actually, Claudia, would you mind if Juliet

helped me? It doesn't matter if she's busy, but if she isn't I could do with some help to unpack all my things and put my books away. I just need to go and collect those boxes from the downstairs landing first."

Juliet's face had lit up again, and Claudia smiled. Maybe this was going to work out.

"Yes, I'm sure Juliet wouldn't mind helping you! And then how about we go and celebrate your first night here with a meal out? There's a new Lebanese place just opened round the corner, and if there is one thing Juliet can eat her bodyweight in, it's houmous and flatbreads!"

Juliet jumped up and down in excitement, squealing with joy, and Daniel smiled agreement.

"That would be fun. Just while I think of it, Claudia, do you need me tomorrow, or can I make plans to see my brother?"

"No, of course you're free tomorrow. That's absolutely fine. Weekends will normally be free for you - although I suppose I might ask you to babysit in the unlikely event I ever want to go out on a Saturday night! But that would be over and above. Monday is your first proper day, and I've arranged to go into work late so that I can come to school with you and Juliet, and introduce you to her teacher and so on. Right, I will leave you two to unpack, and go and have a nice relaxing bath, if that's ok?"

Her new nanny and her daughter both nodded, and then Juliet took Daniel's hand and dragged him off downstairs to fetch his boxes as though she'd known him all her life.

***

Lydia ooched uncomfortably in bed, trying to find a cool spot of sheet, missing the reassuring bulk of Dominic beside her. The luminous green numerals on the alarm clock winked mockingly at her, reminding her that she would have to get up for work in five hours time, and hadn't yet managed to get any sleep.

It wasn't the first night she had lain awake, brain spinning, unable to calm down, switch off and let sleep overtake her. Inevitably this left her tired and irritable during the day. Dominic seemed to be coping much better with the situation. They had made an uneasy peace after Lydia's outburst a few evenings ago, but there was an inevitable awkwardness between them. He was spending a lot of time out of the flat - with Daniel, she suspected. And he'd started running again, taking advantage of the longer spring evenings to go for a ten mile run, sometimes on his own, sometimes with Dan. In a horrible way Lydia was aware that she was starting to feel jealous of Daniel. Jealous of his influence over Dominic. Jealous of the time they spent together. And with a niggling, paranoid anxiety that Daniel was somehow persuading Dominic away from her permanently.

As far as Dominic was concerned, the ball was in her court. As soon as she was ready she could talk to his parents, or ask him to. But the decision of how, or whether, to do that, was one of the main reasons she was habitually awake at 3am. Over twenty years of toxic interactions with Delia were now suddenly a deadly precursor to this enormous decision on whether she and Dominic could be happy together or not. And how could she possibly bring it up?

"Oh, by the way, Henry – are you my Dad?"

"Hi Delia, how are you? Am I the result of Henry cheating on you 30 years ago?"

It just didn't seem possible. And then what reason could she give for her sudden determination to find out about her parentage after all these years? The last thing she wanted to do was let them know about her and Dominic – if there even was a 'her and Dominic' any more. It was bad enough having Daniel trying to keep them apart; at least he liked her, and it was only this stupid photo that was bothering her. Delia would have a pink fit at the thought of her precious son ending up with a woman she saw as a complete waste of space. A recent phone conversation with Delia ran through her mind.

"How are things, dear? Any news on getting a proper job? And did you look into that gym membership offer I sent you? Might be nice to get in shape for summer, mightn't it? If it's the cost that's bothering you I'm sure Henry and I could help out."

She of course had been instantly defensive.

"I've *got* a job, Delia! It might not be permanent, but it suits me just fine. And I don't want to join the gym! I'm happy the way I am."

"We just worry about you, Lydia. It's important to be healthy, you know. And wouldn't you like to have a worthwhile career, like the twins? You could always go to university as a mature student, you know."

Lydia gritted her teeth. As so often during conversations with her Delia, she was reminded of the old joke about the fond but sexist mother at her daughter's inauguration as President of the USA.

Clutching the sleeve of the guest next to her, and pointing at the podium, Sexist Mom stage whispered

"See that girl up there? Well, her brother's a *doctor*, you know."

The twins may not be her brothers (or, of course, maybe they were she remembered uneasily) but she had felt the unfavourable comparisons with them every day she could remember. She had learnt at a very early age that whatever she did, she would never live up to her the standard set by Daniel and Dominic, and so in many areas she had simply stopped trying.

"And the thing is, Lydia, Dominic can't go on supporting you forever, you know."

"Dominic *isn't* supporting me, Delia. I pay half the mortgage, as it happens"

"But you can't carry on living together long-term, dear. Sooner or later he'll get a girlfriend, and he won't want you around cramping his style, now will he?"

It had taken all Lydia's self control not to snap back "Actually, he already has a girlfriend. ME. And yes, thank you, we're blissfully happy together, and plan to be together for the rest of our lives."

Lying here now in the dead of night she wondered how Delia would have responded.

She thought longingly again of Australia. If only they could emigrate then all their problems would be at an end. If she could just be with Dominic, away from Daniel and his parents and everything else she could talk him out of his worries about this stupid photo. She'd tried to explain her feelings to Dominic, but he just couldn't, or wouldn't, get it. It was a very male trait, in her experience - if you couldn't immediately solve a problem, then just brush it under the carpet and pretend it isn't a problem at all.

Giving sleep up as a bad job she slid out of bed, pulled her Chinese kimono robe around her, and padded through to the living room. She switched on the reading lamp, and curled up on the sofa, pulling the crochet throw over her, and reaching for her iPhone as she did so.

Without realising it, her sleepless reflections had brought her to a decision. Dominic was wonderful. He was strong but gentle, caring, funny, gorgeous and he would lay down his life for her unquestioningly. But what he would never do was take a difficult decision. For him it would always be the path of least resistance. He had always been the same, from earliest childhood. She and Daniel were the activists, the ones who made things happen, and Dominic would always follow along in their wake, quite content to let them take the lead as long as he could participate and enjoy being with them. Daniel had persuaded Dominic into taking one definite step – moving into the spare room – but unless she took the next one they would remain in this limbo living in this flat, and loving one another from a distance, for another 40 or 50 years. She couldn't tolerate that, so it was up to her to initiate the change. And to do that she had to pull herself together and stop seeing Daniel as an enemy and treat him as an ally instead.

Unlike Dominic, he was prepared to talk around a problem, looking for a solution even if one wasn't immediately apparent. He was also receptive to emotional subtleties and nuance, and she had a feeling that he would understand her frustration at the prospect of a life lived in a state of permanent limbo, but also her apprehension, bordering on terror, at the prospect of talking to his parents.

She texted "Hi Dan, can we meet up one night this week. Need to talk to you asap. How are you? Love Lyddy x"

Then, suddenly overcome with sleepiness now that she had taken some constructive action, she snuggled down on the sofa and fell into a deep and dreamless sleep until a puzzled Dominic woke her the next morning.

10

Claudia sighed with contentment as she slung her bag over her shoulder and pulled the front door softly to behind her. She could not believe how easy her life had become in the few weeks since Daniel moved in, or just how stressed she had been for years without fully realising it.

Part of the change had come from her reduced working hours. The scare over Juliet's illness had given her the courage to approach her boss, and negotiate a late start on a Monday morning, and every Friday afternoon off. She'd always been terrified to have that conversation before, paranoid that she'd be seen as lazy or uncommitted, that it would be career suicide. It had been such a point of pride to demonstrate that she wouldn't let motherhood make any difference, that she had probably gone too far the other way. In fact, when she the time came it had all been effortless.

"Claudia, you must know that you're one of the most successful and effective members of the team. I'd be very surprised if your productivity decreased with a few hours out of the office - and I'm certainly not going to risk you leaving us in pursuit of a better work-life balance."

So now she could take Juliet into school every Monday, and pick her up every Friday for them to give Daniel the afternoon off and spend some mother-daughter time together. That might mean going to the pictures or to the park, but last week they had simply gone home, got very sticky making butterfly cakes and then spent a happy hour re-arranging the furniture in Juliet's dolls' house.

It wasn't just the extra time though. It was the freedom from living in an atmosphere of barely suppressed bitterness and resentment. The freedom from feeling that every moment she wasn't in the office had to be spent with Ethan and Juliet, leaving her absolutely no time for herself. She had previously even felt that she had to apologise for taking a shower at the weekend - forget any chance of a long relaxing bath - because Ethan's attitude was that he sacrificed himself all week, so the least she could do was pull her weight when she was at home.

Reluctantly she had to admit that Ethan might have had a point about her working hours - especially as she had now seen how easy it had been to change them. But he had never sat down and had a reasonable conversation with her about it, it was always just sarcastic little jibes here, hurt looks there, or passive aggressive comments about Juliet's disappointment that mummy hadn't been there for class assembly or nursery teddy bear's picnic or whatever. Although on the rare occasions Claudia did manage to attend something at school, she couldn't help noticing that none of the full-time working daddies were present at these events. And it wasn't as though Juliet was a latch-key kid - Ethan had been just as keen as she that she had a parent at home with her during the early years, and had totally agreed that it made sense for that parent to be him.

Now Claudia got to go to a pilates class on a Friday afternoon between finishing work and collecting Juliet from school, and went for a swim after dropping her off on Monday morning before she went into the office. Those little windows of time for herself made a huge difference, and enabled her to gear up to and then wind down from a weekend of full-on mummying.

And when she was at work she felt 110% confident that Juliet was happy and safe with Daniel. She adored him already, and he was a total gem. Any worries she had about him intruding in their lives had long gone. Some evenings they ate together after Juliet had gone to bed, and she found him excellent company - funny and interesting and, best of all, interested in *her* - not just as Claudia the lawyer, or Claudia the mother or Claudia the soon-to-be-ex-wife, but just as Claudia. They talked about books they'd both read and cities they'd both visited, or sometimes just sat in companionable silence and watched a film.

They had shared some deeper and more personal conversations too. He had opened up to her about just how much pressure he had felt under working at the hospital, and she had understood a little more clearly why this man who was clearly highly intelligent, educated and capable was taking a break from a well respected career to take on a job commonly associated with students trying to earn a few bucks. In return, she had found it surprisingly easy to talk to him about her failed marriage and her worries about the effect it might have on Juliet.

He was sensitive to her potential need for privacy as well, and several evenings a week would either prepare a simple meal to eat up in his room, or go out to see his siblings or other friends. However, on other evenings like this, he was happy to babysit and she could go out, by herself, in the evening, to meet up with a friend - something she couldn't really recall doing since Juliet was born, as the guilt trip Ethan would put her through simply wasn't worth it.

Now, though, it was a Friday night, and she had enjoyed a lovely afternoon with her daughter, then had a relaxing shower and got changed, and was off to meet Lois for dinner, safe in the knowledge that Daniel had everything under control at home. No wonder she had a spring in her step.

Lois let out an exclamation when she saw her

"Bloody hell, Claudia! Have you had Botox or something?"

Claudia laughed.

"Of course I haven't! You know how squeamish I am! Remember when the blood donation people came to college and I fainted? And I made Ethan take Juliet for all her vaccinations, even when I was still off on maternity leave, because I just couldn't stand it. Believe me, hell will freeze over before I volunteer for having needles stuck into my face."

Lois gazed at her searchingly.

"Well, what is it then? You look totally different."

Claudia shrugged.

"I have no idea! I've started doing Pilates - maybe it's that?"

Lois looked sceptical.

"Hmm, maybe. If that's what it does for you then I might have to try and overcome my complete lack of physical coordination and give it a go myself. I'm not convinced that's what it is, though. If I didn't know better, I'd say you were in love?"

She raised an interrogative eyebrow.

Claudia blushed faintly, but her reply was caustic.

"Nope. Not in love. In fact, the exact opposite. I am realising just how much happier I am being single than I was when I was married. Ethan has done me a huge favour."

There was a short pause whilst both women ordered drinks, and then Lois asked

"And how is Juliet coping? I take it she's alright in herself again now?"

Claudia nodded.

"Yes, she's fine. Eating like a horse, presumably to make up for lost time, and all her teddies have been carted off to imaginary hospital at some point now. And as for becoming the child of a broken home, well, that's a bit more complicated. She misses Ethan of course, but they Skype several times a week. The main problem is that every time anything goes wrong, or I say no to something, or try and make her do something she doesn't want I get "I HATE you, I want Daddy, Daddy wouldn't make me do that." Which, incidentally, isn't even true – Ethan was just as strict as I am, maybe even more so. But it's inevitable that she takes it out on me I guess. And at least it *is* me, and she isn't behaving like that with Daniel. Or, at least, he assures me she isn't. And she does love that I pick her up from school once a week now. I'm like Exhibit A in the playground as she announces "This is MY MUMMY" at the top of her voice. And she really has fallen hook, line and sinker for your Dr Dan."

Lois grinned.

"It seems to be mutual. I had a coffee with Dan the other day, and he was full of praise for her. And for you too, as it happens."

Lois looked searchingly at her friend, but Claudia's head was bent as she studied the menu, her face hidden behind a mass of blonde hair.

"What do you think? Shall I have the scallops to start, or asparagus? Scallops, I think. I love the way they do them here. And then lamb, maybe. What are you having?"

Lois looked thoughtful, but decided not to push it. They discussed the menu briefly, and then Claudia turned the conversation round to Lois.

"And how are things with you? Any news?"
Lois took a deep breath.
"Actually, yes. Quite exciting news, as it happens."
Claudia beamed.
"Have you met someone? Oh, Lois, that's amazing. I knew you would. How did you meet her, was it -"
Here, Lois managed to get a word in edgeways.
"No! I haven't met someone. Not like you mean, anyway. Why does everyone seem to find it so hard to understand that Janey was the love of my life, and I'm not going to replace her? It would be impossible even if I wanted to, which I don't."
Claudia looked shamefaced.
"Sorry, that was a bit insensitive. I do understand how you feel. But I guess I just don't like to think of you being on your own for the rest of your life."
Lois nodded.
"I know. I'm not too keen on the idea, either. So I've decided to do something about it. I want to try and have a baby."
Claudia was silent for a moment. She desperately wanted to be a supportive friend, and she desperately wanted Lois to find happiness after everything she'd been through. But, hand on heart, did she think that single motherhood was the best way to achieve that? She thought back to the early days of Juliet's life. The horror of those 3am scream-fests. The days when you couldn't even manage the time to shower or dress and spent the entire day slumped on the sofa in vomit-stained pyjamas. The

bleak cheeriness of mother-and-baby Rhyme Time where you frantically tried to fabricate conversation amongst women with whom you had nothing in common bar a baby of the same age, terrified that if you failed not only would you never again get to talk to an adult you weren't married to, but your child would also be irreparably socially stunted. Her maternity leave had been the hardest six months of her life, and that had been with a supportive partner. On her own, Claudia wasn't sure she would have survived it. So, how, in all honesty could she encourage her best friend to take that path?

On the other hand a montage of images crossed her mind. Juliet's tiny, pure white baby-gro clad body in the perspex hospital cot less than an hour after her birth. Her first smile, which in that moment was more than enough reward for the perineal tear, extreme sleep deprivation and bleeding nipples of the five weeks which had preceded it. The magical moment when she went to get her from her cot one morning and she lifted up her arms, smiled and said 'Mama' for the first time. A tiny, warm hand in hers as they walked down the street together. Watching her sleep, marvelling that this long-lashed, rosy-cheeked vision of cherubic perfection had been grown in her body. The fierce ache of love which was all-consuming and which left her in no doubt that she would die for her daughter. How could she try and persuade her friend out of experiencing all that?

Tears pricked Claudia's eyes at the unfairness of it all. Why, oh why had Janey, who was kind and funny and thoughtful and so very much loved had to die, leaving Lois bereft and denied of her chance to have a family? And if it felt unbearably unjust to her, as a friend and onlooker, how did Lois manage to get through the days at all?

Lois watched the succession of emotions flit across Claudia's face with wry amusement. She had always been the same - the worst poker face in the world. When they were at university she had endured merciless teasing when she had briefly considered a career as a barrister rather than a solicitor, as she was infamous for the transparency of her emotions, and her friends had found the idea of her standing up in court absolutely hilarious.

"So, what do you think?" Lois asked eventually.

Claudia gazed at her, the tears in her eyes starting to well over.

"I think that you'd be an absolutely amazing mum. And I will do whatever I possibly can to support you."

Lois grinned, and reached into her capacious butter-soft tan leather tote bag to pull out a sheaf of papers. "I'm glad you said that. Because I do need your help. I need you to help me find a man."

11

"Daaannn!"

Daniel looked regretfully at the cup of tea he'd just made, and the newspaper, purchased some hours earlier, which he had yet to open. Juliet's school was having an INSET day, which as far as he could tell, meant a random day in the middle of the school term when the teachers decided that they needed a day of peace and quiet. For training purposes. Not that Daniel blamed them. Several weeks looking after Juliet every morning before school and every afternoon after school had imbued him with endless admiration and respect for the people who had to cope with thirty of the little darlings, in a confined space, for six hours solid every day. And they were actually meant to teach them to read and write as well, whereas the standard he set himself was simply to avoid any trips back to see his old colleagues in A&E.

That wasn't strictly true. He had grown very fond of Juliet, and genuinely enjoyed a lot of the time they spent together. They had elaborate games which involved covering the living room floor with a vast assortment of Playmobil and Lego. He took her to the park, or got her paints out for her to spread all over herself, her clothes and the kitchen table. He sat for interminable periods while she laboriously acted out 'plays' for him. Other things were less fun. Coercing her into her reading practice. Trying to ensure that she ate something approaching a balanced diet. Dealing with the tantrums that could blow up out of nowhere at a fairly small issue.

And now it was 4.30pm, he'd been on the go since 6.30am, all creativity and most patience now utterly exhausted, and was thinking back quite fondly to a fourteen-hour shift in A&E. He had settled Juliet in front of Cbeebies and had been counting on a peaceful thirty minutes with his cuppa and the paper before he had to start preparing her evening meal. Barely three minutes later his peace was shattered.

"Daniellllll!"

The shriek came again, accompanied this time by Juliet in person hurtling into the room.

He tried to keep the weariness out of his voice, and partly succeeded.

"Yes, Juliet? What is it?"

"I forgot about my homework! Is tomorrow Wednesday?"

He nodded.

She looked distraught.

"I have to take it back in tomorrow! It was a projy or a progget. Something like that."

"A project?"

"Yes! That's it! You are clever, Dan! We had to do a project about being a child now compared to a long time ago."

Daniel's heart sank. Brilliant. Just brilliant. How had he missed the note about this? Then he remembered picking bits of soggy paper out of the wash earlier that week - the wash that had included Juliet's hoodie. Presumably the note had been rolled up into a ball in her pocket. Too late he remembered Claudia's warning

"Listen, you need to frisk her at home-time. Seriously. You require the skills of a Ninja to recover all school-home communications. Book-bag is classic, but they could be anywhere. Ethan found one in her knickers once when he undressed her for her bath. We never got to the bottom of that, pardon the pun. But if you miss one, you're screwed."

He groaned.

"Can you remember any more about it, Juliet?"

She shook her head.

"Nope. But we need to do it NOW, Dan. Puh-lease?"

She gazed up at him out of the large blue eyes, so like her mother's, and he sighed and reached for his phone.

"Ok. I'll just text Samara's mummy and see if she's got the note."

Hasina's reply was somewhat reassuring.

"They have to bring in three photos of themselves at different ages, and talk about how they have changed, and their favourite things to do at different ages."

"Juliet, do you know if mummy has any photo

albums?"

Much to his surprise, Juliet nodded, grabbed his hand and dragged him through to the living room. There was a vintage trunk in the corner of the room, and Juliet pointed.

"They're in there. But it's too heavy for me to open."

Feeling curiously intrusive, or perhaps intrusively curious. Daniel lifted the lid. Sure enough, piled inside, a number of expensive looking leather photo albums. Daniel breathed a sigh of relief, and pulled some out.

He and Juliet settled themselves on the sofa with the albums piled up next to them. She picked up the first one and opened it across both their laps. He caught his breath at the first photo. A beautiful beach, regulation azure sky, turquoise sea and golden sand, with a bikini-clad Claudia, heavily pregnant, standing in the middle of it. Her hair was being blown across her face by a breeze, and she had raised one hand to her face to sweep it out of her eyes - an impatient gesture he was beginning to know very well. Her other hand was placed protectively across her bump, and she was laughing.

Juliet pointed at the photo.

"That's mummy, with me in her tummy." she informed him proudly. She turned the pages, until they came to the one of Claudia in a hospital gown and a hospital bed, white-faced and exhausted, with a tiny baby crooked in her arms and an expression of radiant tenderness and pride etched on her face.

"And that's me when I'd just come out of her tummy! Wasn't I small? Even smaller than Jasmine. Do you think Mummy will have another baby soon? Can I take this photo into school?"

Daniel responded slightly absent-mindedly to Juliet's incessant chatter, and they continued to look through the pages together. Beaches and birthday cakes, Christmas trees and family dinners, Juliet as a baby, a toddler, a pre-schooler - sitting, standing, first steps, running, climbing, jumping. And then a more recent one, instantly recognisable as the child sitting beside him now, of Juliet standing outside the front door in a slightly-too-big uniform, fair hair in bunches, huge grin in place, and Claudia's arm protectively round her shoulders.

Maybe it was a trick of the camera, or ageing, or wishful thinking on his part, but it seemed to Daniel that the tangible happiness of the pregnant woman and the new mother faded a little every year. With each turn of the page, Claudia's smile looked a little more strained, her face a little thinner, her body language a little more defensive.

And what of Ethan? Juliet's father, Claudia's husband - the conspicuously absent part of the family jigsaw in which Daniel had found himself. He wasn't in many of the photos, clearly preferring a role behind the camera. If Daniel wasn't much mistaken it was also him who had taken the old-fashioned approach of printing the photos and sticking them in leather albums with carefully labelled dates and captions. He couldn't imagine Claudia ever being organised enough for that. He supposed that she must be more together at work, as presumably the legal profession demanded a certain degree of organisational rigour, but that effort must exhaust her, because at home she was chaotic and impulsive and spontaneous.

He gazed at one of the few photos of the three of them together. In the back garden of this house, a couple of years ago to judge by Juliet's size. Ethan had an arm rather awkwardly round Claudia's shoulders, and Juliet was on her mother's other hip, resting her head against her shoulder, and twining a strand of her long blonde hair round her fingers. Claudia was wearing a strappy floral sundress and flip flops, Ethan was in Bermuda shorts and a linen shirt with bare feet. He looked unremarkable enough. Middling height. Middling colouring. Nothing obvious that made Daniel understand what he'd done to get to marry such an amazing woman. Or why he'd been stupid enough to leave her.

Juliet was talking again.

"So, I want this photo of me when I'd just been born, and the one of me with my first birthday cake, and the one of me starting school. Can I?"

Daniel shrugged. By the look of these immaculate albums, Ethan would be horrified at the idea of ripping three photos out and taking them into a primary school of all places. But then Ethan had buggered off to America, and he couldn't believe Claudia would mind. After all, presumably they had digital copies as well somewhere.

"Sure, I don't see why not."

Ten minutes later she and the photos were covered with glitter and pritstick, and Daniel suddenly glanced at the clock.

"Oh my goodness! It's ten past six! You should have had your tea ages ago, young lady! I hadn't realised it had got so late. And I haven't cooked anything, either. Tell you what, you finish sticking those down, and I'll make you some beans on toast quickly."

12

Lois struck her fist on the table in frustration, causing Horatio to emit an outraged miaow and jump off her lap, flicking his tail in her face as she did so. She gave his head an apologetic rub, but he was too annoyed at having his peaceful nap interrupted to forgive her that easily, and just glared at her before stalking towards his cat-flap.

Lois gazed at her computer screen again, and then round the room, hoping for some sort of inspiration. Why was the composition of a simple email proving so difficult? The answer, of course, was because it wasn't a simple email at all. This was an email introducing herself properly to a man she was hoping to have a baby with but knew next to nothing about.

The pile of responses she and Claudia had looked through had not, on the whole, been inspiring. She'd dismissed out of hand any that weren't written to a decent standard of English.

"You're an awful snob." Claudia had teased her.
She'd admitted it.

"Yes, I suppose I am. But I can't help it. And it's intellectual snobbery, not social. I don't care about their background - as long as it's not Wormwood

Scrubbs, and I don't care how they earn their crust, but not being able to use the possessive apostrophe properly is a deal-breaker. And don't criticise me, Madam, you'd be exactly the same."

Claudia had laughed, but she hadn't denied it, and what she called Lois' grammar-Nazi approach had whittled the pile down alarmingly quickly.

The two or three who seemed to think she wanted to date them, and had written a hard sell of their stellar personal qualities were out, as was the gentleman who felt that a photograph of his genitalia - just to prove everything was present and correct - might entice her to choose him as the father of her child.

Then there had been the ones who came across as desperately needy, and Claudia had banned them.

"Sorry, Lois, but they're not interested in helping you become a mother to anyone except them. You don't need to take on someone else's emotional vulnerabilities."

Lois looked thoughtful. In her experience, all human relationships tended to be about taking on someone else's emotional vulnerabilities, but she also saw Claudia's point. After all, a large part of her motivation for not just going it alone was the desire for some support herself.

Unfortunately, these eliminations had only left one response; the print-out on the table in front of her. Lois knew it off by heart by now, but she re-read it in the hope it might trigger an idea of how to respond.

Hi

I found your advert for a partner in a thoroughly modern marriage very intriguing and, potentially, attractive.

I have been part of a very traditional marriage; my wife and I were childhood sweethearts. Sadly she suffered from ill-health for many years, and died two years ago.

Her health problems meant that we were never able to have children, which was a huge disappointment to us both.

Lately I have been feeling regretful that not only have I lost my beloved wife, I have also lost the whole lifestyle which a man of my age (I am forty-two) might expect. My friends all seem to have young children, and it is hard not to feel envious.

The obvious answer is to try and meet another woman, but I still miss my wife so much that I can't ever imagine wanting to re-marry. I have considered adopting a child, but have shied away from taking such a huge step on my own.

I think that most of my friends would consider me to have lost my mind completely if they could read this email, but I feel that perhaps the time has come to take a risk or two. Playing it safe doesn't seem to have got me very far.

I would love to meet you and discuss further.

Best wishes

Michael

It was an intriguing email. Lois certainly had nothing to complain about regarding his standard of English - it was correctly formal to the point of being pedantic. Claudia had wanted to dismiss Michael to the needy pile, but Lois wouldn't let her. His message had a certain dignity to it, and what he described was an uncanny echo of her own feelings. Unlike many of the respondents he hadn't provided much information about himself, no lists of hobbies and interests, or favourite bands, or even what he did for a living. But was that necessarily a problem? Wouldn't she rather discover these things over a coffee for herself, and make a decision as to whether they had sufficient rapport?

So, after promising Claudia that she would meet in a public place, that she wouldn't give her address or mobile number away, that she would tell her where and when she was meeting him, she had decided to respond and arrange to meet him, and take it from there. She had envisaged meeting several respondents, and knew that realistically it was unlikely she would hit lucky first time, but equally she had to start somewhere.

The only problem now was what to say. She had tried describing her own circumstances, but was worried that that would make *her* seem needy. She had a horrible vision of Michael discussing her with one of his friends, and the friend dismissing her

"I wouldn't go there, Mike! Sounds a bit unstable. Her partner only died a couple of years ago, and now she wants a baby with a complete stranger? She'll end up boiling your bunny, believe me."

No, simple and factual was the way forward. She started again.

Dear Michael

Thank you very much for your email.

I am sorry for your loss, and I understand the feelings you describe.

Would you like to meet for a coffee to discuss things further? Perhaps Central London would be best - how about somewhere near Kings Cross? Weekends are easiest for me.

Looking forward to meeting you,

All the best,
Lois

There. Hardly forthcoming, but it probably was best to wait and talk properly in person. She scanned his photo again, looking for signs that he was an axe-murderer, paedophile or UKIP voter. He looked reassuringly normal. Roughly her own age. Mid-brown, slightly thinning hair. Blue eyes. Rather an engaging smile. Open-neck pale blue shirt. The kind of man you could see in their dozens across North London and, yes, more often than not they would be kicking a ball around with their kids in the park, or trying to imprison a furious toddler into their pushchair, or ordering a babycino along with their flat white in some trendy coffee shop. This was a man, like herself, whose dreams of a family had seemed to die at the same time as the love of their life. A man, like herself, who was a grown-up, who knew that life wasn't fair, but had retained enough optimism hope for second chances. A man who understood that you couldn't simply replace your much loved life-partner like you would a jumper with moth holes.

Aware that she might be disappointed, that perhaps she was transferring too many of her own feelings to him, she decided that the time had also come for her to take a risk, and pressed send. Time would tell.

Michael Arncliffe recoiled slightly from his laptop and slammed the lid down with a hand that was shaking slightly. What had he done? Even though he had removed the visual image, in his mind's eye he could still see it his mind's eye with crystal clarity - his email inbox with its usual selection of adverts, scams and special offers, but also the name of that woman, Lois Hargreaves, and the ominous title of her email 'Meeting Up'. What the hell had he done? What, more to the point, had his bloody brother made him do? This was all Jack's fault. Well, he'd got him into this mess, he was going to have to help get him out of it.

He grabbed his mobile, hands still shaky.

"Hey, Mike!" Jack's voice was indecently cheery.

"She's replied and she wants to meet up!"

"Oh that's brilliant, mate. Fantastic. What did she say? Does she sound nice? When are you meeting her?"

"Jack! For God's sake! I can't meet her! I don't know what I was thinking. I'd had too much to drink, you persuaded me. I should never have let you make me send that message. And now this poor woman thinks she's got someone who wants to have a baby with her, and I've got to find some way of letting her down gently. How am I going to do that?"

Jack's voice was puzzled.

"But why can't you just meet her? You're not committing to anything. She's hardly going to leap in and steal your sperm in the middle of Starbucks! Why not just go along and have a chat? She'll be really nervous too I should think."

Michael felt his chest grow tight, his breathing

shallow and panicky.

"Yeah, she might be nervous. Or she might be a lunatic. What if she's a lunatic? What if she's a mad spinster wanting a husband? She might stalk me."

Jack laughed.

"Mike, just calm down. It's fine. She's not a lunatic, she's a doctor, a consultant in paediatrics at the Princess Royal Hospital. I Googled her. She's gay - she was married to someone called Janey Sullivan who was a food writer, apparently, and died a couple of years. She's in the same boat as you."

Michael felt slightly calmer. If this woman's partner had died then maybe she would understand. Maybe it would even work? But what if it didn't? What if he let her down? Let a baby down? What if the world he'd painstakingly built up since Alice died, a world which relied on him maintaining total emotional independence, came crashing down around him?

His brother seemed to sense what he was feeling, and his voice was gentler when he carried on.

"I know what you're thinking, Mike. You're worried about creating some mess in your neat life - physically and emotionally. You're scared of caring about someone again. But you're such a lovely guy. You're too nice to sit in your pristine flat, pushing numbers round a spreadsheet all day, and the only emotional contact being with me and Daph and the kids."

Michael let the words sink in. He didn't like to

think of his life as empty. Clean was the adjective he employed in his internal discourse. But on a day like today, a Saturday when the whole weekend stretched out before him, a weekend which everyone else was filling with family and friends, empty did start to feel a little too apt. Before giving his brain a chance to engage he spoke impulsively.

"Alright, I'll do it. I'll email her back and arrange to meet up. But only for a coffee, mind. I'm not saying that I'm going ahead with this mad scheme."

Jack's voice was warm with relief.

"Good man. Why not try and meet her today? And then you could come over for lunch tomorrow and tell us all about it."

13

Lois stood in bra and knickers looking helplessly at the contents of her wardrobe. On one side were her work clothes - invariably tailored trousers in navy, dark grey or black, worn with silk shirts, and flat, pointy toed leather pumps. In cold weather she slung a cashmere cardi round her shoulders. It was a classic look, never high fashion, but reasonably stylish, more approachable than a suit, but still smart and put together. She hoped. The other side of the wardrobe were her clothes for home - skinny jeans, Converse trainers in a rainbow of colours, and some slightly grungey t-shirts and sweatshirts - many of them sporting political slogans of yesteryear, or proclaiming her loyalty to some long-forgotten nineties indie band.

Neither look seemed particularly appropriate for meeting Michael Arncliffe in a coffee shop on Kings Cross station.

She had to make a decision, though, and quickly. Being late would create an even worse first impression. On impulse she pulled on a pair of jeans, and then a boxy pale grey silk top. She normally wore the top tucked into trousers at work, but she left it loose today. Not bad, but still a little bland. She searched desperately round her room for inspiration, and her eye fell on a gift box on her bedside table. The chunky mustard-yellow necklace inside had been a birthday present from Claudia. She had never worn it because she avoided jewellery at work for practical reasons, and it always felt too dressy for her jeans and tee weekend combo. But, after clasping it round her neck, she saw that it worked perfectly with this ensemble. The vivid yellow lifted the grey top and added some life and focus. She pulled on grey high-top Converse, twisted her thick and unruly dark hair into a messy up-do and secured it with a big clip, before grabbing her trusty tan-leather tote and deciding that, ready or not, this would have to do. Suppressing her nervous qualms with a stern reminder that this was what Janey would have wanted her to do, she headed out of the door.

Half an hour later, Michael was sipping his third cup of coffee, and wondering why on earth he ever listened to Jack about anything. Jack, who was four years younger than him. Jack who openly admitted he had gone to one of his Finals exams drunk after not going to bed the night before. Jack who resisted any suggestion of a traditional career structure and worked as a freelance graphic designer. Jack, who had fallen madly in love with Daphne the day they met, proposed to her a week later, with her giving birth to their first child a year after that. They were not similar in any way. He loved his brother, and he had been a total rock since Alice died, but why on earth was he suddenly taking life advice from him?

Michael was an accountant. He didn't really understand it when people talked about 'dream jobs' or following their dreams. His dream was to have a secure, well-paid job which would enable him to afford a nice house and look after his family properly. That, surely, was what jobs were for? He had met his wife, Alice, at 6th Form college, and although he had known from the start that she was 'the one', he had waited until they had both graduated and saved up a deposit for their first flat before he had proposed. They had had a clear life plan. A two-year engagement while they saved for the wedding. Then another three years to save up so that they could afford a bigger place to live. Then two years saving so that they had some money behind them when they started to try for a baby. They would have their first baby at twenty-nine, and their second at thirty-two.

The first stage had all gone according to plan. They had had their traditional white wedding aged twenty-three, and a fortnight's holiday in Barbados afterwards. They made their next move up the housing ladder, and were all set to try for a baby, when Alice decided to go for a pre-conception health check. Out of the blue, the increasing tiredness she mentioned almost as an aside - after all, she was working long hours building her career, and wasn't everyone tired sometimes? - was diagnosed as leukaemia.

All thoughts of having children vanished, and they embarked upon a decade long nightmare of treatments which could often seem worse than the disease itself. Twice she was declared to be in remission, twice they allowed themselves to hope for the best, but each time the disease returned with greater ferocity than before. Finally, beyond exhausted after her relentless struggle, Alice had died two weeks before her fortieth birthday, leaving him alone and utterly bereft.

He shuddered. Well, he was here now, and for courtesy's sake - not to mention getting Jack off his back - he needed to meet this Lois woman, explain to her that he had made a mistake in responding, and then resume his calm and peaceful life. He glanced at his watch. They'd arranged to meet at 10am, and it was nearly five past. His spirits rose slightly - he'd give her another five minutes and then go. No-one could blame him for not wanting to hang round all day waiting for someone who might not bother to turn up.

He scanned the room. In her last email, Lois had said she was tall - almost 6 foot - so she should stand out. There was no-one he could see who looked remotely like her photo. Then his heart sank as the door opened, and a very tall, dark woman rushed in. She looked intimidatingly chic, sunglasses pushed up on her head, trendy jeans, an expensive bag. She glanced round the room, and then her gaze met his and her face lit up in a warm smile. Despite himself he couldn't help responding. She rushed over, and he got to his feet politely.

"Michael! Hi, how do you do? I'm Lois. I'm so sorry I'm late. It's ridiculous, but I was so nervous about this meeting that I was almost paralysed with it, and it took me about three times as long as usual to get ready! Have you been here long? Let me just grab a coffee, and then we can have a proper chat."

She paused for breath and, to his surprise, Michael heard his voice responding, matching her honesty with his own.

"Don't worry. I totally understand about being nervous. In fact I was secretly hoping you wouldn't turn up so I could give myself an excuse for backing out!"

She laughed, and went to the counter, leaving Michael feeling pleasantly surprised. He didn't know quite what he had been expecting, but this breezy, likeable woman with genuine warmth in her eyes and voice wasn't it.

When she returned she set down her coffee, and a large chocolate muffin, and then covered his hand with her own.

"Before we do anything else, I just wanted to say how sorry I am for your loss. My own partner died a couple of years ago, so although I wouldn't claim to understand exactly what you've been through, I do have some inkling."

Michael nodded, disarmed again by her frankness.

She smiled again, looking a little more uncertain.

"Now, I've never done this before, so I've no idea what the protocol is, but my suggestion is that we share a little bit about ourselves, circumstances, background etc, and a bit about why we want to become parents. And then if we seem to get on, we could meet again in a week or so, and take things from there. What do you think?"

Michael was silent for a moment. When he'd envisaged this meeting he had anticipated starting by saying that there was no way he could make a decision about having a baby with someone on the strength of a single meeting, and that if they were to get anywhere it would have to be a slow process of getting to know each other, and discovering, amongst other things, if they had shared values and motivations. Once again she had taken the wind out of his sails by saying exactly what he had been thinking.

He nodded agreement.

"Good. Right, well, I'll go first. As you know, my name is Lois Hargreaves. I'm thirty-eight, and I'm a doctor. A consultant paediatrician at the Princess Royal. I was married to Janey, who died of cancer just over two years ago. Her death was fairly sudden - only a few months after diagnosis, so I was in a state of shock for a bit. But now, having had a chance to think, I've decided that I want to have a baby, as Janey and I had always planned. I don't believe I'll ever have another romantic relationship, I can't imagine ever meeting anyone who I could love as much as I loved Janey, and I'd rather not settle for second best. But I've always wanted to be a mother. I love children - hence my job - and at my age it is getting to be now or never."

She paused, and Michael chipped in

"That all makes sense. And I totally understand about not wanting another relationship - it drives me mad when people seem to think that's the magic solution. I want to say, no, I don't miss having a generic wife, I miss being married to Alice, and I can't replace *her*, and I don't want to."

Their eyes met in mutual comprehension and she nodded.

"Exactly!"

"However," Michael continued "What I don't understand, if you don't mind me saying, is why you placed that advert at all. I mean, you're a woman, you've got the eggs and the womb, and surely it's relatively easy to obtain anonymous donor sperm, isn't it? And I imagine that, as a consultant, money isn't a particular issue."

Lois smiled.

"Of course I don't mind you asking. It's an obvious question, and the first one my best friend asked me when I told her what I was planning. The reason is, I don't want to do this on my own. I want a partner - not a life partner, but a parenting partner. I want someone to time the contractions, and to take turns at the night feeds, and who I can turn to when there's a problem, knowing that they care about my child as much as I do. And I want my baby to have the love of two parents. And a positive male role model is important too. And then…" she hesitated, tears coming into her eyes "you and I both know that life is unpredictable. If anything happens to me, I want someone left to care for my baby. My parents are elderly, they couldn't cope, and I'm an only child. I want my child to have a real father, not just a biological one."

Michael nodded. That all made perfect sense to him. They were the reasons why he wouldn't have wanted to go it alone himself, even if he had been blessed with a uterus. He realised Lois was looking at him expectantly, and he cleared his throat.

"OK. Well, I'm Michael, and I'm forty-two. I'm an accountant. I do freelance work - I used to work for one of the big firms, but my wife, Alice, was ill for a long time before she died and I needed to care for her. Luckily we had some savings, and I started freelancing because that was easier to fit in around Alice's treatments. And then since she died I haven't really had the motivation to get a full-time job. The freelancing suits me quite well, and there's no shortage of people running small businesses who need some advice, or some help with their tax return."

He paused.

"And have you always wanted children?"

"Yes, very much. Alice and I were planning on having a family before she got ill, and after that it was never an option. After she died…well, obviously I don't have the option of going it alone. I was thinking about becoming a foster carer, or perhaps adopting, but it still seemed an awful lot to take on by myself, even though I have always been sure I want children."

Lois was thoughtful. The similarities between their situations seemed almost uncanny. She liked him, as well. He had a kind and gentle face, and she instinctively trusted him. If she had been describing the ideal co-parent then he would probably have looked an awful lot like Michael. Of course, it was ridiculous to expect that the first person she met would turn out to be the right one, but she couldn't quell the little bubble of optimism rising inside her.

14

Claudia stretched her arms behind her head with cat-like grace, and yawned widely.

"Right, I'm shattered. Think I'm going to have an early night"

Daniel nodded, conscious of the feeling of disappointment he always had when any time spent with Claudia came to an end.

"Cool. Oh, by the way, you didn't need me to babysit tomorrow night, did you? I'm planning on going out with a friend."

Claudia shook her head, conscious as she did so as to a prickle of curiosity as to whether the 'friend' was just a drinking buddy or a date.

"Nope, that's fine. I'll pick Juliet up from school as usual, so you're free from 9am as far as I'm concerned." she paused. Something, possibly that little jab of unidentifiable feeling as she wondered who his 'friend' was, compelled her to add:

"Some friends from the place I used to work did ask me out tomorrow night, but I can't be bothered. It's been such a busy week in work. I think I'd rather snuggle up and watch a film with Juliet, and then have another early night. Besides," she glanced up under her lashes at Daniel "one of the guys who's going out used to have a bit of a thing for me. Since he heard on the grapevine that I'm single again he's been most insistent we all get together."

Daniel felt a sharp stab of jealousy. This was what he was dreading. He knew that anything happening between him and Claudia was impossible for a dozen reasons, but he still couldn't bear the thought of anyone else having her. Fighting to keep his tone casual he asked

"Oh really? And what about you? Do you reciprocate 'the thing'?"

She shook her head, laughing.

"Nah! He's attractive, but my God does he know it! I think his girlfriend would always take second place to his love affair with his mirror. Anyway, I've got no plans to inflict a string of here-today, gone-tomorrow lovers on Juliet - even if I had the time or inclination to!"

Daniel's heart sank further. Claudia was only articulating what was blindingly obvious - she'd only split up with her husband a few months ago, there was no way she would want to rush into another relationship. Especially not one with her live-in nanny. But. But. It was a kind of torture being so close to her, spending so much time together, getting on as well as they definitely did, and yet knowing that nothing else could come of it. He would just have to be grateful for her friendship, and hope that she continued with her intended plan of celibacy for the foreseeable future.

He was still feeling slightly glum when he met

Lydia in a cosy little wine bar the following evening. It was an intimate space, with only six or seven tables, and a pianist playing jazz softly in the corner. It would be the perfect place to bring Claudia for a first date. Lydia was looking wistfully around as well, and voiced an uncanny echo of his own thoughts

"This would be the perfect place for a romantic night out, wouldn't it? I've wanted to come here ever since it opened, but Dominic and I haven't really 'done' dating, and now we can't."

She laughed

"It's ironic, isn't it? I can't come here with Dominic, who I'm in love with, because it's too romantic for a tete a tete and he is still insisting that we keep things platonic, but I can come here with you, even though it's still the same place and totally romantic because there *is* nothing going on between us, and no chance that there could be."

Daniel looked at her affectionately. He still found it hard to get his head round the fact that his brother and their life-long best friend were madly in love. Not in a judgmental way, just in a flatly uncomprehending one. Lydia may or may not turn out to be his biological sister, but he had always thought of her in a sisterly way. He loved her, always would, but the idea of having sex with her was not something that he had ever contemplated. But he hugely admired her strength and her determination, and if the genetic thing turned out not to be a problem, he could actually see that she and Dominic were a perfect match. Dom was so laid-back, he needed someone with Lydia's feistiness to make anything happen. And Lydia clearly needed the stability and security and unconditional love that Dominic would provide. But, and it was a big but, they surely couldn't build a secure future on such an uncertain foundation.

"So, how are things with you, anyway, Dan? Dom said that you have taken a break from work? What's that all about?"

He shrugged.

"I wasn't really given much choice! I must admit I've been struggling a bit the last few months, and dropped a few balls. Lois, my boss, talked me into taking a break. And then she also got me this alternative job working as a nanny to her best friend's little girl, so that's what I'm doing!"

"Wow! That's a big change!"

A slow smile spread across Lydia's face.

"Hey, this is brilliant! When you break the news to your parents that you have quit being a doctor to become a nanny that will totally draw their fire! They won't even *notice* me and Dom snogging at the family barbeque!"

Daniel returned her smile.

"Happy to help!"

"Seriously, though. How are you finding it? Is it weird living in someone else's house? What are they like, the family?"

Daniel hesitated for a moment.

"The little girl is delightful. She's five, in her first year at school, and she's so sweet. Bright and funny and a little bit wilful, but adorable. And her mum, Claudia, is a newly single parent, so I haven't met the dad yet - he's in America."

"Well?" Lydia prompted, as Daniel had fallen silent. "What's she like?"

Daniel grimaced.

"She's a lawyer, for a big city firm. Works long hours, although she is trying to reduce them a bit now that Juliet's dad's not around. She's late thirties, petite, blonde…" his voice trailed away, and then he blushed and grinned.

"And, like her daughter, she's bright and funny and a little bit wilful but adorable. Shit. I can't believe this has happened, or that I'm telling you, but in just a few weeks under her roof I've managed to develop the biggest crush on my new boss! So what the hell do I do about that?"

Lydia thought for a moment. She had wanted this drink with Dan to talk about her and Dominic, and so far they'd only talked about him, but maybe that wasn't such a bad thing. Chatting like this, without Dom around, was helping her re-discover the feelings of warm camaraderie she had always had with Daniel, and that felt a lot better than the resentment of him that had been eating away at her since photogate.

"Has anything happened with this woman? What's her name, Claudia?"

His tone was despondent.

"Nope, nothing. And there never will be anything. She's my boss at the moment, she's best friends with my real boss. She's only just split up with her husband of ten years and she's told me she doesn't want another relationship. I'm in a position of trust looking after her daughter and living in her house. And she's way, way out of my league. There's a few of the many reasons it can never work and I just have to get over her."

Lydia looked at him in sudden concern.

"Oh wow, Daniel! Sorry, I didn't realise. You're really serious about her, aren't you? I thought you just meant a casual crush."

He shrugged.

"Yes, I'm serious. It's bloody ridiculous, given all those reasons why it can't work, but I do really, really like her. Cheesy cliche alert, but I've never really felt like this before. She's absolutely amazing, Lyddy. So sharp and clever, and witty. But then lovely and gentle and patient with Juliet. Plus she's totally hot."

Lydia's eyes sparkled.

"Have you got a photo?"

He shook his head.

"No, why would I, I'm not a bloody stalker!" Then a thought struck him, and he scrolled through his phone "Actually, yes, I have. I took one of her and Juliet with ice-cream sundaes that we'd made the other week."

He handed his phone over, and Lydia found

herself looking at a slightly blurry photo of a woman and a little girl sitting in front of three enormous fruit and cream covered ice-cream concoctions. They were obviously mother and daughter, both with a mass of wavy blonde hair, small, pointed, determined looking chins and tip-tilted noses. They were both laughing, and the woman's arm was round the girl's shoulders. She looked nice, and she was pretty, but not the ravishing beauty she'd expected from Dan's description. It must be love.

She smiled at him.

"Look, Daniel, you just need to be patient. You're right, it's probably not a good time to make a move on her at the moment, but there's no rush, is there? And you definitely don't need to worry about her being out of your league. You're pretty hot yourself, you know! And a gorgeous young doctor who can cook and who's good with children is always going to be fairly popular with women!"

He smiled wryly.

"Hmm, maybe. But she's not most women. And I'm worried that while I'm hanging around being patient and helping with her daughter's homework, some unscrupulous bastard will jump in and sweep her off her feet. She sees me cooking the dinner, and messing around with play-dough, and hoovering. It's not exactly sexy, compared to all the sharp-suited hot-shot lawyers she spends all day with."

Lydia sighed. It was clearly no use trying to

convince Daniel that he was quite the catch, and that very possibly Claudia thought so too - might even now be moaning to one of her girlfriends that she had a crush on the gorgeous male nanny, who, of course, wouldn't look twice at a middle-aged mum!

"We are a pair, aren't we? Unlucky in love."

Daniel looked perturbed.

"I'm so sorry Lydia. I know that I am the reason you and Dom are feeling unlucky right now. I honestly have driven myself mad wondering if I did the right thing, but I just felt that if I knew, or suspected I knew, something about your background that I *had* to tell you. Do you understand?"

Lydia gazed at her hands, noting some ragged skin round her cuticles. She had *hated* Daniel at various points over the past few weeks, hated him for saying what he had said and interrupting her idyllic love story. But actually, her innate honesty forced her to admit that he couldn't possibly have known the impact his words would have, and that she would also have been utterly furious if he had thought he knew something about her and had made the judgement call that she didn't need to know.

"Yes." she said finally. "I do understand. But I need your help, Dan. Because Dom and I are just in complete stasis now. I don't know what steps we need to take next, I don't know how to resolve this. The thought of talking to your parents about it makes me feel physically sick, and I was kind of hoping that Dom might do something. But…you know Dom. He won't, will he?"

Daniel shook his head. He knew as well as Lydia that taking firm and decisive action wasn't Dom's strong point, and he also sympathised with Lydia's reluctance to do this on her own.

"Look Lyds, I tell you what. I'll phone Mum later, and invite us all round for tea on Sunday, what do you think? She'll be in a good mood because she loves us going home and fussing round and baking for us, and then we can tackle them together. Three-pronged attack, and we won't leave until we get some satisfactory answers. What do you think? You don't have to say anything about you and Dom being a couple, just that we found the photo and got curious."

15

Claudia sat at her kitchen table sipping coffee, and watching Juliet watch Daniel flipping pancakes. This process involved a good deal of ultra-theatrical flipping on Daniel's part, and a lot of excited squealing on Juliet's. The sun was streaming in through the French windows. The air was rich with the smell of fresh coffee and the cooking pancakes. Claudia was overcome by such an extravagant sense of well-being and contentment that she laughed out loud. Immediately the two figures by the cooker turned round, Daniel raising a quizzical eyebrow, and Juliet demanding

"What's so funny, Mummy?"

Claudia gazed adoringly at her daughter. Her blonde hair was a riotous mess of curls which, thankfully, as it was Saturday wouldn't have to be tamed into a style suitable for school today. She was still in her shortie pyjamas, pale blue floral ones, and she looked rosy and happy and healthy. And for the last few days there hadn't been any 'I want Daddy' tantrums either.

"Nothing's funny really, sweetheart, I'm just happy."

She smiled, and Juliet ran over and clambered onto her mummy's knee, laying her satiny cheek against

Claudia's.

"I like it when you're happy, Mummy."

Claudia tightened her arms around the little body, a lump coming into her throat. Juliet seemed to have completely lost her baby chubbiness now, and was slim and leggy. How much longer before she also lost her unselfconscious desire for cuddles with mummy? She and Ethan had never been able to agree on when, or even whether, to have a second baby. Now, Claudia found herself wishing passionately that they had. It seemed suddenly intolerable that she would never experience the wonder of pregnancy again, never again hold her own newborn baby, never again breastfeed, spending hours when the rest of the world slept wrapped in a milky cocoon. Aware that she was seeing the whole process through the Instagram soft-filter that five years distance provided, and moreover that her sunny mood risked tipping over into melancholy, she dropped a kiss on Juliet's soft curls and announced

"I think we should have an adventure today!"

Predictably, Juliet leapt up, shrieked a bit, and bounced around the room.

Daniel watched her, grinning, and then placed a plate of perfect, golden pancakes in the centre of the table, along with a big bowl of fresh strawberries, a bottle of maple syrup and the inevitable Nutella.

They all began to tuck in voraciously, and Juliet asked through a chocolatey mouthful

"What kind of an adventure, Mummy?"

Claudia glanced at the weather forecast on her iPhone.

"How about the seaside? We could go to Hastings?"

Juliet bubbled over.

"Yay! Mummy! Yay! Yay! Yay! Yes, let's go to Hastings! Yay! I need to find my flip flops."

She leapt up from the table, and Claudia put a gently restraining hand on her shoulder.

"Hold your horses! You're not going anywhere until you've finished your pancake and drunk your milk."

While Juliet did so, Daniel glanced across at Claudia. As always, she looked beautiful and serene, munching her pancakes more neatly although no less enthusiastically than her daughter, and giving no sign whatsoever that she had any awareness of him at all other than as Juliet's nanny. It was all very well for Lydia to say he was a catch and he should give her time, yada, yada, yada, but it was more than a bit depressing living with her day-in, day-out, sharing meals and spending most evenings together, full of stimulating discussions and occasional emotional heart-to-hearts, but with no indication at all that she felt even a flicker of attraction for him. So, presumably she didn't. He bit his lip, and decided to push his luck.

"So, ladies. Is this a girls only adventure, or can I tag along?"

Of course Juliet replied with a rapturous

affirmative, but he was almost holding his breath as he looked at Claudia. Would he have irritated her by asking in front of Juliet and so basically blackmailing her into a situation where she had to say yes? Her cheeks seemed to grow slightly pinker, and he felt a sinking sensation in his stomach, wondering if it was suppressed annoyance.

Her smile, though, looked warm and genuine.

"Oh wow, that would be great, Daniel! But you're not on Juliet-duty today - don't you have any plans?"

He shook his head, faintly embarrassed. His plan had been to keep the day free in the hope that he might end up being able to spend some of it with Claudia and Juliet, but he could hardly admit to that.

"Nothing that beats a trip to the seaside! As long as we can paddle, and go to the fairground, and eat fish and chips!"

Claudia grinned.

"Duh! Of course! And ice-cream cones and a trip on the miniature railway."

They finished their breakfasts, and Daniel cleared away and loaded the dishwasher whilst Claudia went to get herself and Juliet ready. As a single man, 'getting ready' for a day out at the seaside on a blazing hot late spring day involved finding his sunglasses and his Havaianas. He was already wearing shorts and a t-shirt. As a mum with a young child, Claudia, as well as choosing a pretty, red and white retro-print sundress for herself and finding her sandals, had also to pack her own bodyweight in kit to cover every eventuality. Sun cream. Swimming costumes. Change of clothes for Juliet in case she got wet. Towels. Hoodie in case it got cold. Waterproof in case it rained. Sunhat. Sunglasses. Handbag sized first aid kit. Frisby. A few Mr Men books for the journey. Snacks. Water bottles. Baby wipes.

Finally, having persuaded Juliet to wear sensible sandals rather than the flimsy, bejewelled flip flops which she had bought in a reckless moment and which would undoubtedly lead to Juliet stopping every two minutes with a stone in her shoe and probably result in blisters and/or a sprained ankle before the day was out, Claudia made it back to the kitchen, staggering slightly under the weight of her bulging rucksack. She looked at Daniel in bemusement.

"Where's your stuff?"

He patted his pockets.

"I've got my phone and my wallet here. Do I need anything else?"

"Swimming things?"

"Good point." he ran upstairs, and returned moments later with a pair of board shorts.
"Any chance I can shove these in your bag, Claudia? I'll carry it for you."

He smiled charmingly, and Claudia returned the smile.

"OK, deal. But don't you need a towel or anything?"

He shook his head.

"If it's warm enough to swim, it's warm enough to run round and get dry afterwards."

Claudia shuddered slightly.

"The chances of me thinking it is warm enough to swim are exceedingly remote. Unfortunately, Juliet is made of tougher stuff."

Daniel grinned.

"Aha! Now I see why you agreed to me coming along! You want to lie around working on your tan while I brave the icy waters with your daughter."

Repressing a qualm at the idea of Daniel seeing her in a bikini, and a flicker of an emotion she didn't choose to examine closely at the thought of him splashing around in his swim shorts, Claudia returned the grin.

"Well, I wouldn't have asked you - not on your day off - but seeing as you've offered! Thank you very much."

It was a golden day.

They went by train, Claudia having reacted with horror at Dan's suggestion of driving.

"No way! You spend hours stuck in a traffic jam in an over-heated car, then another hour trying to park, and by the time you find a space you're so far from the seafront you're practically back in South London anyway. All to the accompaniment of a chorus of 'I'mboredarewethereyet' and then a pacifying Thomas the Tank CD. Hideous."

So they'd taken the train, and Juliet had been so engrossed in the *Frozen* colouring book that Daniel had bought her at the station that the adults had actually been able to read the paper for most of the journey, chatting idly as they did so.

It was lunchtime when they arrived, so by common consent they headed straight down to the seafront, bought fish and chips, and sat on the beach to eat them on the blanket Claudia had stowed away in her capacious bag. Daniel had slipped away for a few minutes at the station, and as they settled themselves on the blanket, he produced a carton of strawberry and banana smoothie for Juliet, and two mini-bottles of Prosecco with two straws for him and Claudia.

Claudia remembered that in Sixth Form she and her friends used to drink their ghastly alcopops with straws, alleging that it intensified the effects of the alcohol. She had forgotten what dubious pseudo-science had led to this belief, but sitting here in the sunshine she felt so light-headed and giggly that she idly wondered if there was something in it after all.

After lunch they paddled, even Juliet declaring that the water - icy despite the baking sun - was too cold for swimming. They still got quite wet splashing, and ran around playing frisby to dry off and get warm. Then they headed off to the promenade, and spent a couple of hours on the fairground, Juliet shrieking with delight as she sat sandwiched between Daniel and her mother on the various rides.

Throughout all this, as a niggling awareness beneath the top layer of giddy happiness, Claudia was aware of some sort of shift between her and Daniel. Nothing as overt as long lingering looks, but some subtly flirtatious undercurrent. She knew *she* was flirting a bit, and whether it was the sunshine, the Prosecco, or the unexpected pleasure at being out for the day with a staggeringly attractive man, she just couldn't seem to help it. She was terribly anxious in case she was coming across as some sort of desperate middle-aged almost-divorcee cougar, chasing the attractive young man, but unless she was very much mistaken Daniel was flirting back. It wasn't strictly necessary, surely, for him to put his arm round her waist to help her down from the rides? And had he looked a little lasciviously at her in her damply clinging sundress?

Painfully aware that the last thing she could do to Juliet was to embark on an idle flirtation with her carer, the person who had brought such wonderful stability and reassuring routine into her life at a time which could have been incredibly traumatic, Claudia felt slightly ashamed of her behaviour, but somehow powerless to stop it. It wasn't deliberate, cold-blooded flirting, it was just a sort of overspill of her contentment at this wonderful sunny day with her beloved daughter and the man who was proving to be such a good friend and support to both of them. Tomorrow, when they were back in their normal routine, everything would fall back into place. Maybe until then she should just relax and enjoy the day.

It was nearly 9pm when they finally got back home, tired, sun-kissed and glowing from the pleasure of the day as much as from the sun. Daniel had had to carry Juliet home from the station, and she was seven-eighths asleep in his arms by the time Claudia inserted her key into the front door.

She barely stirred as Claudia slipped her sandals off and her dress over her head, and popped on her pyjamas. She laid her gently on the bed and pulled the quilt over her, checking as she did so that all her favourite soft toys were in position in case she woke later. Then she kissed her forehead and murmured

"Night night, sweetheart. I love you so much. Sleep well."

but there was no reply, as Juliet was already fast asleep.

She ran downstairs to the kitchen. Daniel was already there, and he handed her a large glass of white wine as she came in, and clinked his own against it.

"Cheers. Thanks for a lovely day."

She smiled up at him.

"Thank *you*. It was very kind of you to give up your day off to hang out with me and Juliet. Who is dead to the world, by the way. I decided we could skip teeth cleaning for one night, and I just sponged her hands and face. She'll need a shower in the morning, and probably clean bed linen, because she's bound to be covered in sand and salt and sun cream, but I just didn't have the heart to wake her up tonight."

She was aware that she was babbling, aware that her choice of topic could hardly be called scintillating, but the relaxed dynamic between her and Daniel had shifted at some point that day, and she felt uncomfortable with either silence, or conversation about anything meaningful.

Daniel was looking at her with curious intentness, and she felt her skin tingling as she blushed under his gaze. Suddenly it seemed harder to breathe, and her legs were slightly wobbly. Dan put his own glass down on the work surface, and gently removed her from her grasp. Then before she was really aware what was happening, his arms were tightly around her.

"I'm really sorry, Claudia. I know this is probably a bad idea for a million different reasons, but I've been resisting it too long. If you don't mind, I'm going to kiss you."

Then his mouth was on hers, and she forced her hands up round his neck, and then burrowed them into his thick hair, pulling him into her even more closely. Like Daniel, she knew this couldn't possibly be a good idea, but somehow her sensible lawyer and mummy persona seemed to have been washed away at some point during the sun filled day, and in that moment nothing seemed more imperative than to surrender to delicious kisses which were turning her into a puddle of lust on her own kitchen floor.

16

Daniel stirred sleepily as the early morning sun filtered through his blinds. His mind wondered lazily over yesterday's events - the trip to Hastings, fish and chips, fairground, home and then…he sat bolt upright. Presumably that *had* happened last night? It wasn't just a particularly realistic erotic dream? After all, he'd had his fair share of those since meeting Claudia. But no. Details were flooding pleasurably back.

Where the hell had he got the nerve to make that first move? She'd seemed different yesterday, though. She was always friendly, but slightly remote, whereas yesterday she had been warm and, yes, flirtatious. All he could think about all day was what it would be like to kiss her, and so when they were alone he just hadn't been able to resist the attempt. And it certainly hadn't been rejected. Dan couldn't help a smug smile spreading across his face. When he had kissed her he had more than half expected an abrupt withdrawal, a metaphorical if not literal slapped face. He had not been at all certain of an enthusiastic response, and certainly hadn't hoped for a flood of passion which led to them making love on the kitchen floor.

And then there'd been no awkwardness afterwards. They'd lain, entwined, coming to the gradual realisation that Moroccan porcelain tiles aren't particularly comfortable, even on a warm day. He'd been scared to say anything which might break the spell, but Claudia and been typically forthright.

"God, I'm starving! Do you fancy a takeaway?"

They'd ordered Thai food, and eaten it whilst sharing the rest of the wine, curled up on the sofa in the kitchen. And then it had seemed the most natural thing in the world to have sex again, this time on the comfort of the sofa. The only awkwardness had come after that.

Claudia had kissed him softly and a little dismissively.

"That was amazing. You are amazing. And I know we probably need to talk, but I'm just so shattered now, and I need to go to bed." She paused. "And, as I'm sure you realise, we can't possibly share a bed in case Juliet was to come in during the night."

Of course he had realised that, but hadn't been prepared for how bleak it made him feel. He had watched in silence as Claudia collected her discarded clothes from the floor, pulling the sundress back on, and then getting a glass of water and gathering her things together before heading upstairs.

She'd turned at the door, and given him an apologetic half-smile.

"Night, then."

He'd forced a smile back.

"Night, Claudia."

He'd headed up to bed himself, and lain awake for

a while wondering what on earth happened now. Previously he hadn't thought Claudia fancied him; that doubt had now been well and truly removed, but all the other objections to any kind of relationship between them were still there in force. She was still very newly single, he was still her employee, living under her roof and caring for her daughter, he was still nearly ten years younger than her, and most of all they had to both make sure they didn't do anything to hurt Juliet. And yet despite all this, Daniel knew with absolute certainty that he didn't want this to be a one-night stand.

He glanced at his watch. It was only 7am, and he hadn't heard any stirrings from the floor below yet, which meant that Claudia and Juliet were probably still asleep. He was due to have lunch with Lydia and Dominic before they went round to have the momentous tea with his parents later, but normally he wouldn't have needed to leave for hours yet.

But this wasn't normal. Was it going to be excruciating for Claudia to have to face him at breakfast? Especially with her daughter there, innocently unaware of any undercurrents and needing to remain so. No, better to go out now and give her a bit of space.

He pulled on his running things, and stuffed a change of clothes into his rucksack. He could go for a long run now, rock up early at Dom's, and get showered and changed there, before they had the lunch which was basically a tactics session for how they handled afternoon tea with their parents.

He crept down the two flights of stairs, and gulped a glass of orange juice. Then, on impulse, he tore a sheet off the shopping list pad on the front of the fridge and scribbled a note:

Dear Claudia,
Thank you for an amazing evening. Sorry not to be around this morning - I'm going for a run, and then straight to my brother's for lunch, and then tea at my parents. I shouldn't be late back, though, so maybe we can talk tonight?
Dan xxx

He folded it over, scribbled her name on the front and left it propped against the kettle, before slipping quietly out of the house.

It was the perfect morning for a run. Still cool enough not to be unpleasant, and with a gorgeous floral smell in the air. Claudia lived in the gentrified area of Walthamstow Village, and it looked picture postcard perfect on this spring morning, a slight mist giving an air of mystery, and the streets still very quiet.

As he ran, he forced himself to put Claudia out of his mind, and to concentrate on Dominic and Lydia.

He had established with Lydia that she had never seen her birth certificate, he had suggested that she started by asking for that, claiming that she needed it to renew her passport, or similar.

Lydia nodded, doubtfully.

"I don't think you actually need your birth certificate to renew it, you know."

Dan made an impatient gesture.

"What does that matter? Mum of all people won't know that, I don't think she's ever had a passport. It's just an excuse."

The thought of a confrontation about decades of lies, adultery, false identity and illicit adoption over his mother's Crown Derby tea set was beyond hair-raising but, he reasoned, it was unlikely to happen. Chances were his mother would produce the birth certificate, it would prove Lydia was completely unrelated to them and it would all fizzle out, with the only remaining drama to work out exactly how Lydia and Dominic broke the news of their romantic involvement.

Unbeknownst to Daniel, Claudia had been awake that morning, and had heard his footsteps going downstairs. She'd stretched herself in luxurious abandonment across the full width of her king-sized bed, and wished that she hadn't been quite so adamant about not sharing it with him last night.

Wisdom had it that the cold light of day left you rueful and remorseful about slightly drunken, lust-addled decisions made the night before, but the opposite seemed to be true of her. She had slept brilliantly; a day of fresh sea air followed by some energetic sex and deeply satisfying orgasms seemed just the ticket for beating the niggling insomnia which plagued her occasionally when she couldn't seem to shut her mind down even when her body was aching with exhaustion.

And this morning she could lie, content and well-rested and indulge herself in an orgy of thinking and daydreaming about Daniel. God he was gorgeous. But he was also kind and funny and clever and brilliant with Juliet. And a fantastic lover, managing to maintain exactly the right balance of strength and gentleness. If she was honest with herself, Claudia had been aware for weeks that she was developing a bit of a crush on Daniel, and had worked hard to hide her feelings and maintain some professional detachment. But now, in a fug of post-coital bliss, she let herself ponder whether it really was so impossible. Nice, solvent, successful, single man meets nice, solvent, successful, (newly) single woman, they're attracted to each other, things progress into a relationship...wasn't that was exactly what made the world go round? She would have to be very careful about Juliet, but surely being a single mother didn't condemn her to a life of celibacy? After all, Ethan hadn't even bothered about being off with the old love before being on with the new.

At this point in her ponderings she heard the front door closing softly and smiled to herself. Daniel would be going out for his morning run. She let her imagination wonder again. Maybe he'd buy fresh pastries from the bakery on his way back and they could all have a relaxed breakfast together.

She jumped out of bed, suddenly decisive. She would have a shower before Juliet woke up, blow dry her hair properly, put on some make-up. After all, if you're going to seduce someone nearly ten years younger, you probably do need to make a bit of an effort she told herself.

The weather felt cooler and looked cloudier today, so Claudia pulled on jeans and an over-sized Cos sweatshirt. One thing to make an effort, another entirely to *look* as though you have. CC cream, concealer, a few coats of mascara, blusher. She had a dilemma about her customary bright red lipstick, but rejected it in the end, on the grounds she wouldn't normally wear it for a weekend breakfast at home.

She still hadn't heard Daniel's return, so she decided to go downstairs and start some coffee. She switched on the radio, threw open the French windows to let some fresh air in, and started the usual morning round of picking up the bits and pieces discarded during the previous day. It was only as she was contemplating the collection of ten large pebbles which Juliet had found on the beach, and deliberating on where they could be kept which would be a compromise between Juliet's enthusiasm and her own aesthetic taste, that she caught sight of the note by the kettle.

As she read it, her mood plummeted, and her mouth tightened in anger. All the visions of a cosy breakfast together were disbanded in a flash, and she was facing Sunday alone and rejected. For fuck's sake. She was nearly 39 years old. She should know better by now. Clearly, for a thirty year old guy, the girl you had sex with on a Saturday night was not the same person you had breakfast with on a Sunday morning. She'd thought Daniel was different - her lip curled with scorn at her own self-delusion - but why would he be? And how arrogant was she? All her thoughts had been about whether she should embark on a relationship with Daniel, never really considering what he might want. Handsome doctors weren't exactly short of offers; there was no possible reason why he would want to saddle himself with an almost-middle-aged single mum for heaven's sake.

Suddenly overcome by a wave of despair she hadn't even felt when Ethan left, Claudia slumped at the kitchen table, buried her head in her hands and sobbed uncontrollably for ten minutes. Then she sat up, pushed her hair off her face, and blew her nose hard. This was ridiculous. She couldn't indulge herself with teenage histrionics, even if Daniel had behaved like a teenage Lothario. She was an adult, and a mother, and she had a daughter to think about.

She poured herself a large mug of coffee, and pulled a packet of pains aux chocolats out of the freezer. There would be no home-made pancakes or fresh pastries courtesy of Dan this morning, but that didn't mean she and Juliet couldn't enjoy a bit of a treat.

Right on cue, she heard tumultuous footsteps on the stairs, and moments later Juliet burst into the room.

Appropriately, 'Sunshine on a Rainy Day' had just come on the radio, and Claudia scooped her daughter up and hugged her tightly. When counting her blessings, Juliet would always, surely, be blessing number one.

"Hi Mummy! Where's Dan?" she looked round the room hopefully, and Claudia tensed, carefully schooling her features into a neutral expression.

"He's spending the day with his family today, sweetheart. So it's just you and me. Would you like a pain au chocolate?"

Juliet nodded, but was not to be entirely deflected by the promise of sweet, fatty carbohydrates.

"I want to go and meet his family too! He said I could, one day, do you think I can today? Could you text him?"

Claudia repressed a shudder, and shook her head vehemently.

"No, not today, Juliet. What would you like to do with mummy? Shall we go swimming?"

Juliet shrugged, and thought for a moment.

"I'd rather be with Dan. But if I really can't, can we go and see Auntie Lo and Horatio?"

Claudia considered for a moment. That actually wasn't a bad idea. She hadn't seen Lois for a while, so it would be good to catch up with what was happening with the baby business. And although she had no intention of telling Lois about her idiocy regarding Daniel, she could maybe do a bit of discreet fact-finding about his love life, current and past.

"Alright, baby, I'll phone Auntie Lo after breakfast. Now, shall I get you some milk?"

"Claudia! Hi, how are you?" Lois' voice was upbeat and vibrant. Hearing her, Claudia realised how flat Lois had been since Janey died. Hardly surprising, but she put on such a brave face that it was almost easy to forget that the recent shadowy version wasn't the real Lois at all. It was brilliant that project baby seemed to be cheering her up.

"I'm good, thanks." her own voice sounded flat now, and she tried to inject some warmth

"No need to ask how you are, you sound really happy."

Lois laughed

"I am. I'm feeling really positive. Michael is brilliant. We're getting on so well, and I think we both feel so lucky to have met each other. And everything's progressing very well - in fact we have a follow-up appointment at the fertility clinic next week."

"Wow! That's fantastic, Lois. I'm so pleased for you. How exciting. God, Juliet's going to be beside herself, you know how much she loves babies."

Lois tried to be cautious, but her voice was bubbling with suppressed excitement.

"Well, it's a long road, and there aren't any guarantees, but it *is* exciting."

Claudia felt more miserable than ever. She was clearly an utterly vile person. After the hell Lois had been through she should be thrilled that things were looking up for her at last. And she was, she really, genuinely was. It was just that there's nothing quite like someone else's good fortune and positivity about the future to throw into sharp relief your own feelings of dejection and misery. Ethan loathed her so much he couldn't stand being married to her even for the sake of his precious daughter, and in fact had crossed the Atlantic to get away from her. Juliet was wonderful, but she was growing up and growing more independent each day, and she would never have another baby. And, apparently, she might be good for a quick no-strings shag, but nothing else. And that sense that Daniel had betrayed what she had thought might be the start of something significant was hurting most of all. She shook herself again. These lapses into self-pity had to stop. In the distance she could hear Juliet calling her - some crisis about the toothpaste apparently, so she only had a couple of minutes to wrap up with Lois.

"It certainly is exciting, and I want to hear all about it. To which end - are you free today? Juliet asked me if we could hang out with Auntie Lo and Horatio. I'm afraid Horatio is a slightly bigger attraction than you, but I'm sure you can live with that."

Lois laughed.

"Horatio would be thrilled to see Juliet. She's the only person in the world he feels really fully appreciates him - it's a match made in heaven as there seems to be no limit to Horario's desire for cuddles and strokes, and no limit to Juliet's willingness to bestow them. Yes, I'm free today. Come over for lunch. And we can take Juliet to the park or something if the weather brightens up later. Ooh, I know. Why don't I ask Michael to pop over? I'd love you to meet him. Apart from anything you should probably vet him before I do anything irrevocable with his sperm."

Claudia hesitated. She had been looking forward to having Lois to herself for a bit, but the chance to meet Michael was fairly irresistible. And it didn't sound like Lois was planning on him being there the whole time.

"Sure, that would be great. Right, you can probably hear your goddaughter's yells from here, and patience is definitely not one of her virtues, so I'll go and sort her out and see you in an hour or so."

17

Despite her endeavours to cultivate an air of insouciance, Lydia felt sick to her stomach, and her legs were shaking as she climbed the short flight of stairs from the tube station. She swiped her Oyster card, and then clung to Dominic's arm for support. He smiled down reassuringly, and linked his arm through hers.

"It's ok, Lydia. What's the worst that can happen?"

Lydia shook her head mutely. What was the worst that could happen? There seemed to be any number of answers to that question. Top of the list was the hideous thought of Delia and Henry confirming Daniel's suspicions, and her having to face the reality that she had fallen deeply in love with her own half-brother. Which was really pretty bloody awful.

Daniel linked her other arm, and they began the oh-so-familiar walk from the tube station to their parents' house. How many times had she done this walk. And how many times had she done it with a sick sense of trepidation like she felt at present. It was all very well for Dominic to maintain his *sang froid*. He was the wonder boy. *He* could do no wrong in their mother's eyes. More, even than Daniel, he was her favourite - although Dan's place in her affections wasn't far behind.

But it was different for Lydia. She knew from conversations with her friends that all teenagers go through a phase of feeling unloved and misunderstood by their families, before coming out the other side of puberty to resume normal relations. But she had even had a proper family of her own, not that she remembered, anyway. Had never really felt loved. No, that wasn't entirely true. Henry could be lovely. But he was hardly ever there, working extremely long hours, and when he was he would always defer to Delia instead of supporting her. And although Delia had always taken excellent care of her physically – her meals were home-cooked, her school blouses were perfectly ironed, her shoes were shiny – there had been no emotional support.

The sun had come out now, and the of them walked under a Penny Lane style blue suburban sky, breathing the scent of roses wafting from the carefully tended front gardens. Here and there squeals of laughter cut through the air as children played in their gardens, and the odd trickle of water across the pavement marked where someone was undertaking the traditional Sunday afternoon task of car-washing.

Lydia knew she hadn't had a bad childhood by many standards. But she had always felt had a total absence of emotional succour from Delia who was the only mother figure she knew. She always felt that she was an irritation, a nuisance, in the way. Other little girls in her Reception class had cried for their mummies when they fell over in the playground. She had cried for Daniel and Dominic, and they had never let her down. They had provided her with the love, companionship, and affection she craved, and she had always felt that as long as she had them she would be alright.

As a teenager, her friends would go off to the West End for a day's shopping with their mums, then out for lunch maybe. Delia would give her some cash if she needed new things, but never suggested going together - simply reserving the right to criticise whatever she bought. Lydia had found a perverse satisfaction in choosing the skimpiest midriff-and-cleavage revealing tops, the skinniest fit jeans or briefest skirts. From as young as thirteen she had seen the attention she provoked from boys at school, or even men on the street, when she dressed like that, and attention was a drug. They also ensured attention from Delia, as she berated her for dressing (and, by implication, behaving) like a slut.

The year the twins had gone to university had been the worst of her life. She had grown to hate the very idea of university as it had claimed the time and focus of Daniel and Dominic and rejected totally the idea of going herself. The fact that her long-dead parents had left some money in trust to come to her on her 18th birthday had been a godsend. And that money had been her means of escape. A round-the-world plane ticket. The chance to put on a real show of bravado and demonstrate to the guardians who emotionally neglected her, and the twins who had, as she saw it then, abandoned her, that she didn't need any of them. Delia had gone ballistic.

"Australia? Why in the name of heaven do you want to go *there*? It's a cultural desert."

This, coming from a woman whose favourite author was Danielle Steele, who patronised the West End theatres maybe once a year to see the latest Andrew Lloyd Webber, and who thought that the National Gallery was basically a handily located tea room, did not particularly bother her. In fact, Delia's vitriolic scorn of anything connected with Australia made her all the keener.

Dominic and Daniel's slight hurt that she was going off without them was harder, but they had both promised to come and see her if they could manage to save up enough. Typically, Daniel *had* managed it - getting himself a well-paid holiday job as an au pair, and spending almost every penny of it on a two week trip to Oz before he went back to uni; and Dominic had not. Dominic had spent the summer volunteering as a sports coach and art teacher for a local project which provided a summer school for children from deprived backgrounds. He loved it, but the £40 a week beer money was never going to run to a plane ticket to Australia, and the one thing with which Mrs Nicholls would not indulge her beloved son was the chance to see Lydia.

That pattern was repeated the entire time she was away; she had seen Daniel a few times, but meeting

Dominic when she came home was almost like meeting a stranger. A familiar stranger. A devastatingly attractive stranger. A stranger who made her feel like she was truly coming home. It was that period of several years not seeing him which had somehow transformed him from childhood friend and companion to man-of-her-dreams love interest.

She looked up at him. The set line of his jaw suggested that he wasn't quite as relaxed as he would have had her believe.

"Is it going to be ok?"

It had become her role to stay positive, to comfort and reassure Dominic, but the stifling familiarity of this street had taken her back to being the little girl who cried for the twins. It was Daniel who answered, squeezing her arm reassuringly.

"Of course it's going to be ok. Whatever happens, it's going to be ok. You are strong, and you'll cope with whatever happens."

She shrugged.

"I don't know. I just feel so damned nervous. Your mum always has this effect on me. The closer I get to home, but lower my confidence gets."

She knew the boys didn't really understand. They had always sympathised with her, but they had been petted, indulged, cosseted to within an inch of their lives, and so she knew that they couldn't really comprehend how their childhoods had looked from her perspective. Daniel smiled at her.

"You don't have to do anything much. Dominic

and I are here, we'll look after you. You just need to ask her for your birth certificate. If she gives it to you, great. If she doesn't then we'll take it from there. But it's not a big drama."

Lydia nodded, somewhat reassured. More reassured than she would have been had she been able to foresee the staggering inaccuracy of Daniel's predictions for an evening that would leave none of their lives unchanged.

As her sons and her ward walked up from the station, Delia Nicholls was fussing round her immaculate living room, straightening perfectly placed ornaments, flicking imaginary motes of dust. The warm aromas of scones and ginger cake stole through from the kitchen. Delia sighed again, and checked her watch for the hundredth time.

"They said 4pm!"

Her husband glanced up from the Sunday Telegraph.

"Well, it's only ten past. Anyway, I thought they said 4ish?"

Delia made a dismissive gesture.

"Well, I thought they meant *by* 4pm. Although you know what Lydia is like for time-keeping. We'll be lucky to see them by 5pm if they're all coming together."

Henry sighed. Over a quarter of a century of hearing his wife lay the blame for any chance misfortune at Lydia's door had almost inured him to the injustice of it, but occasionally, as now, he felt the need for a token protest.

"Lydia's not such a bad time-keeper, is she? I always think it's Dominic who's the worst. Do you remember that time when we thought he was coming for lunch, but then…"

His reminiscence was cut short.

"Yes, but that wasn't his fault! I mean they do all these stupid engineering works at the weekend, and how was he meant to know?"

Biting back the response that he could have checked online, Henry gave up.

"Well, I expect they'll be here soon. Why don't you sit down and relax? A watched pot never boils and all that."

Delia sat down on the edge of the beige leather sofa, but almost immediately leapt up again.

"I'd better go and check what flavour jam we have. Daniel loves apricot, but do you think he'd want it on scones? Raspberry would be better, wouldn't it?"

Henry gave her a look of complete bewilderment. Experience taught him that anything he said would be the wrong thing, but that no response would not be tolerated either.

"Erm, yes. Raspberry would be good."

She nodded.

"Yes. And I've still got some of last summer's home-made - the last jar. But I might put the apricot out too, and then they can choose."

"Just relax!" Henry said again. "It's only the kids coming round for a cup of tea, not Her Majesty and Prince Philip paying a state visit."

Delia made an exasperated noise.

"You make it sound like they're here all the time. It's weeks since the last time I had both of them here together, and I just want to make it nice. I'm sure they don't eat properly half the time."

"Three of them."

"What?" Delia looked puzzled.

"Three of them here all together. You said both. It's weeks since last time we had all three of them here together."

She blushed slightly.

"Oh yes, but you know what I meant." She took a deep breath, and was about to launch in, when the doorbell rang.

18

"So, what's the matter with you, then?" Lois asked.

Claudia started slightly.

"What do you mean?"

They were sitting facing each other across Lois' kitchen table. Juliet was ensconced in the living room, curled up with an ecstatically purring Horatio on her knee, and *Sleeping Beauty* on the DVD player. Disney films were strictly rationed at home, but Lois claimed godmother's privilege and kept a stash at her house for when Juliet visited.

Lois raised a sceptical eyebrow.

"Oh, come on, Claudia! This is me! You can't fool me everything's ok when you've got that look on your face. What is it? Juliet seemed ok? Are you missing Ethan more?"

Claudia shook her head, vehemently.

"No! Absolutely not. Although, it's a bit of a pain - he wants Juliet to go and visit him in the summer holidays for a couple of weeks. Of course she can't fly all that way by herself, so I'll need to fly over with her. And then he has to come back to London for a bit anyway, so he'll bring her back."

Lois nodded.

"Well, that doesn't sound unreasonable. You'll miss her, of course, but it'll be lovely for her to see her dad. And you should make the most of it, and have a holiday in America yourself while you're there." She paused. "But I'd still make Ethan bring her back. You don't want to have to do more transatlantic flights with a five year old than are strictly necessary!"

Claudia wrinkled her nose.

"A holiday by myself?"

"Yes! For heaven's sake, Claudia, don't be pathetic. New York, Boston…maybe go up to Cape Cod. What's not to love?"

Claudia thought. Lois was right, it sounded wonderful. And she had the opportunity to do it all without worrying about child friendly restaurants or babysitters or late nights. She could go to the theatre and sightsee and read books on the beach to her heart's content. So why did she feel so lacklustre at the prospect?

"Hey, why don't you come with me? We could do a Thelma and Louise road trip, it'd be a blast."

Lois shook her head, doubtfully.

"Hmm, I don't think so. I'm not sure what stage I'll be at with Project Baby, but I don't think planning a major holiday is a good idea. Plus I probably shouldn't spend that much money - fertility treatment doesn't come particularly cheap."

Claudia nodded, deflated.

"I'm not sure I'll be able to either really. I'll probably have to save my annual leave for the three weeks of the summer holidays when Juliet is back from America."

Lois looked surprised

"Oh, why is that? Won't Daniel still be with you?"

Claudia shrugged.

"Who knows *what* Daniel will be doing."

She was unable to keep the bitterness out of her tone.

A look of comprehension flashed into Lois' eyes, and she averted her gaze and studied the scratched surface of the heavy old pine table as she replied.

"Ahh. So that's what the matter is. Something with you and Daniel?"

Claudia sat in stunned disbelief.

"How the hell did you know that?"

Lois grinned.

"I didn't really. Lucky guess, based on knowing both of you quite well, you having a face like a long wet weekend, and then practically spitting when I mention his name."

Claudia shook her head.

"Bloody hell. Am I that transparent?"

'Yes! You are! Now tell me, what's going on?"

Claudia glanced nervously at the communicating door to the living room, but Juliet was totally engrossed by her cat cuddle and princessy treat.

"I can't really tell you anyway. You're his boss, for god's sake."

"So are you! Now look, don't be ridiculous. I sincerely hope that by this stage in my career I'm professional enough to maintain a good working relationship with Daniel whatever might be going on in his private life. I would never have suggested him as a nanny for you if I wasn't confident of that. So tell me what the hell is going on - have you fallen for him, or what?"

To Claudia's horror, tears began to leak out of the corner of her eyes. She blinked them furiously away, and blew her nose.

"No, of course not. Well, not really. Maybe a bit. Oh, I don't know." she stopped and thought for a moment.

"It's all crept up on me. If you'd asked me a couple of days ago I would have said there was nothing to it. He is attractive, and probably a bit too attractive for a live-in nanny really, but he is so brilliant with Juliet and she adores him."

Sensing Claudia's discomfort, Lois got up and busied herself making some fresh coffee. More to break the awkward silence than for anything else she asked

"Are you ok with more coffee, or shall I open a bottle?"

Claudia grimaced.

"Oh, god, don't tempt me. What time is it?" she glanced at the big old station clock on the wall, and brightened.

"We-ell, it is 12 o'clock. And it is the weekend."

Lois grinned, and took a bottle of white out of the fridge, uncorking it and pouring two glasses.

"I suppose I'd better start making some lunch. Is pasta ok?"

Claudia nodded, and Lois pottered around taking bacon out of the fridge, tinned tomatoes out of the cupboard, garlic out of a bowl on the worktop, while her friend took a gulp of wine and continued.

"We went to the seaside yesterday. And somehow the mood between us just changed. I felt really flirty, and he seemed to respond. Or maybe he was flirtatious and I responded. I don't know. But it was such a lovely day, and then we rounded it off by having passionate sex on the kitchen floor!"

Lois spun round, a rasher of raw bacon in one hand and the kitchen scissors in the other

"Are you joking?"

Claudia shook her head, ruefully.

"Nope. And this morning I got a Dear John note on the kitchen table."

Lois' eyes widened in disbelief.

"No! I don't believe it! Surely Dan wouldn't do a thing like that?"

Claudia shrugged.

"Well no, I didn't think he would, obviously. But how would you know, Lois, really? I mean you were his boss. You know he's a good doctor, we can both see he has a fantastic rapport with kids. He loves his family. He's a decent bloke, but that doesn't mean he can't regret having inappropriate sex with his live-in employer and try to extricate himself from the situation!"

Lois trimmed the fat and rind off the bacon slowly, thinking.

She hadn't been crass enough to try and matchmake Daniel and Claudia, but it had crossed her mind that they could be perfectly suited. It seemed pretty unbelievable to her that the Daniel she knew would treat a woman like that, but of course, as Claudia had pointed out, her knowledge of him would hardly extend to his behaviour in that situation.

"What exactly did the note say?" she enquired

Claudia shrugged.

"I dunno. Can't remember exactly. Just that he was going for a run, and then to his family for the day, and he'd see me later."

Lois stirred the bacon and garlic, now giving off their gorgeous savoury aroma, and then tipped in the tin of tomatoes.

"That doesn't sound like a Dear John letter to me. Did you know he was going to be with his family today."

Claudia made an impatient movement.

"Yes, he had mentioned it. But Lois, he's always there for breakfast. He goes for a run first thing, then showers, then we have breakfast. I'm sure he didn't mention he wouldn't be around this morning. He obviously just couldn't face me after what happened."

Lois left her sauce simmering and came over to the table.

"Get a grip!" she told her friend sternly.

"You're 38 not 13! He is probably just trying to give

you a bit of space, and he said he'd see you tonight. My advice is, forget about him for now, have a relaxing day, and then go back this evening to have a proper talk with him. Be honest with him."

Claudia felt a slight dawning of hope. She'd been so hurt and disappointed that Daniel wasn't there this morning that she hadn't been able to consider it as anything other than a complete rejection. But maybe, just maybe, Lois was right.

"Hmm. Perhaps. But god, being honest with him. That's a bit risky. Plus I'm not even totally sure what I want."

Lois groaned.

"So tell him that, then! Honestly, Claudia, I really think you're making this unnecessarily complicated. Now, changing the subject, I guess Juliet won't eat pasta with chilli in it? Does she like garlic bread?"

The two women and the little girl tucked into their plates of spaghetti and sauce, garlic bread and green salad. Lois and Claudia shared the wine, and Juliet enjoyed a glass of also-forbidden-at-home apple juice, and they chatted about school and cats and princesses.

As Lois started to clear the plates, Juliet asked bluntly

"Is there anything nice for pudding, or just fruit?"

Claudia put her hand over her eyes in embarrassment.

"Juliet! That's not a polite question!"

Juliet raised big eyes to her mother.

"Isn't it? Why not?"

Claudia was saved from an explanation by Lois.

"No sweetheart, I haven't got anything particular for pudding - though you're welcome to have an apple if you'd like. But I thought maybe we could go to the park this afternoon, and perhaps have an ice-cream in the cafe there?"

Juliet nodded vociferously, and Lois carried on slightly hesitantly.

"And I've asked a friend of mine, Michael, if he'd like to meet us at the park. I want him to meet you and mummy. Would that be ok?"

Juliet nodded again.

"Is he your boyfriend, Auntie Lo?"

Lois hesitated again.

"No, he's not. You know that if I fall in love with anyone, it's a woman, like Auntie Janey was, not a man. He's just a good friend."

Juliet gazed seriously at Lois.

"Oh yes, I'd forgotten that you fell in love with girls. Mummy did tell me. Tabitha in my class has two mummies, so I think her mummies must fall in love with other girls too."

Her gaze became suspicious, and she turned to her mother

"He's not *your* boyfriend, is he?"

Claudia choked slightly on her wine.

"No! Whatever gave you that idea? He's Auntie Lo's friend, I've never even met him!"

Juliet seemed satisfied.

"That's ok then."

Conscious of a sinking feeling, Claudia couldn't resist asking

"Would it be a problem if I ever did have a boyfriend?"

Juliet shook her head.

"No, it wouldn't be a problem, as long as it's Dan."

Lois unsuccessfully smothered a giggle, and Claudia glared at her. This taught her a lesson for asking leading questions. Change subject, quickly.

"Right, well if you want to go to the swings and have ice-cream, you'd better go to the toilet and then find your shoes, hadn't you?"

And then as Juliet looked like she was about to say something else

"Quick, quick, quick! Or we might change our minds and go shopping instead."

Juliet scarpered as the two women met each other's eyes and collapsed in helpless laughter.

19

Claudia, Lois and Juliet enjoyed a relaxing afternoon at the park. Lois's local park was amazing, with a fantastic playground complete with huge adventure climbing frame, sand pit and playhouse, and Juliet quickly made friends with another little girl and played happily with her, leaving Lois and Claudia free to sit on a bench in the slightly watery sunshine, chatting happily.

Claudia had been somewhat sceptical about Michael. Not that she had anything against him in particular, but she still found Lois' 'modern marriage' concept slightly bizarre, and was yet to be convinced it was the answer to Lois' baby dilemma. Her own recent experience seemed to demonstrate that it was hard enough sustaining an adult relationship and bringing up a child when you started the whole process in love with each other. Doing it as almost total strangers seemed to be asking for trouble. Although, she supposed, you could argue that without the emotional complications of a romantic relationship it would be easier to navigate the ups and downs of family life. She and Ethan were certainly arguing less now, although having the Atlantic Ocean between them probably helped with that.

The other thing that troubled her was what would happen if Lois fell in love again. Although she was adamant she never would, she was still young, and still in the first throes of grief. She might feel very differently in ten years' time, and how would that work if she was in a bizarre platonic menage with a child involved?

In person, though, she found Michael utterly charming. He was kind and gentle, full of old-fashioned courtesy like holding doors open, and carrying their tray in the cafe. He also had an unexpectedly dry sense of humour, and Claudia could feel herself really warming to him. She knew from Lois that he wasn't gay, but realised that if she hadn't known she would have assumed he was. She couldn't quite put her finger on why; he seemed to possess a sensitivity she had seldom encountered in straight men, but there was something else too.

He was sweet with Juliet too, and she took to him in a way she didn't often with strangers. All in all, a meeting which she had feared could be awkward and uncomfortable felt surprisingly relaxed. Lois' opinion on Daniel's note had cheered Claudia up more than she admitted, and she felt pretty upbeat as she and Juliet shared a theatrically gigantic knickerbocker glory. Lois and Michael had stuck to coffees, and there was a lot of good-natured teasing as she managed to get herself covered in whipped cream and chocolate sauce.

Eventually it was time to go.

"Do you want to come back for supper?" Lois asked "Michael's going to."

Claudia hesitated.

"You can stay over, if you're worried about Juliet having a late night on a school night. I've got pjs and things for her you know."

Claudia was tempted. At the thought of going home and having A Conversation with Daniel her stomach filled with butterflies, and a cosy and undemanding evening with Lois felt rather tempting. Then she shook her head. As she so often seemed to be reminding herself these days, she had to be a sensible grown-up.

"No, thank you. It's really kind, but I haven't got Juliet's school uniform here, and it would end up being a logistical nightmare in the morning. I should get her home and have an early night, she's had a busy weekend. Plus, you know…"

Her voice trailed off, and Lois nodded understandingly.

"That's fine. Listen, hope everything goes well. Let me know, ok?" she gave her friend a quick hug, and then bent down to embrace her goddaughter.

Juliet returned the hug enthusiastically, and then surprised everyone by hugging Michael too.

"I like you." she informed him. "You're funny. And if you were a girl I think you'd be a good person for Auntie Lo to fall in love with."

They all laughed, and then Claudia took her

daughter's hand and headed off towards the tube station, listening to Juliet's chatter whilst internally planning what she would say to Daniel later on.

***

Whilst Claudia, Lois and Juliet were having fun in the park, things were a good deal less relaxed at the Nicholls family reunion.

Some rather awkward light chit chat had led into the first bombshell of the afternoon; that Daniel was not currently working as a doctor and had taken a job as a live-in nanny instead.

"But *why*?" Delia was asking, "and why didn't you tell us?"

Daniel had known this conversation wouldn't be easy, and wasn't particularly fazed by it.

"I just have told you." he pointed out. "And as for why, well, I just felt I needed a break from medicine for a while. I guess I was getting a bit burnt out."

His father snorted.

"Humph. When I was your age I had a mortgage to pay, and a wife to support. And you then you two arrived not long after. It's a good thing I didn't get 'burnt out', isn't it? Honestly, you young people haven't got much backbone."

Dominic immediately leapt to his brother's defence.

"To be fair Dad, you weren't working fifteen hour shifts saving children's lives, were you? A cosy office job doesn't exactly compare to what Dan's been doing."

It was the nannying that Delia couldn't comprehend.

"Honestly dear, I suppose Dominic's right, and I can understand why you might need a little rest. But working as a *nanny*? It's not exactly making the most of your skills, is it? Couldn't you maybe have gone travelling for a bit, something like that?"

Now it was Lydia's turn to snort.

"Delia! When I went travelling you told me I should get a proper job! You even suggested *I* should get a qualification in childcare, if I remember rightly. It's one rule for girls and another for boys with you, isn't it?"

Delia smiled, tight-lipped.

"Maybe I did. But the circumstances were slightly different. Daniel has qualifications, a career, he's made something of himself. If he wants to take a sabbatical to travel for a while then I can understand that. But what worried me about you was that you *had* no qualifications, no plan, no focus, and that you'd just drift through life without achieving anything. And, frankly, I wasn't far wrong, was I?"

Lydia took deep breaths, trying to calm herself, too upset and angry to answer. As usual, Dominic leapt into the breach again - as he always had, pouring oil on troubled waters. Or, so he hoped.

"Oh by the way, Mum, speaking of travel - Lyddy said I had to remind her to collect her birth certificate off you. She needs a new passport, don't you Lyds?"

Lydia nodded, still not trusting herself to speak. The heads of all three turned to Delia as she flushed and stammered slightly.

"Umm, yes, she did mention it. Unfortunately I seem to have misplaced it. Are you sure I haven't given it to you previously, Lydia? It would be just like you to lose it in one of your 'flat shares'."

Lydia shook her head.

"No. I am absolutely certain that I've never even laid eyes on my birth certificate. Surely you must have all those kind of things together, the things that were my parents'? I mean, my birth certificate, their marriage certificate, their birth certificates and so on?"

She suddenly felt a surge of confidence.

"I think I should probably take all of it now."

Delia shot a panicked glance at Henry, who shrugged.

"Well, umm, I don't know what we've got really. I'll have a look for you at some point, when I've got time. But honestly, I do have better things to do than hunt things out for you, you know! Why this sudden urge to have all these documents – you have never shown the smallest interest before!"

Lydia spoke calmly and firmly.

"That's not totally true, Delia. It's just that you have always shut me down when I have tried to ask any questions about myself or my background or my parents. But as I get older, I find more and more that I want to know."

Delia rolled her eyes.

"Oh for heaven's sake! You're always so melodramatic, Lydia! I haven't tried to 'shut you down, or hide who you are'! You are Lydia Manders, the daughter of Andrew and Ariadne Manders. You parents sadly died in a car accident when you were little, and Henry was named as your legal guardian so you came to live with us."

"Yes, I know that's what you have always told me. But I am at a point where I would like to have all the documents so I can see for myself. Is that ok?"

Daniel chimed in

"It's fair enough, Mum, for Lydia to want these things. Do you have them? You're always so organised, I can't believe you don't have them stashed away safe somewhere. If you haven't got time shall I go and have a look for you? Where would they be? In the attic? Or in the box of paperwork you keep in the study?"

He started to his feet as he spoke, and Delia cried out almost in panic.

"No! There's no need!"

Dominic frowned.

"But there is need, Mum. They are Lydia's things, and she wants them."

Dominic was frowning.

Despite Daniel's suspicions, he hadn't really believed deep down that Lydia could actually be his sister. It just seemed impossible to reconcile the way he felt about her with a blood tie. It had seemed sensible to keep things platonic while they got it all sorted out, but it had seemed very much a 'just in case', and after today's tea party he had been looking forward to going home with Lydia and resuming their normal lives, secure in the absolute knowledge that Lydia was exactly what she had always been – his parents' ward, his best friend, the woman he had fallen in love with.

But he had to admit that he had never seen his mother behaving quite like this before. She was normally so calm and self-assured - maddeningly so according to Lydia. Now she was flustered and clearly on the defensive. Was that just because she was feeling guilty about losing Lydia's documents, or was there more to it than that? A feeling of total panic gripped him, and he spoke sharply.

"Come *on* Mum! Dad! Where are Lydia's things? She wants her birth certificate, and her parents' birth certificates, and their marriage certificate! And anything else you have! You must have it – those things must have been given to you when you took on guardianship, so where are they?"

It *wasn't* his imagination. The look Delia gave his father was one of pure panic. He shrugged his shoulders and glared at her. Daniel leapt in, as Lydia didn't seem as though she was going to.

"Dom's right, Mum. We need to find it for her. I'm going to check. Is the box with all that stuff in still under the desk?"

Delia jumped to her feet and with surprising agility managed to position herself between her son and the living room door and shouted at him.

"No! Daniel! I will not have you rooting around in my house and searching through my things. How dare you try! It's nothing to do with you and Dominic anyway, you should mind your own business."

This outburst was met with stunned silence. In all her twenty-nine years Lydia couldn't remember hearing Delia speak to one of the boys like that. In fact she rarely raised her voice at all. Lydia came in for plenty of criticism, but it was usually delivered in faux-honied tones under the guise of concern. And the boys could generally do no wrong at all. It was all very odd and disconcerting. So much so that she felt slightly sick and shaky.

God, it really did seem that there was some mystery about her birth certificate. All she could feel was that the certainties of identity which were the foundations of her life were crumbling. She felt powerless, even to speak, let alone to work out how to push Delia into revealing the truth. She caught Dominic's eye and gazed pleadingly at him. I know, she implored him silently, I know you don't like confrontation. I know that taking action is my role through all our lives together, but I need you to do something now.

Dominic could feel the fear and uncertainty coming off Lydia in waves. She had turned white, and he could see her hands were trembling. Daniel too was strangely quiet, the shock of being the recipient of his mother's anger, and indecision as to what to do next, having temporarily silenced him. Dom drew a deep breath. All his life he had coasted, had relied on other people, usually Daniel or Lydia, to push him when push was needed. Yes, working in a big modern comprehensive was challenging, but he got through by being totally laid-back and letting the storms of Ofsted, parental complaints and challenging teen behaviour wash over him. Now, though, his and Lydia's entire future and happiness might be dependent on how he handled this conversation.

He rose to his feet and went over to where his mum was standing, guarding the door. He reached out and took her hand.

"What's going on, Mum? There's clearly more to this than a lost birth certificate. Are you hiding something from us? What is it? Is there something about Lydia's identity that we don't know?"

He'd done it. He'd spoken the fateful words. He felt a sense of exhilaration. Lydia felt her stomach turn over queasily. Daniel stared in amazement as the colour ebbed totally from Delia's cheeks.

"Why would you think that?" her voice sounded totally different, high, squeaky, breathless.

Daniel pulled the photo from his pocket with a flourish.

"Well this, for a start! This photo was in the box you gave me. It's of Granny Nicholls when she was young, and she is the living image of Lydia."

At this point Henry stepped in unexpectedly.

"No, Delia. This has to stop. I never agreed with it, as you know. I thought we should have told them years ago. But now they've worked it out for themselves we owe them the truth."

20

Lois and Michael were curled up on the sofa in her living room, Horatio asleep between them, and the remains of a Chinese banquet scattered around. Lois still couldn't believe quite how relaxed she felt around him. Other than with Janey, and Claudia, she didn't think she had ever experienced this level of trust and intimacy with anyone. Part of it was, undoubtedly, that he got it. He understood exactly what it was like to watch the love of your life suffering and then slipping away from you, and the confusing cocktail of emotions that remained. Fury at the injustice of it all. Sadness so overwhelming that just getting out of bed and getting dressed felt like a major achievement some days. Guilt, always guilt - guilt that it was them not you. Guilt that you hadn't been able to help them, save them. Guilt, sometimes, that you resented them for leaving you all alone. Irritation at well-meaning friends and family who thought that encouraging you to 'move on' would somehow be helpful.

Not that they talked about their bereavements all the time. They had discovered a shared delight in 1970s and 1980s sitcoms, and so an evening in with a *Hidey Hi* box-set was a guilty pleasure they could enjoy together. They had talked about careers - Lois' passion for what she did, her determination to succeed, her conviction that helping and healing children and families was her vocation, but also Michael's growing disillusionment with accountancy, his irritation with clients who simply saw his role as reducing their tax burden to the minimum they could get away with. They discussed their shared values, and how they might apply to bringing up a child, and the practicalities of child-rearing in the modern marriage they were creating.

It made sense, they agreed, that after taking a few months maternity leave, Lois should return to work full-time, while Michael took over the day-to-day responsibility for caring for the baby. Perhaps as the baby got older he or she could go to nursery a couple of days a week, and Michael could continue his freelance accountancy, but Lois was the one who loved her job, and she earned more than enough to support a family, whereas Michael felt he would be entirely comfortable in a caring role.

They were planning to have the top floor of Lois' three-storey townhouse turned into a self-sufficient flat for Michael, with its own bathroom, bed-sitting room and kitchenette. Obviously he would spend a huge amount of time in the rest of the house, and hopefully they would normally eat together as a family, but they both felt it made sense for them to be able to have some space apart and a little bit of independence if they needed it.

Lois shifted position now, took a mouthful of beer, and turned to Michael who, like her, looked half asleep.

"We ought to start getting some quotes for the building work, you know."

He nodded.

"Yeah, I guess we should. Although there's no major rush. We've got this six month delay to get through first, not to mention a nine month pregnancy."

Much to their frustration, they had discovered that the fertility clinic they had chosen had a policy that donor sperm from a 'known donor' such as Michael would be had to be kept for six months before being used, in order to minimise the risk of an illness like HIV being passed on. Lois had been so annoyed she had considered lying and saying that they were in a relationship, or even forgoing the clinic entirely in favour of the good old turkey baster method, but after her initial anger her cool common sense and scientific judgement had taken over. They had already explained their circumstances to that clinic, so if they were going to pretend to be in a relationship they would have to go elsewhere- and she had selected that particular clinic on the basis of its stellar success rates. There would also be the awkward issue to get over of why, if they were a couple, they weren't going down the traditional 'having sex' route to conceiving a child. And at her age proper clinical IVF would have a far higher chance of success than

A Thoroughly Modern Marriage

syringes at home.

Lois giggled suddenly, and Michael glanced at her. "What's the joke?"

"Oh, nothing really. I was just thinking about this bloody six month delay, and ways around it. And wondering, if we pretended to be a couple, how we would explain we needed IVF when, as far as we know, we're both perfectly fertile. And then I thought that maybe we could say that you were totally impotent, and so IVF was our only hope, but I wasn't sure that the red-blooded male in you would agree. Which is what made me laugh."

There was a silence, rather an uncomfortable silence. Lois began to curse herself for her tactlessness. Michael had become a good friend, and she felt she could discuss most things with him, but clearly jokes about his sexual prowess were a step too far - as she imagined they would be for most men.

"Sorry, Michael. I didn't mean to offend you."

He grinned at her.

"You didn't. But it's made up my mind - I am going to talk to you about something I never thought I'd discuss with anyone again after my wife died, but it might reassure you about our future."

The casual laid-back atmosphere had changed subtly, and Lois turned to Michael, prepared to put all her doctor's good listening skills into practice.

"Go on, what is it? I'm pretty unshockable!"

Michael took a deep breath, and looked down at his hands, and then started to stroke Horatio as a displacement. He couldn't believe that he was about to have this conversation, but instinct seemed to be telling him that it was the right thing to do.

"Well, it's no big deal, but I guess I'm not totally normal. Although I had a very happy marriage I am largely asexual. I mean, prior to meeting my wife I had never been in a relationship, and never wanted to be. And then I fell very much in love with her, and although sex and physical intimacy *was* part of our relationship, it was never even close to being the most important part. And since she died, I haven't been attracted to anyone else. I'm telling you, because an obvious complication to our plans would be one of us falling for someone else, so I just wanted to be clear that from my side that is vanishingly unlikely. "

Lois was silent for a moment. Relieved, mainly that he hasn't confessed to some hideous perversion involving children or animals or something equally vile that would have meant she would need to run far and fast. But no. Not wanting to have physical relationships at all, that felt manageable. She smiled at him.

"Well, no-one is entirely normal! I mean, I only want to have sex with women, and famously that is so abnormal that Queen Victoria couldn't even consider it as a possibility."

He laughed.

"Yes, I know. And these days homosexuality, and bisexuality are quite rightly considered completely normal, as are a whole range of fetishes and predilections. But it sometimes feels that not wanting to have sex at all is still something of a taboo."

Lois shrugged.

"Well, it's certainly no big deal to me! Thank you for telling me. And I guess it is reassuring that you are unlikely to be chatting up the au pair or something, but otherwise it's none of my business. And if things change for you, and you *do* meet someone you want to be in a relationship with, well, we would work it out. And same if I did, although like you I also think it's an incredibly remote possibility."

He laughed.

"I certainly won't be chatting up the au pair! And I agree, if either one of us did meet someone, then we would work something out like lots of blended families do with step-parents and so on these days. I just wanted you to know it wasn't likely to be an issue we faced."

Lois nodded. His reference to chatting up the au pair had reminded her of Claudia and Daniel, and she wondered how they were getting on with their big conversation this evening. Michael's revelation, now she was processing it, made total sense. The feeling she had of being totally relaxed with him so early was presumably because there was absolutely no possibility of sex becoming an issue between them. She never fancied men, and he never fancied anyone. It also was reassuring for their future, as one of the points Claudia had raised was what would happen if and when Michael met another woman and wanted to have kids in a more conventional way with her. Knowing that was unlikely was good news for her, and made his enthusiasm for her modern marriage concept even more understandable.

"So that's why you want to have a baby with me."

It was a statement rather than a question.

"Yes, I think it is. I can't imagine meeting and falling in love with anyone else after Alice, and because sex isn't really a big deal for me it has to be a real meeting of minds for a relationship to work. I think what Alice and I had was truly a once in a lifetime occurrence."

Lois let her glance wonder round the familiar room. Squashy sofas in rather battered brown leather, bay window with slightly faded curtains drawn back to show the twilit street outside. Mantlepiece a jumble of cards and invitations and photos, and a wood-burning stove underneath. Scuffed-up old floorboards and a couple of threadbare antique Persian rugs. How many evenings had she and Janey spent here, curled up on this sofa with a takeaway, just like she was now? It suddenly felt slightly jarring, doing this, sharing secrets, making plans with someone who wasn't Janey. The uncomfortable thought that she hadn't just wanted a baby or just wanted a family, she had wanted those things with Janey struck her.

She let her gaze fall on Michael who met her eyes with some anxiety and trepidation, and she felt a rush of warm affection for him wash over her. He looked unremarkable, really. Tallish, light brown hair, receding slightly on the temples. Blue eyes, slightly accountant-y glasses, nice smile. But as she had noticed back in the coffee shop when they first met, the thing that really struck you was the almost tangible aura of kindness and warmth which seemed to surround him. Maybe it would be ok after all. Maybe this could work.

Lois laid her hand on top of his where it was resting on Horatio's back.

"Thank you for telling me, Michael. It doesn't make any difference, obviously."

She felt him relax.

"We have both had a tough time, and we've both learned from it what is really important to us, and we're going to create our own family that works for us and our child. That's it, all we need to know, and all we need to focus on."

21

Lydia was still shaking, whether with cold or reaction she barely knew. Dominic tucked a throw tenderly around her shoulders, and then sat down next to her, taking her small cold hand in his large warm one. The revelations of the evening, the fact that all three of them were possibly estranged from Delia and Henry forever, Lydia's obvious shock and distress - all of those combined should have left him stressed, overwhelmed, reaching for the gin bottle. Instead he felt like he could fly. Ecstatic, omnipotent, filled with an unshakeable conviction that everything was going to be alright now.

Daniel came out of the kitchen area with a tray on which balanced three steaming mugs of hot chocolate and a packet of biscuits. He handed one each to Lydia and Dominic, and then sat on the leather arm-chair opposite and cradled his own mug. They looked at each other in silence, and sipped the sweet, reviving drinks. Lydia felt her shallow, panicky breathing slow, and she reminded herself that, whatever had happened, she was safe now. Home now. With Dominic and Daniel, who had proved beyond doubt that she could rely on them utterly.

Daniel broke the silence first.

"Well! When I saw that photo, I knew there was something odd going on, but I never in a million years expected all that."

Lydia nodded, and shuddered, and nestled in closer to Dominic, reflecting on the events a few hours earlier.

After Henry's assertion that the children should know the truth, Delia had turned a nasty shade of greenish white, and almost collapsed onto the sofa. As she was clearly not going to be particularly informative, the three of them had turned enquiringly to Henry.

He had sighed heavily, and then begun his tale.

"None of you know this, but I was not an only child. I had a half-brother, who died twenty-six years ago when Lydia was just a toddler. He died in a car-crash, and his wife died with him, so their little girl was left an orphan overnight."

He paused. The tension in the room was tangible. A million questions were forming in Dominic, Daniel and Lydia's minds, but they were scared to vocalise them in case it somehow shut the floodgates of information which miraculously seemed to have opened.

Eventually Daniel risked it.

"You said half-brother? But weren't Granny and Grandpa Nicholls only in their early twenties when they got married? Was one of them married before?"

Henry shook his head.

"Not married, no. But when Granny Nicholls was about eighteen she got pregnant. It was towards the end of the Second World War, and the father was an Australian, who was serving with the RAF over here. Granny was a WAAF at the time, and she met him, and I guess things were different in war-time…she had been engaged to Grandad Nicholls, but he had been reported missing, believed dead, and she turned to this man for comfort I expect. She discovered she was pregnant, and the family were devastated. Unmarried motherhood was still a real stigma then."

Lydia was silent, trying to take it all in. She still couldn't totally work out how this related to the mystery of her birth certificate, but her imagination was caught by the story. She had always loved Granny Nicholls, who only died a couple of years ago, and had always called her 'Granny' as the twins had, even though she was no relation. Having seen the photo Dan had found she could trace a likeness to that young girl, even though the woman she knew had been grey-haired and stooped. She thought of Granny, a young girl of eighteen, believing the love of her life was dead, seeking comfort, but then bringing disgrace on herself.

Henry was continuing, not meeting the eyes of the younger generation, but staring down at his good quality navy suede carpet slippers as though they alone contained the answers to life, the universe and everything. Delia, in her corner of the sofa, was almost rocking backwards and forwards, clearly intensely distressed, but ignored by everyone as all eyes were focussed on Henry.

"It turned out that Percy, her lover, was already married to an Australian woman, so he couldn't do the decent thing and marry Granny. But, he and his wife didn't have children, and he offered to take the baby and bring it up as their own. I don't think Granny wanted to let the baby go, but she didn't have any money of her own, and her family put her under a lot of pressure, so I don't think she had much choice. She went to stay with relatives in another part of the country so that no-one knew she was pregnant, had the baby, and then Percy took him – the baby - back to Australia with him. Then, much to everyone's delight, at the end of the war Grandad Nicholls came home, not dead after all, he'd been taken a prisoner of war, and survived. He and Granny got married as they'd always planned."

Daniel interjected again.

"Did she tell Grandad Nicholls about the baby?"

Henry nodded.

"Yes. In fact, Grandad Nicholls offered to adopt the baby himself, and bring him back from Australia. But the baby was two by this time, and settled with his Australian parents, and apparently his adoptive mother wrote Granny a heart-rending letter, begging her not to take her baby away. Granny felt that she had wronged her enough, even though she hadn't known Percy was married, and decided to leave the child where he was. Then afterwards I was born."

He paused again, and took a gulp of tea from his delicate china cup.

"When I was old enough, Granny told me about my brother, and we became pen-pals. The adoptive parents sent photos of him every year on his birthday, and he used to write to Granny sometimes as well. When I was in my twenties, before I married your mother, Granny and Grandpa Nicholls and I went on holiday to Australia and I met my brother."

The eyes of all the children were round.

"Henry! I didn't know you'd ever been abroad! Let alone Australia! Why didn't you tell me when I went there?"

Henry shrugged.

"I wanted to, Lydia. But things had got complicated by then." He glanced in his wife's direction.

"I kept in touch with my brother, and over the next couple of years we both got married. He married an English girl he had met while she was travelling round Australia, and they moved back over here, and lived up in Yorkshire, near where she had grown up. You boys came along" he smiled at his sons "and then not long after my brother told me that his wife was pregnant. We met up a few times, although it wasn't particularly easy, with one thing and another, as none of us had much money in those days, and the twins weren't the easiest of travellers…And then my brother and his wife were killed."

By this time the truth was dawning on Lydia. Her head reeling, she almost shouted.

"Go on, Henry! What happened? What happened to the baby?"

He smiled at her.

"It turned out that my brother and his wife had made a will leaving me as guardian to their daughter. Andrew's parents were dead by then, and Ariadne wasn't close to her family. Neither of them had any siblings. So, when Dominic and Daniel had just turned four, I became guardian to my little niece, Lydia."

Lydia had felt the blood rushing from her head, engulfing her in a wave of dizziness. Then she thought she was going to be violently and humiliatingly sick. She rushed from the room, and raced upstairs, locking herself in the bathroom and bending over the lavatory retching. After a moment or two the cold sweat on her forehead abated, and the wave of nausea receded. She got up, splashed her face with cold water, smeared on some of her mother's expensive face cream, and opened the door. She met Dominic on the landing, and he put his arm round her.

"It's ok, Lyddy. It's all going to be alright. I love you, you know that?"

She nodded, and relaxed into his embrace for one blissful moment.

"I know. And I love you. But, oh my God, Dom. I feel sick. How have they kept this from me all this time? I don't even know who I am."

"Well, you're not my sister! Which is helpful. I was seriously worried for a few minutes back there. You will, however, always be the love of my life. Wait until we break *that* news to them!"

The nausea rose again.

"Dominic! No, you can't!"

He laughed, grimly.

"Oh can't I? Just bloody watch me. If there's one thing I've learned today it's that unknown amounts of trouble are caused by secrecy. No more."

22

Lydia took his arm, and they made their way back downstairs. The tableau in the living room was much as they had left it. Henry still staring at his feet, Delia wrapped in sullen, silent misery, Daniel almost self-combusting from the effort of keeping his questions to himself until Dominic and Lydia returned.

Lydia went straight over to the man she had never known was her uncle.

"Why did you never tell me, Henry? Why? I don't understand."

Henry sighed.

"I don't know. There were lots of reasons. I think none of us wanted to make a big deal of it. Or upset Granny by raking up the past."

Lydia threw up her hands in exasperation.

"Oh for God's sake! All that time I thought I had no family, thought that you didn't really want me, thought I was living with you on sufferance…"

"Oh, Lydia love…"

Henry started, but suddenly Delia cut in over him.

"Damn right, Lydia! Damn right you weren't wanted! How *could* I want you? I had toddler twins! Do you, in your lazy, pampered little existence, have any idea how much work there is in looking after baby twins? I was exhausted! I hadn't had more than two hours consecutive sleep for about three years. And just when I was starting to get the boys in a routine, just when I was starting to enjoy them, just when it was starting to feel a bit less like an endurance test and more like a life I might actually want, then I get landed with another toddler! And not even my bloody toddler! The baby of some godforsaken bastard Australian I'd barely even met, and I'm suddenly expected to bring you up as well. And getting stuck with you meant I never got the chance for another baby, never got the chance to have a little girl of my own! I didn't want another child thrust on me just then, but later, maybe when the boys were at school, I would have loved another one *of my own*. But I couldn't, because Henry said three was enough, that we couldn't afford more."

Dominic gazed at his mother in horror, unable to believe the force of bile and hatred spewing from her lips, and desperate, somehow to stop her before she hurt Lydia even more. It was Daniel who stepped in, though, recognising the symptoms of near hysteria. He went and sat by his mother, handing her a glass of water.

"Drink this, Mum, and be quiet for a bit." he instructed her firmly. She obeyed, and, temporarily at least, was quiet.

Lydia, face pale, eyes wide gazed unflinchingly at her guardians.

"So, why did you take me, then? If you really didn't want another child living with you? I mean, presumably there are children's homes I could have gone to?"

Henry stood up and moved over to his niece, enfolding her in his arms, where she stood passive and unresponsive.

"Darling girl! We did want you! Well, I wanted you. I hadn't ever got to spend much time with my brother, but I cared about him, and I wanted to do my best for his little girl. And Granny Nicholls couldn't bear the thought of her granddaughter being alone on the other side of the world with some distant Australian relatives you had. It was bad enough she'd lost her son, she didn't want to lose you too. So, Granny and I went up to Leeds to bring you home."

Lydia felt tears prick at her eyelids, and for a moment she let herself luxuriate in the feeling that she *had* been wanted. Then her mother's voice broke in again.

"Yes, your 'uncle' and your grandmother sorted it all between them. I was left at home alone with the twins while they went off to 'rescue' you, without anything I said being considered at all. It became quite a pattern, actually."

Clearly this was nothing Henry hadn't heard before. He carried on talking to Lydia as though his wife had never spoken.

"You were the most adorable little thing, Lydia, so tiny and so pretty. The foster carers who'd been looking after you since your parents died were really worried about you – you hadn't been eating properly, or talking at all, since your parents died. But when Granny took you in her arms and you just sort of melted into them, and from that point you started eating and talking again. You obviously remembered her, and felt safe with her."

Lydia gave up any attempt to hold her tears back then. She stepped away from her uncle's awkward embrace, and sank down on the edge of the sofa, burying her face in her hands and sobbing as though her heart would break.

Henry looked away to hide the tears in his own eyes, consumed with regret that he had allowed his wife to over-ride his natural instincts all these years, and prevent him having this conversation many years earlier.

Dominic had sat next to Lydia, his arm round her shoulders, waiting until she looked up. He handed her a tissue and she blew her nose ferociously and then subsided against his shoulder.

"Why didn't you tell us, Dad?" Henry reeled visibly. He had never guessed that such icy, steely tones could emanate from his laid-back, easy-going younger son.

"Do you have any idea how much harm you have done with your insane secrecy?"

Henry shook his head.

"I'm sorry, son. I always thought we should, but your mother thought it was best not. And after she'd agreed to take Lydia in, to bring her up almost as though she was her own, I didn't feel I could go against her wishes."

Dominic was shaking his head.

"No, Dad. That's not good enough. Hiding behind Mum isn't a sufficient reason. You must have known she didn't truly love Lydia, so why would you think she had Lydia's best interests at heart in not telling her? You didn't. You just opted for an easy life, in the same way you opted for an easy life in not really sticking up for Lydia when she needed you growing up. I know that's true, because we're the same, you and I. I have always opted for the easy life as well. I have let other people - mainly Lydia and Daniel - make the tough decisions, and I've gone along in their wake. Well no more. Now I've seen the damage weakness like that can do I am going to change. I am going to be strong. I am going to follow what *I* believe is right, stand up for what *I* believe in, not hide behind my brother or my...girlfriend."

Neither Henry or Delia seemed to notice Dominic's implied revelation, although Dom had felt Lydia's body tauten against his as she prepared herself for a fresh onslaught.

Delia glared at Lydia as she sat in the protective circle of Dominic's arm.

"Oh yes. Lydia has always had you two just where she wants you, hasn't she? She'd barely been in the house a week before she had you running round in circles after her, and that's never changed. She's even inveigled you into putting a roof over her head now, although she's too lazy to get herself a proper job and a place to live, acting like a teenager even though she's knocking thirty. Even though when I was her age I was bringing up three children, and she can't even take responsibility for herself. *That's* why I didn't want to tell anyone. Think of it from my point of view, Dominic."

She gazed pleadingly at her son, seemingly oblivious to the disgust etched on his features as he met her eyes.

"I took Lydia into my home, brought her up as my own, nearly killed myself with the work of three children under four, gave up my chance of another baby of my own. And what thanks do I get? None. Any affection she had to give went to you and your brother, or to your father, or your grandmother, never to me. I just got sullen resentment, or downright defiance. But your father wasn't the one to change the nappies and do the potty training, or get up to her in the middle of the night, or deal with the tantrum in the middle of the supermarket. She adored you two, and she'd be so happy and excited when Granny came round to see her, but I barely got a smile. If you'd all known the back story then she would have milked it for all she was worth. Tragic little orphan girl. Long-lost niece. Wicked step-aunt. She'd have wrapped you all around her finger even more firmly than she already had. She's always acted like she was something special, different to the rest of us, so if she'd known the backstory she would have been unbearable. She *isn't* part of our family, not properly, not legitimately, and I didn't want to give her the reason to pretend that she was."

Henry was looking horror-struck. All these years he had believed, or told himself he believed that Delia was putting Lydia's best interests first in keeping the story of her birth a secret, when all along it had been nothing more than spite. For the first time he made himself confront just how hard Lydia's life must have been growing up, how much of the love she deserved she had missed out on. He had known that she and Delia weren't close, would have to have been deaf and blind to miss it, but had always told himself that mothers and daughters always argued, and this was a similar sort of thing, it was nothing unusual, and not for him to butt in.

In some ways Lydia was less shocked than the twins. Unlike everyone else in her family, she had always known that Delia's feelings for her often seemed closer to resentment than anything else. Now at least she knew why. She ignored the prickle of conscience that Delia's words awoke, suppressing the fact that she *had* been a difficult child and teenager. That she *had* taken her anger and grief at not having her own parents out on Delia. That she had, at times, consciously charmed the men in the family, as she always could, and inveigled them into taking her side when necessary.

Dominic could barely speak for rage.

"I cannot believe that you would play games with someone's life like that. Poor Lydia has spent her whole life feeling unloved - clearly because you didn't love her - and not knowing why, blaming herself. It's incredible she's turned out the warm, loving, generous, kind-hearted, amazing person she is. No thanks to you two!"

"Unloved! Ha! That's a joke! With you two boys continually fawning over her. Bloody spoilt little madame, that's what she is. Unloved!"

Daniel opened his mouth to speak, fearing for what his brother might do next, but Dominic was too quick for him. His voice was deceptively soft now.

"You're right, Mum. I do love Lydia. Very much indeed. More than life itself, in fact."

He squeezed her tighter, and dropped a soft kiss on her pale cheek.

"But because of your perverse, selfish secrecy I have been torturing myself, feeling that my love, our love, was wrong. Daniel found that photo, and we all recognised Lydia's likeness to Granny Nicholls, and came to the wrong conclusion. We thought that she was *Dad's* illegitimate daughter, and Granny Nicholls' granddaughter that way. I should have listened to Lydia. She was right all along - as usual. She said that nothing as good, as pure, as strong as our love for each other could possibly be a sin or a crime, and she was dead right. But I have been through *hell!*"

His voice rose again.

"I have been to *hell* because of you. Because you didn't tell us the truth properly you left me find out part of it and believe Lydia was my sister. I thought that I had fallen in love with my sister. I thought I was wrong and dirty and perverted. I thought I was going to break up our family and break your hearts, and it drove me to drink, literally. If it wasn't for Daniel's support I'd probably be a complete raving alcoholic by this time."

Delia and Henry were both silent, dumbstruck, brains whirring as they tried to take in the implications of what Dominic was saying.

He hadn't finished.

"God. You were giving Dan a hard time for quitting his job – part of that was so he could look after me! Because I was in such a state over being in love with my potential sister!"

Daniel threw Dominic as look of stunned surprise - he had certainly never mentioned that part of his motivation for leaving the hospital to either Dominic or Lydia. Despite the tension, Dominic grinned at his brother.

"Oh, come on mate! You're my twin brother. I know you better than anyone in the world. I knew what you were up to, and I'm bloody grateful."

Delia had found her voice at last.

"Are you trying to tell me that you two" her appalled glance travelled between Dominic and Lydia "are *lovers*?"

She almost choked over the last word.

Dominic nodded cheerfully.

"Yep. That's right. We have been for a few months now. Until we thought that we might be siblings! Thankfully today's revelations have straightened that out at least!"

Delia transferred her gaze to her eldest son.

"And you knew about this, Daniel?"

He nodded.

"Right. That's it. Get out of my house NOW. All of you. You vile little slut, Lydia. I always knew you would damage my family, but I didn't know quite how comprehensively you'd manage to totally destroy it. Get OUT NOW!"

Dominic stood up, pulling a shaking, trembling Lydia with him.

"Don't worry, we're going. And until you give Lydia a full apology you won't be seeing me again."

Daniel nodded.

"Dom's right, Mum. You have behaved appallingly to Lydia, and we won't stand for you talking to her like that. I don't want to see you again until you've apologised either."

And with that, they had all walked out, Dominic half carrying Lydia out and to the taxi Daniel quickly ordered.

23

While Daniel, Dominic and Lydia raked over the shattered remnants of their stable, secure, respectable suburban family, half a mile away Claudia was cleaning an already spotless worktop. She hadn't been able to settle to anything all evening, not work, not television, not reading, and so had cleaned to take her mind off things, with the result that the entire house gleamed more pristinely than it had since the day they moved in.

She glanced at the clock for the thousandth time. 10.30pm. Daniel had said he was going out to tea with his parents. It seemed pretty implausible that this tea-party would still be carrying on at 10.30pm on a Sunday evening. Although, of course, she didn't know Daniel's family. Perhaps, instead of the sedate china teapot and homemade scones she was picturing they actually all let their hair down with tequila shots and drinking games when they got together. Perhaps. Or, perhaps somewhat more likely, Daniel was regretting their night of passion, and because of the awkwardness of their situation and living arrangements was simply taking the coward's way out and avoiding her until she got the message.

Well, she'd got it, loud and clear. Thank God she

hadn't given herself away too badly. Thank God she could get out with her pride more or less intact, without him having realised how much she cared, how much he was beginning to mean to her. Her heart and footsteps were leaden as she plodded upstairs. She may as well have a hot bath in a vain attempt to relax, and get an early night. Tomorrow was another day, and all that. Her footsteps quickened. Now she had made the decision, she wanted to get upstairs and into her bedroom before he came home, and not give him the satisfaction of seeming to have waited up for him. Almost running now, she got to the top of the stairs and bolted into her bedroom, shutting the door quickly behind her.

Thank heaven for en-suite bathrooms - no need to leave the room until breakfast time tomorrow. By which time, Claudia promised herself, she would be recovered. Ice maiden lawyer would be back on duty, and Daniel would have been relegated very firmly back to his position as live-in nanny. She didn't want to disrupt Juliet's life again; she had suffered enough recently from the actions of grown-ups who ought to put her happiness and wellbeing first. Daniel, if he was willing to, would stay on as nanny, but she would never waste another thought on him.

Wallowing in the warm, fragrant water, Claudia resisted the almost overwhelming temptation to let her thoughts linger on last night's blissful sex. How long, she wondered, before she experienced that again? If she ever did. She couldn't recall ever enjoying sex quite as much - what if she never did again? Always supposing she ever met anyone she wanted to sleep with, and that they weren't as put off as Daniel clearly was by a practically middle-aged single mum. She sighed. It was probably best to remove herself from the sensual atmosphere of a warm bath before the memories of Daniel's large, strong, sensitive hands or his warm lips, or his thick blond hair, gorgeous blue eyes, deliciously muscled torso and broad shoulders became too intrusive. A cold shower was the traditional remedy, but Claudia couldn't quite face that, and settled for buttoning herself into comfortable and resolutely unsexy pyjamas and climbing into bed with a Barbara Pym novel.

She was just drifting off to sleep when she heard a faint click which could be the front door, and just the faintest suggestion of footsteps. Did they pause outside her bedroom door? If so, not for long. She sighed again, blinked back the tears which threatened, and her last conscious thought before sleep overtook her was a repeated resolution to be so icily polite that Daniel could never pierce her defences again.

***

It was about 10.30pm when there was a pause in the conversation. Lydia asked sleepily if Daniel was going to stay the night.

"I can easily put clean sheets on the bed in my

room, if you want to. And I'm sure we've got a spare toothbrush."

Daniel shook his head.

"No. You two probably need some time on your own. Plus, I need to be back for Juliet's breakfast time - I didn't tell Claudia I'd be…" his voice trailed off, and he turned pale.

"What is it?" Lydia sat up and turned to look properly at her brother.

"Oh shit. Oh fuck."

"What?!"

He looked at her, wild-eyed.

"I left Claudia a note this morning, telling her I'd be back this evening so we could talk. Oh fuck. What time is it?"

"Just after half ten. But don't worry, I'm sure she'll understand when she hears the story of family crisis. Were you meant to be looking after Juliet?"

He shook his head.

"No, Sundays are my day off."

"Well then. No big deal."

He pulled at his hair.

"No, you don't understand. It is a big deal. Oh bloody hell. I can't believe I forgot!"

Dominic and Lydia were both staring at him in confusion now.

"Forgot what?"

Daniel was doing up his trainers as he spoke, all fingers and thumbs, fumbling with the laces.

"Look, the thing is, we, erm, had sex for the first

time last night. It was amazing. You know, Lyddy, how I feel about her, and I feel it even more now. But I was worried about crowding her, you know, in the circumstances, with living in the same house and everything. So I sneaked out early, just leaving a note saying I'd see her this evening. But now I haven't showed up, and she's going to think I've walked out on her, or that I regret it or something. I can't believe I finally had my chance, and I've messed it up. I'm such an idiot."

Dominic slapped his shoulder gently.

"Give yourself a break, Dan. It's been a fairly unpredictable day all round. I don't think she's going to hold it against you when you explain. Just go home now, get some sleep, and have a proper talk with her tomorrow. At least you know where she is, given that you live together!"

Daniel looked at his brother, a flicker of hope in his eyes, and then at Lydia.

"What do you think, Lyddy?"

She nodded.

"Dom's right. I'm not saying she won't be feeling a bit pissed off right now, but you have got a pretty good excuse. You just need to explain properly tomorrow. Use that famous Nicholls charm! She clearly likes you - given last night - so I'm sure it'll work out."

Daniel nodded, feeling slightly better.

"And do you two mind, if I tell Claudia everything? I'm sure she's trustworthy."

Dominic hesitated slightly, looking at Lydia, but she nodded vehemently.

"Of course I don't mind! I don't what I'll say, if anything, to anyone else, but I know how much Claudia means to you, so you owe her a proper explanation. And, after all, none of us have done anything to be ashamed of."

Daniel nodded gratefully, wrapped both of them in a bear hug, and set off for home.

Now the drama of the day was over, he became aware of how utterly exhausted he was. Nonetheless, he formed a plan in his mind as he dragged himself home. If Claudia was awake when he got in he would tell her everything, there and then. Throw himself on her mercy. But what if she wasn't? He could hardly pour out a tale of love and betrayal, illicit sex, concealed hatred and family breakdown over Juliet's breakfast Cheerios. No, if he couldn't see Claudia tonight, then he would need to deal with things slightly differently.

He let himself in softly, not wanting to wake Juliet, even if Claudia was still up. Downstairs was in darkness, and he crept up the stairs. No light under her door, although he could catch an intoxicating whiff of the scented bath oil she used, which suggested she hadn't been in bed long. He paused outside her door. Dare he knock and go in now, offer his explanation before things got even more convoluted? Regretfully he decided not. It wasn't fair to Claudia to wake her up with such a complicated story when she had to work tomorrow. And she would hardly be at her most receptive either. No, it was time to put Plan B into action.

24

After Daniel left, Lydia and Dominic sat in silence, nestled into one another. Lydia was feeling calmer now, but her mind was racing with questions. She was half Australian! That perhaps explained her strong affinity for the country. Did she have relatives there? Dad had said that her parents had both been only children, but what about other relatives? Were her mother's parents still alive? She suddenly felt overwhelmed by what she had lost, and tears started seeping again.

Dominic pulled her closer into him and, yet again, she soaked the front of his shirt while he stroked her hair.

"My mother…" her voice choked "my mother, my real mother, loved me, Dom. Didn't she?"

"Oh Lydia, baby. Of course she did. Who wouldn't love you? You are innately loveable."

She grimaced.

"Delia doesn't love me."

Dominic almost snarled.

"No, well, she's an idiot. But my dad loves you. And Granny Nicholls did, and Daniel does, and your parents did. And I love you to the ends of the earth, Lyddy."

She smiled.

"I know. I'm so lucky to have you. And I love you so much. But I can't help feeling weird. Rootless. Familyless. Orphaned. I mean, I always was all those things, I know, but somehow, knowing how close I came to having a proper family, makes it all feel even weirder."

Dominic gazed down at her lovely face, almost overwhelmed by the surge of love and protectiveness her was experiencing. Suddenly he knew he couldn't hold back, he couldn't wait for the perfect moment or create a romantic memory to treasure for a lifetime. The words which had sprung to mind the second he heard his father's revelation sprang from his lips.

"Will you marry me, Lydia? I know this isn't a big romantic moment, and obviously I haven't got a ring, because until this afternoon I wasn't even sure we could be together, let alone get married, but I love you so much, and *I* want to be your family. I want to look after you like you've always looked after me. I want you to be one hundred percent certain that you will always have me, I want us to put down new roots together."

Yet more tears flowed from Lydia's eyes.

"Yes! Oh Dominic, yes, I would love to marry you. And you're wrong - I think that might be just about the most romantic thing I've ever heard. You are amazing. And if there is one good thing to come out of all this mess today, it's that I get to be your wife!"

She paused, and a mischievous smile crossed her face

"Hey, shall we call your mum and dad to tell them the good news?"

***

After struggling to get to sleep, Claudia was dead to the world when Juliet bounced onto her bed at 7.30am.

"Mummee! Where's Dan? What's for breakfast? Is it Monday? Are you taking me to school? Where's my book bag?"

Claudia groaned.

"Woah, one thing at a time, love! And give mummy a chance to wake up!"

She stretched sleepily.

"Isn't Dan up?"

Juliet shook her head, blonde curls flying.

"No, and his bedroom door's shut, and you said I shouldn't disturb him when it was."

Claudia dropped a kiss on the blonde curls.

"Quite right, good girl. Right, listen, sweetheart. Mummy needs to have a quick shower to wake herself up, and then I'll come and sort breakfast. Dan was late home last night, so he's probably still asleep. And yes, I'm taking you to school today because it is Monday. So, you go and look for your book bag whilst I get sorted. It's probably either on the hook in your room, or in the cupboard under the stairs. I won't be long."

She forced herself out of bed and into the shower, liberally applying the grapefruit and lime shower gel which claimed to 'awaken and energise'. If it didn't work, she'd bloody sue them. Or make coffee. The thought of coffee propelled her out of the shower to get towel dried, dressed in a sober black legal-chic shift dress with zebra print pointy sling-backs, make-up applied and hair tamed. Fifteen minutes after Juliet came bouncing in she was in the kitchen, putting coffee on and rifling through the cupboards for a breakfast cereal Juliet considered acceptable.

"No, you're not just having Nutella on toast for breakfast. Look, I tell you what, how about I slice a banana on as well?"

Compromise reached, Juliet sat down with her chocolate spread and banana toast and a mug of milk, while Claudia practically inhaled coffee and toyed unenthusiastically with a bowl of granola and yoghurt. The butterflies in her tummy were making her feel nauseous. No matter how many times she had told herself that she was totally indifferent to Daniel, she was utterly disconcerted by his non-appearance at breakfast for the second consecutive day. Was he out this time? No note today. As she considered the matter, whiles replying automatically to Juliet's cheerful chatter and filtering out the Today programme's interrogation of some hapless politician, she felt anger start to rise.

Ok, so she had been incautious and indiscreet in

sleeping with the nanny, but what kind of point was he trying to make with these ridiculous avoidance tactics? She was hardly going to leap on him and demand a repeat performance over Monday morning breakfast. She was going to have to confront him somehow, else how could she trust that he was going to be there to pick Juliet up from school that afternoon?

They finished eating - in Claudia's case with the bowl of cereal largely untasted - and Claudia turned to her daughter.

"Right, sweetheart, you pop upstairs and clean your teeth and start getting dressed. I'll come and do your hair in a few minutes, but I just need to have a quick word with Daniel first."

"Ooh, can I come and see Daniel with you? I want to tell him about seeing Horatio yesterday."

Claudia shook her head firmly.

"No, Juliet. You can go and clean your teeth and get dressed like I just asked you to. You'll see Daniel later."

Silently she crossed her fingers behind her back, ignored her daughter's pout, and shepherded her up the stairs. After ensuring that Juliet had vanished into the bathroom, she continued up the stairs to Dan's room.

She listened at the door for a moment, and then knocked sharply.

"Hello?"

Her lips tightened.

"Hi Daniel, it's Claudia. I just wanted to check that you were definitely ok to pick Juliet up from school today, seeing as I didn't see you yesterday to confirm."

There. She was proud of herself. She had sounded cool, calm and in control.

The door suddenly flung open, and Daniel stood there, towel wrapped round his waist and drops of water still gleaming on his shoulders. She averted her eyes firmly from his delectable torso.

"Yes, of course I'll pick Juliet up. Listen, Claudia, I'm so sorry about yesterday, I honestly planned to be back yesterday evening so we could have a proper talk, but something major came up…I can't really explain now, because it's complicated, but maybe this evening after Juliet's in bed…?"

His voice trailed off as he took in the look of icy disdain on Claudia's face.

"There's absolutely no need for explanations, Daniel. Sunday is your day off, and what you do is no concern of mine whatsoever. I was simply confirming arrangements for today. Now, if you'll excuse me, I must go and help Juliet get ready."

She turned and walked away, head held high, heels tip-tapping on the laminate floor, and although she knew her legs were trembling, she hoped that to Dan she conveyed entirely the ice-maiden impression she had been aiming for.

She did. So successfully that he closed his bedroom door and sank down on the bed in bleak despair. Last night, in his post-adrenaline rush exhausted haze it had all seemed quite simple. Lydia was right, he just needed to explain the circumstances. She must like him, because the explosive chemistry of Saturday night had surely been mutual. But this morning, in the cold light of a grey Monday morning, the idea that he and his icily polite employer had ever been on ordinarily friendly terms seemed unlikely, let alone that they had rolled naked on the floor bathed in each other's sweat. He fancied her like hell in her fitted black dress and sexy heels, but again, they seemed to belong to a different person to the carefree barefoot girl in a crumpled sundress. It was all very well to say that he needed to explain, but how the hell do you convey sixty-odd years of intensely emotional family history to someone who is barely giving you the time of day, when you're naked apart from an irritatingly skimpy bath towel?

And how would he ever be able to start the conversation and get her to really listen? Always supposing she would listen. Best case scenario was that she was pissed off at his defection yesterday and he could bring her round, but worst case was that she'd submitted to a slightly drunken lustful impulse on Saturday night and had been regretting it ever since, in which case pouring out his heart and soul to her was going to be just plain embarrassing.

His mobile started ringing, and he glared, tempted to ignore it, get back into bed, pull the covers over his head and not come out until it was time to collect Juliet from school. Then he saw that it was Dominic, and reluctantly pressed the green button.

"Hi."

"Hi!" his brother sounded ridiculously exuberant, and he could hear Lydia's voice in the background too.

"Guess what?"

"What?"

"We're engaged! I asked Lydia to marry me last night, and she said yes!"

"Wow!" Dan's head reeled slightly. In the past few weeks Lydia had gone from the friend he had always thought her, to a potential half-sister, to a half-cousin, and now to a future sister-in-law. It was a lot of big shifts.

"That's fantastic. Congratulations to you. And commiserations to Lyddy. Though I suppose no-one can say she doesn't know what she's taking on."

Dominic laughed.

"Thanks, mate. Listen, are you free today?"

"Yep, pretty much. I have to pick Juliet up at 3.15pm, and then I'll have her for the rest of the day."

"Oh great!" Dominic's voice was warm with relief.

"Listen, could you spend the day with Lydia? She's not in work today, but I've got to go in, and I really don't want to leave her on her own after yesterday."

He could hear Lydia protesting faintly, but Dominic ignored her.

"Would you mind?"

Daniel thought. A very large part of him wanted to hunker down and indulge in self-pity. Or go for a run in an attempt to shake it off. However. Dominic was right. Lydia certainly shouldn't be on her own today, and being a better brother and friend was one of the reasons he had finally decided to quit his hospital job in the first place. And actually, given the mess he was making of things, getting some advice from Lydia might be quite useful.

"Sure, no problem. I'll just get dressed and head over - tell her I'll take her out for breakfast. Now, you get off to work, you're going to be late!"

25

Lydia looked pale and tired, but her smile as she opened the door to Daniel was radiant.

"Hi! Thanks for coming over. Dom is such a fusspot, I would have been absolutely fine, but it's made him feel better about going to work, and it's lovely to see you anyway."

He gave her a quick hug.

"You look knackered! Do you want to go out and get something to eat, and some strong coffee?"

She nodded emphatically.

"Yep. That sounds great. We didn't go to bed until about 2.30am, there was so much to talk about."

Daniel's grin was wry.

"Just a bit!"

Despite her evident tiredness and the emotional maelstrom she was living through, Lydia looked as beautiful as always in a short, loose denim tunic dress, long hair twisted into some kind of elaborate updo, and bright pink lipstick. The weather was glorious again, so she only had to slip her feet into flip flops, grab her cotton flamingo print tote bag and she was ready to go.

They cut through Lloyd Park. Despite the fact that it was barely 9.30am, the playground was already full of laughing, shrieking pre-schoolers.

Lydia suddenly cut across Daniel's idle chatter.

"Can we have a baby, now?"

It took him a moment to adjust.

"Well, yes. I mean first cousins can legally marry, and you're only half cousins, so you can definitely have children."

She shook her head impatiently

"Yes, I know legally. But is it *safe*? Would the baby be ok?"

Daniel shrugged.

"God, Lydia. I don't know. It's not my area of expertise at all. My understanding is that the child of first cousins has a slightly higher chance of some kind of genetic problem, but it is only a slight increase, and the chances are pretty low to start with. Plus, being half cousins makes a difference as that's a whole extra pile of different DNA thrown into the mix."

He tucked his arm through hers.

"Look, Lyddy, there's nothing certain in this life. I've seen that time and again at work. You and Dominic would be great parents, and if you want to have a baby I think you should go for it. I don't think it would be irresponsible, and I think the overwhelming likelihood is that it would all be fine."

He felt the tension ebb from her body.

"That's ok then! We can go ahead. I just wanted to check, because I know how badly Dominic wants children, and if he couldn't have them with me then it wouldn't be fair to marry him, would it?"

Daniel shrugged again.

"I dunno. My impression is that Dom wants you more than he wants a baby. But I really don't think it's something you need to worry about."

She laughed.

"Well, in that case, what are you doing on the 28th July?"

He was bewildered.

"Umm, I don't know. Looking after Juliet I guess, if Claudia hasn't sacked me by then. It's the summer holidays, isn't it?"

"Yes, it is. And after checking the website this morning, it's also the first available slot at Waltham Forest Register Office, so it's our wedding day!"

For the first time, Daniel was shaken out of his anxiety about the situation with Claudia.

"Wow! That's pretty quick! Are you sure? Don't weddings seem to take years to plan for most people?"

Lydia grinned.

"Yup, they seem to. But don't think our wedding is going to be quite like everyone else's in the circumstances! Dom and I want to get married, it's really important to us, but we can't exactly have a huge white wedding. In fact, you're the only definite person on the guest list at the moment. And we can't agree whether you should be Dominic's best man, or giving me away!"

Daniel stopped walking and pulled her to him for a tight hug.

"If you want me to, I'll do both. But what about my dad? Won't you ask him?"

She shook her head vehemently.

"No. Even if we asked him to the wedding, you're the one who's always been there for me, Dan. For both of us. I don't know what state Dominic would have ended up in this spring without your love and support and non-judgemental friendship.

He gave her another squeeze, and they resumed their walk. Over the little wooden bridge, and through the arrangement of formal flowerbeds towards the lovely Georgian house which had once been William Morris' family home, and was now a museum and gallery dedicated to him.

"Where do you want to go for breakfast anyway?"

Lydia shrugged.

"I don't know. I'm not that bothered. How about the cafe here?"

Daniel agreed, and they wandered into the conservatory built onto the back of the house, which was now a sunlight flooded cafe.

Lydia sank down at a table by the window looking back over the park and lake, conscious even the short walk from her flat had left her totally exhausted.

Daniel went up to the counter and ordered two plates of poached eggs on sourdough toast with spinach and slow-roasted tomatoes, two glasses of freshly squeezed orange juice and two flat whites.

"You need some proper food."

He announced as he sat down opposite Lydia.

"I bet you haven't eaten a thing since that hot chocolate I made you last night!"

She blushed slightly.

"Well, maybe not! I am actually starving now I come to think about it. And there's so much to do! I feel completely over-whelmed."

She pulled a notebook and pen out of her bag and began to scribble, murmuring as she did so:

"Right, so I need to confirm the booking of the registry office, and make an appointment for us to take our passports in and fill in all the forms. And I suppose I should get a dress - not a big meringue, but something pretty. And get Dom's best suit dry-cleaned. Oh, and rings! Dom wants us to go together to choose a vintage engagement ring, but we'll need wedding rings too. We're not exactly going to have a reception, but I thought we'd book a table in Eat17 afterwards - you know, that lovely restaurant in Walthamstow Village? Just for us, and anyone else we ask to be witnesses, oh, and Claudia of course if you'd like to invite her...OH MY GOD! I totally forgot to ask! Oh, Dan! I'm so sorry! What a selfish idiot I am! I've been so wrapped up with the wedding thing that I completely forgot to ask you how it all went with Claudia last night."

The food arrived at that moment, and Daniel paused for a swig of coffee and a couple of mouthfuls of egg before he replied, ignoring Lydia's obvious impatience.

He sighed.

"Nothing happened, really. She was already asleep when I got home, and I didn't think waking her up to talk about it would be a good idea. And then this morning I couldn't decide what to do, because a proper conversation with Juliet around isn't exactly easy. So I just skulked in my room, and she came up to check I was still doing pick up today, and she sounded really ratty, to be honest, and I wasn't dressed and my mind just went blank and I bottled it. Epic fail. I just don't know how to row back from this."

It was Lydia's turn to eat her eggs ruminatively.

"You have to talk to her, properly. Without Juliet around. Preferably not at the house, somewhere neutral."

He raised a sceptical eyebrow.

"Yuh huh. Sounds great, Lyds, but there's the little matter of not being able to leave a five year old girl on her own while I chat up her mum!"

Lydia frowned.

"There must be someone who can babysit! Oh, what about Lois? You said she was really close to Juliet."

Daniel was shaking his head.

"No way. I do not want to have a conversation about me and Claudia with Lois. That is a bad idea on so many levels. And before you suggest it, I'm not asking the mum of one of Juliet's friends either."

Lydia thought again.

"I know! What time does Claudia normally finish work?"

"About 7.30-8pm. She doesn't get home for Juliet's bedtime except on a Friday."

"Perfect! I'll look after her then. You can put her to bed as normal, and I'll stay until you get home. You can Uber into town and meet Claudia outside her office and whisk her off to some lovely bar to have a proper talk."

Daniel patted her hand.

"That's very kind of you, Lydia. But I can't leave Juliet with someone she's never met. Even if she's theoretically asleep. She might wake up, and she'd be scared if she didn't know the person who came to her."

"No problem. I'll pick her up from school with you, and spend the evening with both of you, and get to know her. Then there's no problem."

Daniel sighed again, feeling very tired himself. Lydia in full flow was a pretty much irresistible force. And while he could see a dozen niggling little objections to the plan he had to admit that the idea of being able to have a proper conversation with Claudia in a neutral setting was appealing.

"What about Dom? You've just got engaged, surely you want to be with him this evening? And doesn't he want to take you to buy a ring?"

"Not tonight!" Tone and look were both

triumphant.

"It's parents evening tonight, he won't be home until at least 10pm, probably later. And, in fact, some of them sometimes go for a drink afterwards, and if he knows I'm out he can go without feeling like he's abandoning me."

Daniel capitulated.

"Oh alright then. Thank you. Now, what do you want to do until then?"

26

Claudia glanced at her watch. 7.30pm. She'd absolutely had enough for the day. She stretched, shut down her laptop and heaved herself to her feet. However hard she had focussed on work, however many times she had told herself that Saturday night had been a temporary aberration and that Daniel meant nothing to her, she had felt weighed down all day by sadness and regret. She grabbed her bag, and automatically pulled out her compact mirror. God, she looked rough. Pale, tired, drawn. Re-applying her make-up felt like a huge effort, but she was damned if she was going to let Daniel see her like this when she got home. She spritzed on some perfume, re-applied her red lipstick, and swept a little blusher onto her cheekbones. There, that was better.

As she crossed the glass and steel lobby of her smart office building, she was already imagining the hot bath she would sink into, and the caress of her crisp cotton sheets. So deep was she in this fantasy that she jumped out of her skin when she felt a hand on her arm and a man's voice in her ear.

"Claudia!"

She blinked. What the hell was Dan doing here? Then her heart started to race.

"Daniel! Oh my God, Juliet, is she ok?"

"Yes, she's fine. Sorry, I didn't mean to scare you."

Her breathing slowed.

"Well, where is she? And what are you doing here?"

Dan's heart sank, and he cursed both Lydia's advice and his own naivety in accepting it.

"She's tucked up in bed at home, fast asleep. My very good, totally reliable, friend is looking after her. Don't worry, she is brilliant with children, and 100% trustworthy. And she's been with us all afternoon getting to know Juliet, and Juliet was thrilled to have Lydia looking after her. She's been nagging me for ages to introduce her. I put her to bed as normal, but she knows that Lydia is there if she needs anything."

Claudia was frowning.

"O-kaay. I'm sure that's fine. But, Dan, I'd appreciate it if you let me know if someone different is going to be looking after Juliet, please. And I still don't understand what you're doing here."

Daniel looked acutely miserable.

"Oh God, I'm sorry, Claudia. It was a really stupid idea. It's because I feel so bad about Saturday night, and then being tied up with family stuff yesterday, and not getting a chance to talk to you properly, to explain, and then I thought maybe if I could take you out properly, like a proper date, then you might at least hear me out, give me a chance…but it was probably a really stupid idea. All I did was give you a fright about Juliet. I'll leave you alone."

All this came out in a rush, and then Daniel turned as though to walk away. Claudia listened in amazement, the icy feeling which had enveloped her chest since she first saw Daniel's note the previous morning beginning to thaw. God knows what had happened yesterday, but Daniel had come to find her today. He wanted to take her out. It seemed as though he didn't consider her as an embarrassing one-night aberration after all. She exhaled the breath she was scarcely aware she had been holding, and reached out to grab Daniel's arm.

"Wait! Dan!"

He turned round, and she smiled at him. He caught his breath at her radiance.

"I'd love that! It's about ten years since I went on a proper date, so I must warn you I have no idea of the modern mores, but I'm willing to risk it if you are!"

He returned her smile, and tentatively took her hand.

"Thank you, Claudia. That's amazing. Look, I've booked at table in the bar at the top of Tower Forty-Two, but if there's somewhere you'd rather go..."

His voice was hesitant.

Claudia was impressed.

"Wow! That would be wonderful. I've never been up there. Excellent. Let's go."

It was only a short walk from Claudia's office building, and so a few minutes later they were seated at a table for two, gazing down at London Town spread below them like a model village, the river glistening in the evening sunshine, and a bottle of champagne and two flutes on the table between them.

Daniel raised his glass, and she clinked it.

"Here's to you."

"Hmm." Her tone was sceptical, but she was still smiling. "Go on then. Champagne, flattery, a night out with babysitting laid on…what are you trying to soften me up for?"

He took a quick gulp of champagne.

"I wanted to explain what happened this weekend. I feel like I've made a real hash of things - some of it through stupid decisions, and some of it through circumstances spiralling out of control."

Claudia surveyed him coolly.

"Ok. Explain away. I have to say, what it looked like from my perspective was a classic case of morning after regret."

"No!"

Daniel's exclamation was several decibels too loud, causing people on neighbouring tables to glance round curiously. He lowered his voice, but continued urgently.

"God, that's exactly what I was worried you would think. On Sunday morning - yesterday - wow, I can't believe it's only yesterday! I left the note and snuck off without seeing you because I wanted to give you some space. I'd kind of got the impression on Saturday night, when you went off to bed, that maybe you had some regrets, and obviously it's an unusual situation with us living under the same roof, and I didn't want to crowd you. But believe me, I have no regrets about what happened on Saturday night. The very opposite!"

Claudia blushed slightly.

She knew she had cold-shouldered him somewhat on Saturday night, using Juliet as a screen for her sudden desire to protect herself from the intimacy of sharing a bed. It wasn't that she didn't want to, it was that she wanted to a little too much. How honest dared she be?

"I'm sorry about that. I was worried about Juliet finding us in bed together, but also I was worried that you might have some regrets, and I guess I wanted to protect myself by being the first to take a step back."

He smiled, feeling a surge of renewed hope. She was here, she was listening, she had implied that she wanted to protect herself from his rejection, which surely implied she wasn't entirely indifferent to him?

"I honestly intended to be back for Juliet's bedtime last night so we could have a proper talk, but then we had a massive family crisis yesterday afternoon, and it pushed everything else totally out of my mind."

Claudia raised her eyebrows enquiringly

"Oh yes?"

Her tone had cooled again as she remembered her obsessing yesterday evening - where he was, what he was doing, why he hadn't come home, whereas apparently she had slipped his mind completely.

He grinned, and she felt her heart and her stomach

flip a little.

"Just wait. Just wait until you hear, and then you can decide whether or not it would have pushed things out of your mind!"

And then it all came out, the story of illegitimacy, adoption, secrecy, bitterness, family breakdown and finally an engagement. Claudia listened, leaning forward, chin propped on her hands, mouth slightly open and eyes fixed on his face. This was infinitely better than a box set.

Finally, he drew to a close. The bottle of champagne had long gone, and he signalled to the waiter to bring another.

"Wow! Is that really all true?"

Daniel laughed

"If I was going to make up an excuse for being home late, I don't think I would have managed to be quite that original!"

"It's just unbelievable. Wow. That poor girl - what a thing to discover!"

Daniel shrugged.

"It is pretty unbelievable. I just can't understand why my parents thought keeping it a secret was a good idea! But, you know, I think Lydia is going to be alright. She's incredibly strong, and of course the huge positive is it means that she and Dom can now have a proper above board relationship, get married, have kids if they want. After the panic that they might actually be siblings!"

Claudia nodded, thoughtfully.

"And what about you, Dan? How do you feel about it all? It's a pretty big deal for you, too, isn't it?"

Daniel felt a subtle warmth creep through him at her question. Obviously it was mostly about Dom and Lydia, it was their story, their drama, but it *did* affect him too. How much remained to be seen. He stood by his assertion the previous day that he wouldn't see his mum again until she had apologised to Lydia, and he had no idea when or even if that would happen.

"It's weird. I've been seeing everything through the prism of what it means for Dominic and Lydia. But it is weird for me too, I guess. I'm not close to my parents in one sense - I mean, I'm not round there all the time or anything, and we've got pretty different values and lifestyle. But it's one thing being like that, and another to be estranged completely."

Claudia stroked his hand tentatively.

"And do you think you are? Estranged forever?"

"Who knows? I hope not. I hope mum will see sense and apologise. I think dad will make her - although it doesn't seem like he's done a great job of standing up to her so far! But if she doesn't…"

He shrugged.

"I think her behaviour to Lydia has been atrocious, and I can't imagine wanting to see her again until she acknowledges that. And acknowledges Dominic and Lydia as a couple."

She smiled at him and, emboldened by the

champagne, reached forward to run her hand down his cheek. He put his own hand up to hers and held it there, smiling back at her.

"You're very close to Dominic and Lydia, aren't you?" she asked softly.

"Yes. Very. Clearly not as close as they are to each other, mind you! But yes, Dom is my twin, and my best friend, and Lydia has been part of our lives and another really good friend for as long as I can remember. From my point of view it's actually really nice to discover that she is my half-cousin, because that's kind of how I have always subliminally felt about her I think."

They sat and stared at one another, her hand still held against his face. The atmosphere between them was suddenly electric.

"What were you going to say?' she asked suddenly.

"When?"

"If all the...family stuff hadn't happened. Last night. What were you going to say?"

Daniel took a deep breath. He thought of Lydia's bravery in dealing with the very foundations of her life shifting beneath her. Of Dominic's in confronting their parents and declaring his love for Lydia. Of both of them in prioritising their love for each other over all other considerations."

"I was going to say that I like you. Really, really like you. That I've had the biggest crush on you pretty much ever since we met. That I couldn't believe my luck on Saturday night, and I still can't. That you are so bloody beautiful and sexy and lovely and clever and funny. And, given all that, I wonder if you might consider me for the position of boyfriend as well as nanny? I know that you're still married, technically, and that it's an unusual situation, but I really think that if we…"

Claudia moved her hand across his mouth to stop the flow of nervous chatter.

"Yes. Yes. I'd love you to be my boyfriend. Apart from anything, it makes me feel ten years younger! A husband is terribly ageing, whereas a boyfriend makes me feel, mmm, kind of teenage, and a bit naughty…"

Daniel was already on his feet, credit card out.

"If feeling naughty is what you want, believe me, I'm happy to oblige."

The waiter was at his side instantly, and five minutes later Daniel and Claudia were snogging on the back seat of a black cab speeding down the Kingsland Road towards Walthamstow.

27

Lois sat in the sterile splendour of a Harley Street waiting room, inwardly comparing her surroundings of thick pearl-grey carpet, leather arm chairs in a slightly darker grey, polished wood tables covered with glossy magazines and a state-of-the-art bean-to-pod coffee machine in the corner, with the waiting room of her outpatients clinic. There the chairs were scuffed plastic in an assortment of colours, the floor was hard-wearing rubber, covered with spilt drinks, muddy footprints, or worse, more often than she cared to consider, and to one side was a riot of brightly-coloured, extremely battered plastic toys.

Lois had always refused to consider private work as she was such a staunch believer in the NHS. When Janey became ill, friends and family had assumed that they would go private as they were a comparatively wealthy couple and would surely want to maximise her chances in any way possible. Which, of course, Lois would have done. But it hadn't been necessary. Janey had seen one of the top consultants in the country, received the latest drugs, and the most compassionate of care all on the NHS. They had used their money to smooth the rocky path of cancer treatment in whatever ways they could - taxis to and from the hospital, spa treatments like facials or massages to try and relax Janey and make her feel like a woman as well as a patient, a stash of cashmere jumpers and bed socks as the chemotherapy made her permanently cold.

Now though, there wasn't much option. Lois knew that time was not on her side, and if she wanted to pursue this course then languishing on an NHS waiting list was not the way to go - even if the treatment were authorised in the first place. She felt surprisingly nervous. Nothing much was going to happen at this visit, it was simply to get the results of the various tests they'd had at their last appointment - her hormone levels and potential egg reserve, his sperm count - and discuss the treatment options in more detail. Still, though, being on this side of the waiting room door, waiting for a nurse to call you in, brought back more troubling and unpleasant memories than she cared for. Glancing at Michael, his face pale and set she guessed she wasn't the only one. She nudged him gently with her elbow.

"The waiting room game, huh?"

He forced a smile.

"Yep. Been there, done that, not a fan."

She smiled sympathetically, and opened her mouth to reply when a smartly uniformed nurse came out of a room to the left.

"Dr Hargreaves, Mr Arncliffe, if you'd like to step this way please."

Lois' stomach churned as he got to her feet. She held out her hand, and after a second's hesitation

Michael took it, his own icy cold.

Ms Symons, the specialist, was about Lois' age, wearing a pencil skirt, blouse and heels which emphasised her curvaceous figure. Her long dark-red hair was swept up into a chignon, and her pale, freckled skin and the green eyes behind the severe black-framed glasses hinted at Celtic ancestry. In other circumstances, Lois privately acknowledged, she would have found her extremely attractive - although the fact that the fourth finger of her left hand was weighed down with both a wedding band and an emerald and diamond eternity ring indicated that she was very much spoken for. Lois twisted her own wedding band, trying to draw courage from it as she remembered the look on Janey's face as she placed it on her finger. Something about the look on the consultant's face warned her that things were not going to be entirely straightforward.

The doctor gave them a warm, but professional smile.

"Hi, how are you both?"

Lois and Michael murmured polite nothings, and then there was an expectant silence.

Ms Symons shuffled some papers and then gazed directly at them.

"Right, well, as you know we did a couple of tests last time you were in, to determine whether your respective sperm count and ovarian reserves were in the normal levels. Unfortunately, the test results do show that things aren't quite as straightforward as we would have liked. Mr Arncliffe - the tests do show that your sperm count is on the low side. It wouldn't be at all impossible for you to conceive naturally, but it would be unlikely. However, with IVF we can use a procedure called ICSI whereby we select an individual sperm and inject it directly into the egg."

Michael and Lois both nodded. Lois was well aware of the procedure and knew that it had good results, although it was more expensive than conventional IVF. She sneaked a sideways glance at Michael, wondering how he was taking the news of his potentially compromised fertility, but he looked as calmly imperturbable as ever.

Ms Symons took off her glasses.

"I have to say, though, it is a somewhat unusual situation for a sperm donor to have such a low sperm count. I understand that you are not a couple?"

Lois felt anger rising. She was well aware that a doctor's besetting sin can be a tendency to play God - it irritated her when she encountered it in colleagues and she fought to avoid it herself, but it was more than irritating when you were sitting on the other side of the desk as a patient.

"We're not a traditional couple, no."

Her voice was colder and harder than she had intended, and it was Michael's turn to glance sharply at her. "We are good friends who have both lost our chances to have a family in a more conventional way due to both being widowed at an early age. Michael is not my 'sperm donor' he is the person I've chosen to have a child with, and our lack of romantic involvement makes no difference to that. We can proceed using the ICSI method."

The doctor on the other side of the desk compressed her lips, and, to Lois' horror, she saw that she was looking at her with something suspiciously like sympathy.

"Yes, that is a potential option. However, unfortunately, the Day 3 FSH test and the AMH test indicate that your ovarian reserve is fairly poor."

Lois could dimly hear the clinician's voice going on and on, recounting numbers, statistics, options, treatments, drugs, but she couldn't take any of it in. Blood was ringing in her ears and her heart was pounding. All she could think was "it's not fair". Hadn't she suffered enough? How was it possible that the first thing since Janey's death which had enabled her to feel positive about the future was going to be snatched from her before she had even had it?

All through Janey's treatment Lois had used her medical qualifications to try and facilitate things. Although gynaecological oncology was very far from being her specialist area, she knew the resources to access, she understood the terminology, and she could read up beforehand enabling her to ask relevant and pertinent questions, and persist until she got the answers they needed, even if they weren't the answers they wanted to hear. She had promised herself that she wouldn't do that with her pregnancy, she wanted to experience it like a civilian. Her information would come, like every other mum-to-be from Mumsnet or the NCT rather than articles published in the National Journal of Obstetrics. She had read up on fertility treatments, but had done so on regular websites like Fertility Friends, rather than medical ones. Now she realised that Ms Symons was expecting her to react with professional calm, to ask sensible questions and discuss options in a rational and adult manner, but she knew she was utterly unable to do so. She pushed her chair back abruptly and got to her feet.

"I'm sorry." Her voice was thick with unshed tears. "I'm afraid I need a little time to adjust to this. Excuse me."

She turned and fled to the door, fumbled to find the handle and managed to get out and into the sterile opulence of the waiting room. Like a cornered animal, her only thought was that she had to be by herself, at home. The idea of talking to anyone was literally intolerable. She sped down the corridor, trying to remember the way to the front entrance, desperately hoping Michael wouldn't follow her. A vain hope. Just as she spotted the main entrance she heard hurried footsteps behind her and felt a hand on her shoulder.

"Lois!"

"Leave me, Michael. Please. I need to be on my own right now."

She tried to shake his hand off, but his grip was surprisingly firm. She turned to face him.

"You can't run away from it, Lois. Sure, it's not good news - for either of us - but we need to have a proper conversation with Ms Symons and work out the best option like adults."

The metaphor seeing red took on a new and vivid resonance for Lois at that moment. She pushed at Michael, wanting him away from her, and opened her mouth to let sarcastic invective roll out unchecked.

"Oh can't I? I think you'll find running away is *exactly* what I can do. I don't want to sit and discuss 'options'. I don't want to hear some supercilious bitch telling me it's unlikely I'll ever have my own baby. And don't tell me it's the same for you - low sperm count is easily treated. In fact you don't need to be here at all, there's no need for you to be trying to make it work with an elderly infertile lesbian! As for behaving like an adult - well, I think I've done the most adult thing I ever want to do, I've sat down and agreed a Do Not Resuscitate agreement on my beloved wife, and I've held her hand while she died, and I've stood up to give the eulogy at her funeral. I'm sick of being a grown up! All I fucking wanted was to have a baby with the woman I loved, and now she's dead and I can't even have a baby. And I've just HAD ENOUGH!"

She almost screamed the last words, then turned and ran out of the door without giving him a chance to respond.

Luckily there were a plethora of black cabs in that part of London, and she hailed one and collapsed shaking and sobbing on the back seat, not allowing herself to look back to see if Michael had tried to follow her or not.

28

Claudia stretched herself out luxuriously. In a minute she would get up, have a shower, get dressed and go and join her boyfriend and daughter for breakfast, but right now it was blissful to just relax and savour her feelings of total contentment. Contentment the like of which she couldn't ever remember feeling before. She had been happy with Ethan, at the beginning - obviously, she would hardly have married him otherwise. But she couldn't remember ever feeling so totally relaxed with him - or, frankly, fancying him quite so much. It was very early days, just three weeks since that momentous evening in Tower 42. She and Daniel had woken up the next morning in a hungover, hedonistic, post-coital sprawl in each other's arms, and hadn't looked back.

Claudia had been worried about telling Juliet - not worried that she would resent Daniel, but worried that she would break her heart if things didn't work out. But it was clearly impossible to keep their relationship a secret when they all lived together, so Claudia decided that she would just have to trust in her daughter's innate good sense and resilience. She had been totally matter of fact about it.

"That's good. I always thought Daniel should be your boyfriend. Auntie Lois thinks so too."

Claudia had caught her breath

"Juliet! I don't believe Auntie Lois said that to you!"

Juliet looked at her mother pityingly

"Nooo! Of course she didn't *say* anything, but I could tell from the look on her face when we had lunch with her that day. I'm not *stupid*!"

She had also braved the hideous conversation with Ethan, not wanting him to hear the news from Juliet first. His dismissive shrug had somehow transmitted itself across the Atlantic, even though they were having an ordinary phone conversation because Claudia detested FaceTime and Skype.

"It's no skin off my nose what you do, Clauds."

Her skin crawled. She had always hated being called 'Clauds' and he always did it, however often she asked him not to.

"I mean, this Daniel guy was looking after Juliet anyway, and I was quite happy with that - she likes him, Lois likes him, he's clearly trustworthy. So it's pretty immaterial whether shagging you comes as a perk of the job."

His tone suggested he was somewhat doubtful it could be considered a perk, but she chose to ignore that, just relieved that a potential source of conflict had been removed.

Juliet was counting down the days until she flew to America to see her father, and Lois was getting increasingly excited too. What would have been a tedious chore - having to take a transatlantic flight with a child who had an inbuilt aversion to sitting still, followed by the misery and loneliness of a fortnight without Juliet for the first time in her life - was now shaping up to be a blissful break with her new lover. She would miss Juliet hugely, of course she would, but the New York-Boston-Cape Cod itinerary which Lois had outlined a few weeks earlier was now looking set to be a reality, *and* she would have Daniel with her. Two heavenly weeks of sightseeing and great food and amazing sex. She shivered in delight, but then frowned slightly. There was just one niggling worry on the horizon. Which would hopefully be resolved today. She got out of bed and went to the bathroom. Nope, nothing. Her frown deepened. There was no two ways about it, her period was now a week late.

She reminded herself how vanishingly unlikely it was that she was pregnant. True, after Ethan left she had become rather haphazard about her pill taking. But as soon as she and Daniel became an official couple she had started taking it religiously again. She was nearly thirty-nine, an age when fertility famously declined anyway, and she hadn't missed *that* many pills. It was probably the erratic pill-taking which had caused the problem, and played havoc with her hormones. Deliberately ignoring her sore, swollen breasts - they were always a little tender when her period was due - she decided that, unlikely or not, she should do a pregnancy test later so that she could put the worry out of her mind. Thinking of pregnancy reminded her of Lois as well - she really must make another effort to talk to her and arrange a meet-up. They hadn't actually spoken since that lunch just before she and Dan got together, there'd been the odd text, but Lois sounded busy and distracted, and Claudia was having such a wonderful time staying in with Daniel that the last thing she really wanted was to arrange an evening out without him.

Dressed and showered she ran downstairs to where Daniel and Juliet, looking TV advert perfect, were playing *Charlie and Lola* Snap at the kitchen table. She kissed both of them, and started to look for breakfast ingredients. Noticing the claw of blackening bananas in the fruit bowl she asked

"Juliet, when you've finished that game do you want to help me make banana muffins for breakfast?"

Juliet thought

"Can we put chocolate chips in?"

"Yep!"

"Yay! Yes, I'd love to Mummy."

They pottered around the kitchen together, Daniel still sitting at the table with his long legs stretched out, cradling a cup of coffee.

"You haven't forgotten Dominic and Lydia are coming to dinner tonight, have you?" Daniel asked.

Juliet became practically apoplectic with excitement as Lydia was officially her new favourite person.

Claudia could understand why - Lydia had the closest looks to a Disney princess she had ever seen in real life, but she was also a natural with Juliet, warm and funny and engaging, and prepared to spend hours crawling round the floor pretending to be a cat if required. Dominic she was yet to meet, hence this evening's dinner.

She wrinkled her nose.

"Are you cooking? I think these muffins are going to pretty much shoot my cooking bolt for the day, and delicious though I'm sure they'll be, we can't really serve them for a dinner party!"

Daniel laughed.

"Well, they're ten times better than anything you'd get if you relied on my brother to cook dinner! But yeah, I'm happy to cook. I'll need to pop to Waitrose in a bit, though - do you mind if I take the car?"

Claudia shook her head.

"No, that would be fine, but actually I'm happy to go, there's a few bits and pieces I need."

He nodded.

"Well, shall we all go, and I can take Juliet to the park while you shop and then we can have lunch out?"

Claudia nodded happily. Just the kind of relaxed family Saturday she had always imagined, but had never experienced with Ethan because she was drowning under waves of his poorly suppressed resentment and insistence that she did everything connected with looking after Juliet, the house, cooking, cleaning and so on because he was exhausted and needed a break. Which she understood, but equally she just wanted to enjoy spending time together with her husband and daughter sometimes, without all the resentful subtext.

The day was every bit as relaxing as Claudia had hoped. They had a pub lunch, sitting outside in the sunny beer garden, and then headed home. Daniel pottered round the kitchen making some complicated aubergine dish and an elaborate chocolate roulade whilst she sat at the kitchen table with Juliet and helped her make a poster about the importance of recycling – her homework for the weekend. By that time she was aware of feeling completely exhausted. Daniel noticed – God, she loved his sensitivity and perception – and offered to give Juliet her tea and put her to bed so she could have a lie down and rest before the evening. She kissed him briefly on the mouth, dropped another kiss on Juliet's curls, and accepted gratefully.

She hadn't intended to fall asleep, just to lie down and read her book for half an hour, but within moments of getting into bed she was fast asleep. Her sleep was so deep and instantaneous that when she awoke she was momentarily disoriented. She glanced at her iPhone and realized it was already 7.15pm. She leapt up in horror. She was still wearing the poster-paint spattered jeans and t-shirt she'd been wearing to help Juliet, and she didn't need to look in the mirror to know that her hair would be a frizzy bird's nest. Shit. This was not the image she wanted to portray to Daniel's brother, who would be arriving in quarter of an hour. And Lydia was incredibly beautiful and always impeccably dressed and groomed. Not to mention being a decade younger.

Claudia swiped cleanser over her face, removing the smears of that morning's mascara from under her eyes, and then splashed her face with cold water, and patted on some allegedly radiance enhancing tinted moisturizer. A dab of touche eclat under each eye, fresh mascara applied quickly, and a sweep of rosy pink blusher over the apples of her cheeks. Then a coat of confidence boosting red lipstick. She smoothed serum over her hair to ease the frizz slightly, and then twisted it up and pinned it, letting a couple of curls fall loose to frame her face. Then she grinned at her reflection. Hmm. Not too bad. Either that tinted moisturizer really was worth every penny or else the effect of a two hour nap and a brand new love affair was giving her a natural glow.

She pulled on a denim shirt dress and then stopped, frowning. The buttons just about did up, but there were unsightly gapes over her bust. With a sinking feeling she remembered the Clearblue test sitting, still pristine and unused in its box, shoved in her bedside drawer. The day had been so relaxing she'd completely forgotten about it, but her period still hadn't started. She flipped quickly through her wardrobe looking for something with a bit more stretch. A jersey wrap dress, perfect. Navy, with a print of small white seagulls all over, which wasn't very exciting, but this bloating or whatever it was had given her a fairly impressive cleavage. Tan-coloured wedges, and then her last Christmas present from Juliet, assisted she was fairly sure, by Lois – a silver chain with a pendant made of a collection of turquoise and blue semi-precious stones and a silver letter C. It was now 7.25pm. She had just enough time, and decided not to procrastinate any longer. Do the test, get it out of the way, get on and enjoy the evening. She retrieved the paper bag from her bedside table, bolted herself into the en-suite and began to read what seemed like unnecessarily complicated instructions.

29

Daniel frowned slightly. On paper, the evening seemed to be going perfectly. Everyone was getting on well, and the food was a triumph. Claudia looked more beautiful than ever, and he was almost bursting with pride as she sparkled and scintillated and charmed everyone. Juliet had behaved impeccably, coming down to say hello and goodnight in her little floral pyjamas, but then allowing her mother to carry her away and tuck her in without a fuss. And yet, there was something not quite right. Some air of unresolved tension. Claudia seemed a little *too* animated at times. He could have suspected her of being slightly drunk, except that she had had one glass of wine and then stuck to sparkling water, claiming she had a slight headache. And Lydia and Dominic seemed strangely keyed up as well, exchanging quick, furtive glances when they thought no-one else was watching.

Daniel doled out second helpings of pudding, and then asked if anyone wanted coffee or liqueurs. Dominic and Lydia both accepted a glass of brandy, and Daniel poured himself one too, but Claudia got up to make peppermint tea, joking that her digestion needed all the help it could get after the impossibly rich roulade.

When she was seated again, he saw Lydia and Dominic share another of their conspiratorial glances.

Lydia raised her eyebrows, and Dominic nodded almost imperceptibly.

"So," Lydia began "You know we're going to Australia for our honeymoon?"

Daniel and Claudia both nodded. Lydia and Dominic were planning a shoe-string wedding – now only a few weeks away – but they were blowing their savings on the trip of a lifetime to Australia afterwards. Getting married at the beginning of the school holidays meant that Dominic had a whole six weeks off, and Lydia had already handed her notice in on her job and would be working her last day just before the wedding and then applying for something else on her return.

"We-ell, we've decided to make it a bit of an extended holiday."

Daniel laughed.

"I thought five weeks *was* extended! What do you mean?"

Lydia looked uncomfortable, and Dominic was staring down at his hands, refusing to meet his brother's eyes.

"Sort of not a holiday, holiday. We're going for a year."

"Bloody hell!"

"How amazing!"

Daniel and Claudia's exclamations were simultaneous.

Daniel glared at Claudia, irritated by her spontaneous enthusiasm. The sinking feeling in the pit of his stomach told him that he really didn't like this idea at all.

"Are you serious?"

Lydia nodded, gaining courage now the news was actually broken.

"Yes. We are serious. We're going to Sydney. I *loved* Australia, and I've always wanted to go back. And now it turns out I *am* Australian, so I want to even more. I can catch up properly with some friends I made when I lived there, and even trace some family maybe. I know I don't have siblings or parents, but maybe I have aunts and uncles and cousins. I want to find out. I want to see where I was born. I want to find out everything I possibly can about my parents. And I want Dom with me while I do that."

Daniel's face had softened.

"I understand that totally, Lyddy. Of course I do. But a year! That's a huge decision. I mean what about the flat? And Dom's job?"

Dominic spoke up at this point.

"We're doing a home swap. Actually with an Australian girl who Lydia met when she lived there. She and her boyfriend are coming to London for a year, and they were looking for somewhere nice to live, and they have a flat in a suburb of Sydney. We can even use their car while we're there."

The sinking feeling was back. It started to look as though this was more than a madcap scheme or impossible dream. He played his final card.

"But your job?"

Dominic met his brother's gaze full-on. He knew exactly how Daniel felt. He felt it himself. They'd never been apart for more than a few fortnight long holidays in their life. He knew he would miss him hugely, but he also knew that Lydia needed to do this, and that they both needed a break, and some proper time away from the toxic family situation.

"I've taken a year's sabbatical. And we have a twinned school in Sydney, so I can do some supply work there. Lydia will get some temping work, probably."

Daniel was silent. Always fair-minded he could see that this made total sense for Dominic and Lydia, but that realisation did nothing to ease his sense of abandonment. He'd missed Lydia when she went travelling, but that wasn't remotely the same. Dom was his twin. Literally his other half. He'd *always* had Dom. And now he wouldn't for at least a year. And whereas a year would be ok, he could see that it could very possibly be for much longer, even forever. It was all too easy to see how Lydia, already a huge fan of Australia, could discover relatives, renew old friendships and make new ones, and be in no hurry to ever return to grim and grey old Blighty where her closest family had lied to her and rejected her. And sporty, easy-going Dominic seemed tailor-made for living the Australian dream. He foresaw a bleak future where his twin was a grainy face on Zoom, an unfamiliar figure you saw every couple of years, where his nieces and nephews would be virtual strangers.

He sighed deeply. There was absolutely nothing he could do about it. Somehow he would have to put a brave face on it.

He forced a smile to his face which didn't deceive anyone else sitting round the table. Claudia had been watching him closely, and her heart ached with pity for him, and she also felt a flash of surprisingly strong resentment against Lydia and Dominic for hurting Daniel. The rush of compassion and protectiveness confirmed what she already knew deep down; for her at least, this was not a fling, she had fallen deeply in love with him.

The silence threatened to become uncomfortable.

Dominic broke it.

"Dan? It's not forever, you know. We're not emigrating. I haven't sold the flat, or quit my job. We just need a break. You can come and see us – you and Claudia. I bet Juliet would love Australia!"

Daniel nodded.

"I know. It'll be great. I can see it's totally the right thing for you both."

Claudia and Lydia moved the conversation on with a flurry of light chit-chat, but it did a fairly poor job of covering the somewhat morose silence of the two brothers. It wasn't long before the party broke up early; it was barely 10.30pm as the final goodbyes echoed round the tiled hall and the front door was gently but firmly shut behind their guests.

Daniel and Claudia flopped wordlessly down in the sitting room. Claudia, despite the peppermint tea, feeling slightly sick. That was just nerves. Her realisation of the depth of her feelings for Daniel made how she handled this conversation, how she comforted him and showed him she understood, critically important. Actually it was Daniel who spoke first.

"I feel really weird, Claudia. Sort of…abandoned. I mean, I know all this has been ten times worse for Dominic, and particularly for Lydia, but still. First of all finding out that they were in love, which totally shifted the dynamics between us all. And then that my parents have basically been lying to us our entire lives. And now that my twin, who was the one person I thought I could unquestioningly depend on, is moving to the other side of the world."

Claudia crossed the room and curled up at his feet, laying her head against his knees.

"I totally understand why you might feel that way, Daniel. But, you've got to remember, Dominic will always be your twin. Nothing can break that bond between you, certainly not a few thousand miles. These days, distance doesn't matter nearly so much, with Zoom and everything. And you know, it's obviously different for children, but look how well Juliet is coping with her dad moving to another country. He was her main caregiver for five years, and now she only sees him electronically, but she's fine with that."

Daniel nodded, feeling comforted not so much by Claudia's words as by the loving warmth in her voice.

The voice carried on, slightly smaller now, muffled by his leg.

"And I know it's not the same thing, I don't think we're a substitute for Dominic and Lydia, but you've got me and Juliet now. And we love you. I mean, you know she adores you." A pause. "And so do I. I love you, Daniel."

He pulled her up onto his lap and kissed her, pushing his hands into her soft blonde hair, uncaring of the damage he was doing to her up-do.

"I love you. I love you too, so much. And I know how bloody lucky I am to have you, and Juliet."

Claudia looked up at him, eyes dilated.

"There's something else, Dan. I don't know how to tell you, and it might be the most inappropriate time when you're still trying to process Lydia and Dominic's news. But I just don't feel comfortable with you not knowing. I did a test this evening, just before the others arrived, and I'm pregnant."

30

Lois opened her eyes and groaned. What time was it? Oh God, Claudia was meant to be coming round in half an hour or so. Was it too late to text her and cancel? She just didn't feel like talking to anyone – that was why she had ignored the numerous texts, emails and voicemail messages from Michael. He seemed to have got the message now, because she hadn't heard from him for over a week, but funnily enough that didn't make her feel any better. Instead of feeling plagued and pressurized she felt lonely and abandoned.

Thank heavens for work. Just as in those dark early days immediately after Janey's death, work had been her saviour. It gave her a reason to get out of bed in the morning, a sense of purpose, and while she immersed herself in other people's problems she could forget her own.

Today, however, was one of the Fridays she didn't work, and so she hadn't bothered getting out of bed. She'd staggered downstairs to feed Horatio, and make herself a cup of tea, but then she'd scooped him up in her arms and headed back upstairs to bed. Horatio of course was in seventh heaven. He wouldn't be pleased when she moved, but she really did have to have a quick shower, brush her teeth and put some clothes on before Claudia arrived, or she'd be dragging her off to the GP for anti-depressants.

Lois knew she wasn't depressed, not clinically depressed anyway. She was miserable because she was trying to come to terms with another setback, trying to work out what the new way forward might be. She was starting to have the glimmerings of an idea, but she had wanted a bit more time to think it out on her own before she spoke to Michael. She was uncomfortably aware that she owed him a bloody big apology for her behaviour at the clinic and the hurtful words she had thrown at him. It wasn't going to be easy, but it had to be done. Even if he wouldn't forgive her, she knew that she couldn't forgive herself and move on until she had put things right as far as she was able.

First things first, though. Right now she had to get ready to see Claudia, and probably to relate the whole sorry saga of her antique eggs to her.

By the time the doorbell rang at 1.30pm Lois was showered, hair still damp around her face, and dressed in very old, very comfortable jeans and a very old, very soft t-shirt. Horatio was indeed sulking.

Claudia bounded in looking enviably radiant. Lois made them both cups of herbal tea without saying much, and then they sat down across the table from each other.

"So, how are things going?" Claudia asked.

Lois shrugged. Suddenly she really didn't want to

talk to Claudia about the test results, the row with Michael, what it all meant, her fragile new plans. Claudia just looked too happy, too radiant, too contented. The reason she and Michael had bonded so quickly was their shared vulnerability, and when that shared experience was missing it could make you feel less close to a friend.

"Oh you know. Not too bad. Very busy at work."

Claudia looked thoughtfully at her, but that was a closedown if ever there was one. She wondered briefly if she should push her friend to talk, but equally she didn't want to upset her, and she did have an awful lot of news she wanted to get off her own chest.

She made one more attempt.

"Is everything ok, though?"

Biting back the sarcastic response that yes, apart from being a friendless widow who could never have her own children everything was fine, Lois forced a smile.

"Yep. All fine. But what about you? How are things going with Daniel?"

A huge grin spread across Claudia's face.

"Quickly! I think you'd say things are going quickly with Daniel."

It's only just over a month since we first slept together and now not only are we living together but I've told Ethan about us, Juliet knows and is thrilled of course, he's met my parents, I've met his brother and his brother' fiancée…oh yes, and I'm pregnant!"

Lois was silent as she tried to fight down the overwhelming wave of rage and bile and envy which threatened to engulf her.

Unable to interpret the expression on her friend's face, Claudia hurried on, talking quickly from nervous excitement.

"It's unbelievable, isn't it? It must have happened literally the very first time we slept together. I hadn't really been taking my pills properly since Ethan left, but I'm so used to being on the pill that contraception didn't really occur to me that first evening. And he just assumed I was too. So, I'm only a few weeks, very early days, and obviously anything could go wrong. But I'm so excited! I'd actually been feeling slightly jealous of you having a baby – I mean, obviously I was pleased for you, but the timing, with Ethan leaving, it just made me feel a bit meh. Like I'd missed my chance to ever have another baby. And I wouldn't have planned it like this, clearly, but Daniel actually seems really happy. Thrilled, to be honest. So after an initial panic I'm letting myself be happy about it. And the best bit is that you and I can have our babies together! You need to hurry up and get that IVF going so that we can go through the whole thing together – the NCT classes and the baby groups, God it will all be so much better with a friend to do it with…"

Claudia's voice trailed off, as she began to take in that the expression on Lois' face was registering something distinctly more sinister than surprise. Her friend still hadn't spoken. Claudia racked her brains to think what she had said to upset Lois so much. Was she feeling protective of Daniel? Did she think Claudia had tried to trap him?

"I wouldn't have planned this, you know, Lo. I admit that I was careless, but to be fair, I didn't exactly plan to seduce Daniel against his will. He could have insisted on using a condom. He might be younger than me, but he's an adult. A doctor, for God's sake. He knows all about the birds and the bees." She giggled, nervously. "It's unbelievable. When Ethan and I decided to try for a baby we read up on everything. I took vitamins and temperatures and scheduled sex, and made him wear loose boxers and stop having Jacuzzis at the gym, and it still took me 9 months to get pregnant with Juliet! And now, with a bloke I wasn't even in a relationship with, when getting pregnant couldn't have been further from my thoughts, wham bam, first shag and I'm up the duff."

There was still an uncomfortable silence. Then, very slowly, an icy suspicion crept up on Claudia. She felt her stomach clench with tension and regret. Shit. Those tests that Lois had been going for the results of. It was just after that when she went quiet. She'd said she was busy, and she often did have very busy phases at work when Claudia would barely hear from her for weeks, but she should have connected the two things this time. What an unspeakably rubbish friend. She had been far too wrapped up in her little bubble of love with Daniel, and too involved with his family dramas to spare Lois more than a passing thought.

"Oh shit, Lois. Have I just been the most monumentally tactless person in existence? Did the tests show some sort of a problem?"

Lois nodded grimly.

"Yes, actually. They did. How kind of you to ask. And so promptly too. It's less than three weeks since the appointment!"

A heavy lump of guilt settled in Claudia's chest.

"I'm *so* sorry, Lois! I'm so, so sorry. What did they say?"

Lois shrugged.

"Oh, you know. Just that my eggs are really rubbish and I probably won't be able to get pregnant without a donor egg. Apparently it's not uncommon with women in their late thirties, although that doesn't seem to be a problem you suffer from, little Ms Oops-I-accidentally-got-pregnant."

Her voice was hard, cold, flat.

Claudia reached out a hand to touch the other woman's arm, but Lois pulled away sharply.

"Oh, Lois. I'm so, so sorry. If I'd known I would never have…"

"Never have what? Never had unprotected sex? Never told me about it? Never have ignored me for weeks because you're too busy having delightful fecund sex with your lovely lover, or hanging out with the daughter *you already bloody have*?"

Claudia felt the first faint stirrings of anger herself. She had been insensitive, true, but she hadn't really done anything wrong. She *had* texted Lois after the tests, several times, it wasn't her fault if Lois chose to lick her wounds in private? OK, so maybe she had been a little bit distracted with Daniel, but Lois had always had a tendency to do this, retreat from the world and ignore any attempts to communicate with her, but then get narked because no-one seemed to care what she was going through.

She took some deep breaths and deliberately summoned patience in the way she did when Juliet was being particularly trying.

"Look, Lois. I am really, really sorry that the news wasn't good for you. And I'm sorry about the bad timing of my news. I do know how lucky I am, I really do. Have you been back to the clinic and talked about other options? I mean, I don't know much about it, but could you try egg donation, or surrogacy or something?"

Lois glared at her friend.

"Oh don't fucking patronise me, Claudia. I'm a bloody doctor, I know what the options are – I just don't much like them! I'll sort things in my own way, but in the meantime why don't you just go back to your perfect little life and your perfect little family and leave me be."

Claudia failed to keep her temper this time.

"I wasn't patronising you! God, I can't win, can I? If I don't talk to you I'm callously ignoring you, if I try and engage then I'm being patronising. I know that the real problem as far as you're concerned is that I'm pregnant and you're not, but I can't help that. Me not having another baby wouldn't mean you could have one. I'm going because I need to collect Juliet from school. I'll phone you in a few days when you've calmed down!"

With that she clattered her chair back from the table, grabbed her handbag and stalked out, slamming the front door behind her. It was only on the other side of the door that she realized that, as per 85% of the time at present, she was desperate for a wee, and there was no way she would make it as far as Juliet's school without a very nasty accident. Swallowing her pride and knocking on Lois' door claiming pregnancy related discomfort seemed like a very bad option indeed, so she clenched her pelvic floor muscles and hobbled off towards the big chain coffee shop on a nearby corner. Thankfully the toilet was vacant, so she dived inside, hitched up her skirt and pulled down her cotton briefs, heaving a sigh of relief, before she noticed the red stain on her knickers and a wave of panicky nausea engulfed her.

31

Lois was still sitting, head in hands, at the dining room table when her phone rang. She was awash with self-pity, jealousy and guilt. The injustice of Claudia's effortless fecundity stung, but a small, rational part of her knew that she hadn't done anything wrong. She *had* tried to contact Lois after the test results, and Lois had shut her out because she wanted lick her wounds and do her thinking in private. Now, though, she wanted to talk to someone about her thoughts, get another opinion, some advice, have a discussion. It wasn't fair to contact Michael until she knew for certain what she was saying, and anyway, it was Claudia's viewpoint she wanted – Claudia who had known her since she was eighteen and had assured her with tears in her eyes that she would do anything she could to support Lois becoming a mother.

She glanced at her phone. It was Claudia phoning. Steeling herself to apologise – never her favourite activity – Lois pressed accept. But before she could begin her reluctant mea culpa, Claudia had launched in.

"Lois? I'm so, so sorry to do this to you, but I need help! I'm in the Costa at the end of your road, and I'm bleeding, and I don't know what to do. Can you help me? Please?"

Lois' resentful jealousy vanished in an instant, melted by a wave of compassion.

"Of course I'll help you! Stay where you are, I'll be there in two minutes."

She grabbed her handbag and keys and was out of the door in seconds, jogging down the street. She pushed open the door to the coffee shop, and saw Claudia sitting at a table, white as a sheet and twisting a ring on her hand nervously. She went over and hugged her.

"Right, firstly, I'm sorry for being a twat earlier. Can you forgive me?"

Claudia smiled faintly and nodded.

"I was pretty twattish too. Sorry."

"Secondly, let's get you sorted out. Any pain?"

Claudia shook her head.

"Not really. I feel a bit crampy, but I have been for a week or two, and I did at the beginning with Juliet."

"And how much blood?"

She shrugged.

"I don't know. More than spotting, but not as much as a period."

Lois nodded.

"Look, I don't know much about obs and gynae, but I seem to remember that a bit of bleeding is quite common early on. Probably best to get checked though. Shall we go to the hospital? There's a walk-in early pregnancy clinic, they'll check you out."

Claudia nodded.

"Ok. I'm so scared, Lois."

"I know. But it's almost certainly going to be fine. Have you spoken to Dan?"

"Yes, I phoned him – he's going to pick Juliet up from school. He said I should phone you, that you wouldn't mind, that you'd help me."

Lois punched her arm lightly.

"Well of course I would, stupid."

Claudia pulled a face.

"It just seems a bit tactless, under the circumstances!"

They were walking outside into the sunshine by this time, Lois hailing a passing black cab.

Lois spoke seriously to her friend.

"I was being an idiot. I'm not saying I'm not jealous in one sense, because I am. But I'm jealous of something that's never going to happen to me! There's no way I can get pregnant accidentally, there wouldn't have been even if Janey hadn't died. It's just one of the biological disadvantages, or advantages depending on your viewpoint, of being gay. Pregnancy for me was always going to have to be test tubes and injections and hospitals. And the problem is, I just don't want to do any of that. I had a major panic attack when the consultant told me it wasn't going to be plain sailing, but I don't think it was because it was bad news about my fertility, I think it was that I have had enough of hospital waiting rooms and test results and exploratory operations to last me a lifetime and beyond. I don't want to have a baby like that. I don't want to do all that. So I'm jealous of you not just because you're pregnant, but because you got pregnant naturally having sex with someone you love. And that's such a privilege."

Lois paused for breath after her long speech. They were bumping along in the back of the taxi, Claudia still looking pale and drawn.

"God, Claudia, I'm sorry. I should stop blathering on about me when you're so worried about your baby."

Claudia shook her head, smiling.

"No, don't be silly. There's nothing we can do about my baby until we get to the hospital and find out what's going on. It helps, it takes my mind off things, to talk about something else.

I totally understand why you would feel like that, about the medicalisation of it all, but what other options do you have?"

Lois was quiet for a moment before replying.

"Adoption. I've been doing a lot of thinking, Claudia. I think I leapt into the IVF project with Michael too quickly. I was so determined to be positive and move forward and get on with things, that I didn't really consider a lot of the implications."

Biting back a desire to say 'I told you so', Claudia asked instead:

"Adoption sounds like a good plan. But isn't it really difficult to adopt a baby? And would you and Michael be allowed to adopt together, seeing as you're not a proper couple?"

Lois winced.

"That's one of the problems. No, I don't think we would be. I've had a couple of initial conversations with a social worker on the adoption team, and she was really positive about me adopting as a single woman, but couldn't really see a way a single woman and a single man could adopt a child together."

Claudia breathed an inward sigh of relief.

She had liked Michael, very much, far more than she had expected too. She had trusted him instinctively too, and could completely see why Lois felt he would be a good person to have a child with. But she had never been able to feel in her heart of hearts that the arrangement Lois was proposing would work long-term, for all sorts of reasons.

Lois was speaking again.

"And as for adopting a baby – you're right, that is difficult. But I don't want to. You know, the reason I wanted to do this with Michael in the first place was because I couldn't imagine coping with a pregnancy or a birth or a new baby by myself, and because I didn't want to have to give up my career, but was really worried about being a single working parent to a little baby. But if I adopt an older child, that will all be different. I will get a year's adoption leave from work, so we could spend that time really getting to know each other and establishing a routine. But then I could cut back my hours a bit more, and an older child would be at school during the day. It would be a totally different prospect."

Her eyes sparkled with tears.

"And, Claudia, through work I've seen some of the older children in care or foster care. They've had such a terrible start in life, and it's often really difficult to find permanent homes for them. I could do that. I've got so much love to give…and I know that I get on well with children."

Claudia embraced her friend, blinking back the tears in her own eyes.

"Oh Lois, I know you have. You will be such an amazing mum. I wanted to support you with the baby plan, and I would have done, but this feels like a much better fit for you. But what's Michael going to say?"

Lois's look of excitement faded.

"I don't know. I'm not looking forward to that conversation, but I'm going to have to have it soon. Anyway. Enough. We're here. Let's find out what's happening with you."

***

Nearly five hours later, Claudia wearily turned her key in the door. Daniel had been hovering around looking out for her, and she practically fell into his arms, relishing their warmth and strength. Daniel exchanged glances with Lois over her head.

"She's fine. As I said on the phone, the baby looks ok – they're the right size, and a good strong heartbeat, and her blood hormone levels are high. They'll do regular scans for the next few weeks to check progress. The gynae we saw was Miriam – do you know her?"

Daniel nodded.

"She said Claudia needs to rest for a week or two, and a bit of TLC. But her hunch is that it's all going to be fine."

Daniel nodded again. Lois had told him most of this on the phone, assuaging the worst of his anxiety, but he still felt surprisingly shaky after Claudia's panicky phone call earlier, and the hours of uncertainty. He had known he was excited about the baby, but hadn't realised quite how much it meant to him, or how worried he would feel about Claudia. She was still snuggled against his chest. He loosened his hold on her slightly, and looked down at her.

"Come on then, if you're meant to be resting, we should get you sitting down. Lois, can I get you a cuppa, or something stronger?"

Lois shook her head.

"No thanks, Dan. I've got a taxi waiting. I didn't want to send Claudia home on her own, but I've got some important stuff of my own to sort out this evening, and I know she's in good hands now!"

Claudia detached herself from Daniel and hugged her friend warmly.

"Thank you so much, Lois. I would have totally gone to pieces without you. Good luck with Michael. I'll catch up with you tomorrow."

The front door slammed behind her, and Daniel and Claudia surveyed one another.

Claudia still looked pale, with deep shadows under her eyes, and she was shivering slightly in her thin cotton dress. A ball of cotton wool taped to the crook of her arm showed where she had had blood taken, and the feisty, bubbly, confident woman he had fallen in love with suddenly seemed terribly fragile.

He put his arm round her, guided her down the steps to the kitchen, and she sank down on the sofa.

"Juliet's in bed and asleep. She was shattered after gymnastics, so she settled really quickly. Listen, I'm just going to run up and get you a cardi because you look cold, and then I'll get us something to eat, and we can talk properly. Ok?"

Claudia nodded wearily, and sank back into the sofa cushions.

Two minutes later Daniel was back. Her tenderly helped her into a chunky cardi, and eased her feet into fluffy slipper socks before putting her legs up on the sofa and arranging a cushion in the small of her back. His tenderness warmed her as effectively as the blanket he had tucked round her.

"Right, now what do you fancy to eat?"

Claudia shrugged. Now the drama was over, for now at least, she was over-whelmed by bone-aching fatigue.

"I don't know. I feel a bit sick, but starving, and it's really hard to decide what I want. Sorry, I'm being a pain."

He grinned.

"I'm used to trying to feed your five year old daughter, my darling. Believe me, you've got a long way to go before you register as a pain on my fussy-eater scale!"

She laughed.

"Look, I made a veggie lasagne with Juliet. If you don't feel like that I can freeze it, but if you would like it I can heat it up in 20 minutes or so. What do you think?

Claudia nodded, enthusiastically. The thought of Dan's home-made lasagne with richly garlicky tomato sauce and layers of roasted vegetables and oozy cheese was suddenly just what she wanted.

"Ok." Daniel lifted the lasagne from the fridge to the oven, and then handed Claudia a glass of water and some crackers. "This will keep you going and help with the nausea."

He sat down on the end of the sofa, stretching out his long legs, and taking her feet onto his lap.

She smiled warmly at him.

"How did I get so bloody lucky with you, Daniel? Seriously? I love you so much, you know."

He smiled back, reaching out to stroke her hair.

"I know, because I know how much I love you. Now, do you want to talk about what happened, or not?"

Claudia nodded.

"I'd rather tell you. Although, there's not much to say really. Lois told you the headlines. I was so frightened. When I saw that blood, I just thought that was it, and I realised just how much I want this baby."

Daniel squeezed her hand.

"I know. Me too."

"Anyway, Lois was brilliant. I don't know if everyone gets such good service on the NHS, but I think I'll make sure I take her to the hospital with me for all my appointments, just in case. She was amazing when Juliet was ill too. And there was some other doctor there then too, young, gorgeous guy, who was pretty helpful."

They exchanged smiles again, marvelling that their first meeting had only been a few short, though eventful, months ago.

"I had some blood tests, and then they decided to do a scan. An internal scan." She winced. "Not the most comfortable or dignified of proceedings I have to say, and the suspense while they were doing it before they told me they could see a heartbeat nearly killed me." She paused. "Anyway, they could. But, listen. This is the bit Lois didn't tell you. They could only see one heartbeat, but there were two yolk sacs. It's a twin pregnancy, but it looks like maybe one twin hasn't made it. Although it could just be the position – apparently it's still really hard to see the heartbeat still at this stage anyway, and harder with twins."

Daniel tried to assimilate this information.

"Whew! So that's why they want to scan you again,

anyway?"

"Yes. And why I'm supposed to rest as much as possible. They want me to go to my GP and get signed off work for a couple of weeks, until we can see what's happening."

They gazed at each other.

"So, it might be twins?"

She shrugged.

"It *might* be. I just don't know what to think or feel. On one hand I'm so thrilled and relieved that one baby, which is all we hoped for, is ok. And actually, if you'd told me apropos of nothing I was having twins I would have freaked out completely. I mean, how the hell would we cope with twins? But now I know it's a possibility I can't help but hope that the other little one does make it, and to feel sad that they might not."

Daniel nodded slowly. That pretty much summed up his own feelings too. The idea of twins was simultaneously terrifying and thrilling. His own twins, growing up best of friends like he and Dominic! But then *two* newborn babies, as well as a school-girl, to be responsible for, when a few months ago he had been a carefree bachelor.

Claudia continued.

"My hormone levels are very high. High enough to support a twin pregnancy, but of course that could be because I've only just lost one of them. And the high hormones are why I have been feeling so sick and tired. They're going to keep on measuring those as well."

Daniel nodded, remembering all this from his obs/gynae rotation. He also vaguely remembered that losing one twin could make it more likely you lost the other, but he decided to keep that to himself for the time being.

They ate their lasagne and salad snuggled together on the sofa, and then Daniel tucked Claudia up in bed. She was asleep almost instantly, even though it was barely 9.30pm. He stayed awake, reading, and occasionally glancing at her beautiful face, open and vulnerable in sleep, marvelling that this amazing woman was carrying his child, and wondering very much how the next few months were going to pan out for all of them.

32

The house was as immaculate as always, the only sound being the dishwasher humming away in the background, but the atmosphere could no longer be described as peaceful. It was several weeks since the eventful Sunday tea party which had seen Daniel, Dominic and Lydia storm out in fury, and Delia and Henry had barely been on speaking terms with each other since.

Henry was as angry with himself as anyone. He knew, had always known deep down, that he had let Lydia down. That she had deserved honesty and support from him over the years, and that he had been wrong to deny her this in an ultimately futile to keep the peace with Delia. He was angry with Delia too, though. He had always believed, or tried to believe, Delia's alleged reason for keeping the children in the dark about Lydia's true parentage – that it was about protecting Lydia and not raking up the past unnecessarily – and so the forced realisation that she had been motivated by jealousy and resentment all along had unleashed his own resentment towards her.

Delia had initially been wrapped in a sense of rectitude and smugness that she had been right all along. Hadn't she always said that Lydia was trouble? Well, here she was carrying on a secret love affair and alienating Delia from her precious sons, which proved her fairly conclusively to have been right all along. After a couple of days, however, this began to seem like cold comfort. Neither of her sons would take her calls, and her husband was barely speaking to her above a few stiff formalities. It was hardly the kind of thing she could discuss with her friends at the golf club, and so Delia had begun to feel desperately lonely.

So when Henry opened a conversation over breakfast one morning with the words

"There's something I need to talk to you about." Her spirits rose. True, his brusque tone didn't seem particularly promising for a reconciliation, but at least he was communicating, which had to be an improvement.

She smiled hopefully at him, but there was no answering warmth in his eyes.

"I'm meeting Daniel for lunch today."

Delia's eyebrows shot up.

"Here?" the hope in her voice was palpable, but Henry was totally unmoved by it.

"Don't be ridiculous, Delia. Have you made a full and proper apology to Lydia? No? Well, in that case there's no way that any of the children are going to be coming here, is there?"

Delia shook her head. Apologising to Lydia still felt like a ridiculous thing to be expected to do. How had she ended up being the villain of the piece? She'd taken her in and brought her up out of the goodness of her heart, and she'd repaid her by seducing her son, but somehow *she*, Delia, was the one who was said to have behaved badly and needed to apologise. It was ridiculous. A faint hope still persisted though. Daniel was famously fair-minded and conciliatory. If he'd asked to meet Henry, then maybe he was trying to build bridges.

"So you're meeting him in town, then? Did he ask to meet you?"

Henry shook his head, and his voice was still cold as he replied.

"No. I'm meeting him at his house – the house where he is living now and looking after this child – and it was me who asked to meet him."

In answer to her unvoiced question he continued.

"I don't want to approach Dominic and Lydia. I can't imagine how hurt and furious they must be right now, and I don't blame them. But I don't want to lose my children, Delia, even if you don't care. I'm going to try and have a proper conversation with Daniel, and I'm going to give him my mother's letter to give to Lydia."

"But surely..."

"No buts. Mother left that letter with her will, and a note saying that it should be given to Lydia when we told her the truth, and recommending that this was sooner rather than later. At your behest I ignored the later part of her request, but now Lydia does know I am going to carry out my mother's last wishes. I'm also going to give Lydia the other things she has a right to – her birth certificate, the other information we have about her parents and remaining relatives, all the other things we have denied her all these years. Do you have a problem with that?"

Delia shook her head, meekly. Henry went out shortly afterwards, and she was left alone with her thoughts as she went round the house hoovering non-existent crumbs and polishing already immaculate surfaces.

***

Claudia shook her head firmly.

"Nuh-uh, Daniel. I just don't think this is a conversation I should be part of. Not the first time I meet your father! I'll stay and say hello, and then I will clear off and leave you to have lunch together and do the talking. And I'll pick Juliet up from school, so you have plenty of time. You might want to go round to see Lydia afterwards anyway."

Daniel nodded reluctantly, and bent to bury his head in her soft blonde curls.

"I know. You're right. I just like having you with me. Also, you're meant to be resting – are you going to be alright – going out all afternoon, and doing the school run?"

"I'll be fine. The nausea is clearing now. All I'm going to do is sit in a squashy sofa and sip peppermint tea and read my book in that nice café on

Barrett Street. Very undemanding, but it gives me a little walk, and I'll go mad if I never escape from these four walls!"

There was a knock on the door. Daniel took a deep breath, conscious of butterflies in his stomach. Claudia hugged him tightly.

"Good luck, darling. But remember, it isn't your responsibility to sort everything out for the whole family!"

A couple of minutes later, Claudia stood up as Daniel led a very tall, stocky man with greying hair into the kitchen.

"Dad, this is my...girlfriend, Claudia."

Henry's eyebrows shot up, but he replied with calm friendliness:

"How do you do, my dear?" and bent to kiss her cheek.

Claudia replied lightly, and they exchanged a few pleasantries before she made her excuses and left.

Daniel had been busying himself making drinks, and handed Henry a G&T as they heard the door bang behind Claudia.

He took the glass, and looked round the sunny kitchen with approval.

"This is a nice place."

"Yes, it is, isn't it? Shall we sit in the garden?"

They crossed the kitchen to the French windows which stood open, and settled themselves at the little wrought iron table on the patio. Daniel had placed a dish of olives there earlier, and for a few minutes the two men sat quietly, sipping their drinks, listening to the drowsy buzzing of the bees around the big tubs of French lavender.

It was Henry who spoke first.

"Thank you for agreeing to see me, Dan. I know you and Dominic and Lydia are angry – rightly so, but I really do want to try and sort things out."

Daniel shrugged.

"Look, Dad, I am angry at the way Mum spoke to Lydia, and I think you guys made the biggest mistake by lying to us all these years, but really I'm the least affected of anyone. It's Lydia and Dominic you *and Mum* really need to be talking to, and apologising to."

Henry nodded.

"I know, you're right. And I want to. I want to build bridges. But I don't think Mum is ready to yet, and I wasn't sure if Lydia would want to speak to me. I wanted to find out from you how the land lay. And I've also got some things I'd like you to pass on to Lydia, if you don't mind?"

Daniel sighed.

"Right, Dad. You've asked for this. You want to know how the land lies? I'm going to tell you.

"Dominic and Lydia are engaged, and they are getting married in about a month's time. After that they are going to Australia for a year to try and track down some of Lydia's birth family.

I am in a relationship with Claudia, who you just met. She is, or was, kind of my boss, as I've been acting as nanny to her five year old daughter, Juliet.

Claudia is in the process of divorcing her husband, who left her for another woman a few months ago. She is also pregnant, with our twins. It's early days for the pregnancy, and we're still not sure if both babies are going to be ok, but it's looking more hopeful now.

I can't answer for Lydia and Dominic – you need to talk to them yourself – but I can say that I love you and mum. I always will, and I will always be grateful for the chances you have given me. But, I am horrified at the way you have treated Lydia, and if you want us to have a relationship with me, and with your grandchildren in future, then you need to sort that out. I need to feel that you understand why what you did was wrong, and that you have properly apologised before we can move forward.

And yes, of course, I will pass things onto Lydia if you would like."

There was another silence, Henry sitting slightly open-mouthed. His hand groped for his glass, and he downed the rest of the gin. Daniel stood up, took the glass, and went inside to re-fill it. When he returned, his father clapped him on the back.

"Thanks, son. I really appreciate your honesty. It sounds like quite a lot has been going on recently! First of all, congratulations! I hope and pray that both the babies are ok. Twins are quite the adventure! Claudia seemed lovely, and I'd really like to get to know her better – and so would your mum.

I can't deny, though, that the idea of Lydia and

Dominic getting married is going to take some getting used to. I had no idea at all that she and Dom had become romantically involved."

Daniel smiled.

"I know what you mean. I found it strange at first, because to me, even before I knew, Lydia was more like one of the family rather than a potential romantic interest. But I have had a bit longer to get used to it, and they're so happy together, Dad. I know it seems a bit strange at first, but they really are so well-suited."

Henry returned his son's smile.

"Yes, I can see that in a funny sort of way. And, at the end of the day, it is my problem to get used to the idea. I don't ever want to make Dominic and Lydia think that I'm not happy for them. All I want to do now is whatever I can to make it right. Or as right as I can. These documents for Lydia might be a start – they should help her to make a start discovering if she has any relatives still living in Australia. And will you ask her, if she will speak to me? If she will, then I can phone or see her, and apologise."

Daniel agreed, and the two men enjoyed a strangely companionable lunch together. The warm sunshine, the temporary respite from some of the complicated emotions they had both been dealing with, the delicious food all combined to create a feeling of deep tranquillity. Daniel realised how few times he had spent alone with his father. Normally Delia was there, bustling around, or Dom or Lydia were there too, and there was that unspoken current of tension running between Lydia and Delia.

Henry was no great shakes at deep and emotional conversations, but he did his best to step up, asking concerned questions about Claudia's health, and the babies, and about Daniel's feelings on the suddenness of his transition to stepfather of one and father of two. He also gave some surprisingly well thought out and sage advice about Daniel's future career, and Daniel was startled to realise that of all people it might be his dad who had actually hit on a workable solution.

33

Lydia answered the door in bare feet, and a short tunic dress with a bright print, looking radiantly relaxed.

She certainly didn't seem to have spent the day worrying, knowing that Daniel was having lunch with Henry.

She kissed Dan's cheek and asked immediately

"How is Claudia? And the babies?"

"No further news, really. Claudia is feeling pretty rough, but she's putting a brave face on it. But like I told you on the phone, the latest scan the other day showed that there *are* two strong heartbeats, and both embryos are measuring to be the right size, so that's really encouraging. It's just really hard maintaining a balance between being positive, and not building our hopes up too much."

Lydia smiled sympathetically.

"I can imagine. Well, obviously I can't, but you know what I mean. It would be *so* amazing if you two had twins! I've got everything crossed for you. Listen, can I get you a drink? A beer? Or I've got some home-made lemonade?"

Daniel grinned.

"Of all the shocks of the last few months – you and Dominic being a couple, you turning out to be my secret cousin, Claudia being pregnant, Claudia being pregnant with twins – I still think the biggest shock is you turning into a domestic goddess! Lemonade would be great, thanks. I had a G&T and a couple of glasses of wine with Dad, so I'm feeling a bit fuzzy."

Lydia poured two glasses of lemonade from the jug in the fridge, and carried them out onto the tiny balcony. Daniel followed her through, and they sat in silence for a few moments, sipping their drinks. Then Daniel put a hand into his beat-up leather satchel and pulled out an A4 envelope which he pushed across the table to Lydia.

"Dad gave me some things for you. Paperwork. I'm not sure exactly what – hopefully your birth certificate."

Lydia opened the envelope.

"Yes! My birth certificate. Wow. Well, that's really helpful as Dominic and I have to go to the registry office with all our paperwork, and I knew I needed this, but I've been bottling actually calling…your parents to ask for it."

She pulled out a couple of photos.

"Oh my God! Dan – look! This is me, with my mother. Oh wow! I've got a few photos of us, but I have never seen this one before."

She sat and stared at the image for a couple of minutes, eyes welling up with tears, and then handed it wordlessly to Daniel.

He looked down at the picture of a young woman, about the same age as Lydia herself, cradling a newborn baby wrapped in a white blanket. You couldn't see much of the baby apart from a tiny red scrunched face, but the expression of rapt devotion on the woman's face was both unmistakeable and deeply moving. Daniel recalled the self-same expression on Claudia's face in the photo he and Juliet had seen in the photo album, and allowed himself a second of imagining her looking like that at their babies. His heart flipped over with hope and longing and fear, and then he dragged his attention back to Lydia.

He smiled, and asked

"Is there anything else in the envelope?"

She turned it upside down.

Some more official looking documentation fell out, and she glanced through them.

"Ok, this is my parents' birth certificates, and their marriage certificate, and their death certificates." She pulled a face. "Not much to show for a life, is it?" she gestured at the papers.

Daniel laid his hand on her arm.

"Maybe not – but you're a pretty impressive result! If your parents could see you now, I'm fairly sure they'd think you were an amazing achievement."

She smiled her gratitude.

"I think that's it. Oh no, wait. There's another, smaller envelope."

This one had Lydia's name written on the front in beautiful, old fashioned script.

"Dan – is that Granny's handwriting?"

Daniel nodded.

"Looks like it to me, yes."

"Why have I got a letter from Granny?"

Daniel shrugged.

"You know what I'm going to say…"

Lydia took a deep breath, squared her shoulders, and carefully opened the envelope.

For a moment her eyes were so blurred with tears she couldn't make sense of the words. She blinked determinedly, and looked down at the closely written sheet of blue fountain pen:

To my very dearest Lydia,

By the time you read this, my darling, I will be dead. Please don't be too sad – I had a long life, and by and large a very good life, and I am ready to go.

One regret I do have is that I have never been able to persuade Henry and Delia to tell you the truth about your own history. If you are reading this, they must now have told you, and I hope that you can forgive them for leaving it so late in your life.

I was little more than a child when I met Percy Manders – your real grandfather. My heart was broken by thinking that my beloved fiancé had been killed in action. Percy was far from home, and lonely, and I was flattered by his attention. He was much older than me, and had money to treat me to little things, and he had a proper old-fashioned chivalry which made me feel cossetted and protected. I realise this all makes me sound very shallow, and I cannot pretend that I was in love with Percy. But I thought that my heart was buried with my first love, and it didn't seem such a terrible thing to take a little comfort where I could.

Then I realised I was pregnant. At first I was quite pleased. I was confident that Percy would do the honourable thing and marry me, and the prospect of starting a new life on the other side of the world was rather exciting. It was clear by then that England and her Allies were going to win the war, but equally clear that life was not going to be remotely the same afterwards. Escaping the drab, grey world of rationing and bereavement for a new life in the sunshine, with a husband who adored me, and a little baby, seemed about as good as I could hope for.

I will never forget the expression on Percy's face when I told him. The colour simply drained out of it, and he sat staring at me, mouth agape. For the first time I felt a prickle of unease – this didn't seem like my confident, worldly lover.

"But, but you **can't** be." He stammered. "We were careful. It must be a mistake. Have you seen a doctor?"

I almost choked at the idea of seeing Dr Hamilton. Seventy if he was a day, he had brought me into the world, and my mother before me. His morals and manners were pure Victorian, and the thought of telling him I was expecting a child out of wedlock was, well, **un**thinkable.

"No, I haven't." I told him. "But I'm pretty sure. I've missed three monthlies now. I have been feeling horribly nauseous, and can't face coffee any more. And my skirts are getting tight round the waist."

He sunk his head into his hands and groaned, while I stared at him in surprise. I was so naïve, Lydia my dear. I couldn't understand his distress. Without meaning to boast, I was considered a very pretty girl in my youth, and Percy had always seemed besotted with me. Why was the idea of marrying me to legitimise his child causing him such pain?

Then he told me about his wife. His wife of over twenty years. His barren wife, sitting in their comfortable home on the other side of the world, anxiously waiting his return. He told me of the years of anguish as they had both longed for a child, and had had their hopes dashed month after month. I listened in growing fear and despondency. How could things happen like this? How could my beloved George die at twenty-one years old? How could I fall pregnant accidentally by a married man, while another woman broke her heart over her inability to conceive?

Percy was unable to meet my eyes as he told me he couldn't bring himself to ask his wife for a divorce so he could marry me. Told me that it would break her utterly. Told me that he knew he was a cad either way, but that I was strong and would survive, and his wife might not. By now I had lost all enthusiasm for marrying him in any case. He had deceived me, and deceived his wife, and I didn't want my bright new future to be built on the ruins of another woman's life.

But I had a terrible problem. In 1944, unmarried motherhood was still a shocking stigma. I would bring disgrace on myself and my family. I would have been happy to put a ring on my finger, declare myself a war widow (as, indeed, I felt I was), and make a life for myself and my child far away where no one knew us. But I had no money of my own, no qualifications, no way of earning my living. I felt beaten into submission by circumstance.

Percy behaved as honourably as he could. He saw my parents, and broke the news to them, drawing their anger onto himself rather than me. He implied that, if he hadn't exactly raped me, he had certainly seduced me against my better judgement. Such were the double standards of the time, that he actually won my father's grudging respect for his 'honesty'. And, my parents' deep gratitude for his offer to adopt the child and take it back to Australia for he and his wife to raise as their own.

Apparently he had confessed all to his wife, Joan, and she was so delighted at the prospect of a baby at long last that she was willing to forgive his infidelity. Everyone saw it as a perfect solution. I was whisked away to my Aunt Emma's in Northumberland, and Percy paid for the most luxurious nursing home a prospective mother could desire. I had six weeks with my baby boy, named Andrew after Percy's father, before he was weaned onto a bottle. Percy hired a top Norland Nanny to accompany him and the baby on the long journey back to Australia.

I am sure you will be asking how I gave in without a fight. I don't really know the answer. Perhaps I was suffering from depression, but no one talked about that in those days. In the space of little more than a year I had lost the love of my life and my firstborn child, and I felt completely numb. I kept telling myself that I was doing the best I could for my baby boy – he would be growing up in a wealthy family, with two parents who adored him, free of the stigma of bastardy. If I kept him then none of that would be true. I decided to train as a nurse, so I could do something useful with my life, and try to atone for my mistakes.

Shortly after came the most glorious news of my life. George had not been killed! He had been a prisoner of war in Italy, but had escaped and had been hiding out in the Tuscan hills ever since, surviving on the scraps of food a kind Italian family were able to pass him, and whatever he could forage for himself. When the war in Europe ended, he made his way back home. He was terribly thin, and looked twenty years older than when I had last seen him, but he was my George, and he was safe. My mother told me on no account must I tell him about Percy and the baby. I ignored her advice, and confessed the whole story. He could not have been more understanding. We got married as soon as possible, and he even offered to get Andrew back from Australia and raise him as his own son.

But I had a letter from Joan, begging me not to take 'her' son away from her. It was heartrending. But, however much I might regret the timing, I knew that I couldn't do that to her. Or to Andrew. I might be his birth mother, but this woman had raised him from a tiny baby to a toddler, she was the only mother he knew. I had sinned, and this was my punishment. And, to be honest, in the ecstasy of my reunion with George, the loss of my child faded to a manageable pain.

When I gave birth to Henry a few years later it brought some of those feelings back, but I was very lucky. I had a wonderful husband and son, and Percy and Joan were very good about keeping me in touch with Andrew. I got a photograph and a letter every year on his birthday – at first these letters were from Joan, telling me of his progress, but as time went on he began to write himself, which was wonderful.

Meeting him as an adult, when George and Henry and I went to Australia, was truly humbling. Any doubts I had had about letting him leave evaporated because he had turned into a wonderful man – intelligent, caring, thoughtful, witty. I couldn't have done better for him than Joan and Percy had done, and although I had no real right to feel proud of him, I still did. It also warmed my heart to see Andrew and Henry together, both brought up as only children, and yet discovering true brotherly affection together.

By the time Andrew met your mother, Ariadne, Joan and Percy had both died. I was so pleased he had found happiness, and absolutely thrilled when they moved back to England, and not long after he told me they were having a baby. The twins had been born by then, so I was already a proud granny, but after two sons and two grandsons there was something very special about learning I had a granddaughter. I loved you from the moment I first saw you my darling Lydia.

I won't write much about your father and mother's death. It was a very bleak time for all of us. The only silver lining for me was the chance to atone for abandoning my son fifty years earlier by offering sanctuary to his daughter. I had a happy marriage, two fine sons, two adorable grandsons, but I don't think any human being ever touched my heart the way you did then, Lydia.

Henry had been appointed your guardian, and he was more than happy to take care of his brother's child. Delia was not so happy. I think we mishandled the situation, Lydia, and I think you were the innocent victim of our mistakes. When I saw Delia's reluctance, I wanted to take you in myself. Your grandfather would have been happy to, but Henry was not. He pointed out that Andrew had named him guardian not me, and that must mean he wanted you to grow up in a proper family with young parents, not grandparents already in their seventies. I had no choice but to concede, and Henry talked Delia round somehow. I resented her for not welcoming you wholeheartedly, and I let that resentment show more than I should, which meant that she felt she couldn't ask me for support when she needed it.

I know you have always had a difficult relationship with Delia. I have always hoped that Henry's affection, and my deep love for you, not to mention your friendship with Daniel and Dominic, has made up for that, but I know it probably hasn't – a girl needs a mother. And if she can't have her birth mother, then she needs a damn good substitute.

Try not to judge Delia too harshly, though. She had a very difficult first few years with the twins, and then had another toddler foisted on her without having any say in the matter, in fact having her wishes directly over-ruled. I am afraid Henry was not a particularly hands-on father, and most of the day-to-day responsibility fell on Delia. I tried to help, but we ended up with a Mary and Martha situation of Delia doing all the mundane chores of cooking, cleaning, potty training and so on, while I swooped in for the cuddles and the fun. Some of that was Delia's fault as she rather enjoyed playing the martyr, but honestly, I probably didn't try hard enough to properly help her with the practical things. I relished the bond between us, Lydia, even though I wasn't allowed to openly acknowledge you as my granddaughter, and perhaps I encouraged it at the expense of encouraging a closer bond between you and Delia.

I also think Henry made a grave error of judgement in refusing to countenance having another child after taking on guardianship of you. Delia had always wanted, and expected she would have, another baby at some point, and unfairly she blamed you for robbing her of that, rather than laying the blame on Henry, where it belonged.

And then, of course, there was your relationship with the twins It was very hard for her to see your closeness when she adored them so much. Whatever the reason, she was always implacably opposed to you being told that you really were part of the family rather than the hanger-on she seemed to try and make you feel. Having opposed her on so much, Henry gave into her on this. And I felt I had no right to tell you in opposition to his wishes, because he was your legal guardian not me. I have taken the easy route of writing this letter, now I know my time is limited, and begging Henry to tell you the truth and give you this letter after my death. Presumably, if you are reading this, he has done so.

Try and forgive all of us for our mistakes, Lydia. Although I suspect you will be inclined to hold Delia most to blame, I think the real responsibility is mine. I let my love for you and my desire to retain your affection prevent me from taking the steps I knew deep down were the right ones. I should have been more assertive, and if I couldn't persuade Henry to agree, I should have told you the truth myself. Perhaps I still should. But I am so tired now, I know my life is coming to an end, and weakly, selfishly, I just want to enjoy you and Dominic and Daniel in the time I have left, and not embroil myself in a family row. I apologise.

I hope that now you know the truth you can use it to help you live the life you want. Find out about your Australian family. Realise that your parents loved you deeply, and that however flawed our execution, Henry and I were also motivated by our love for you and our desire to do what was best. Understand that Delia had a hard time for reasons that were absolutely not your fault, and try to forgive her for taking her frustrations out on you.

The adults in your life got a lot wrong, Lydia. But when I look at the strong, resilient, courageous, talented and beautiful young woman you have become, I can't help but think we must have got something right as well.

I hope that you will be happy, my darling Lydia. Your presence in my life has given me some of my deepest joy.

God bless you and watch over you always.

With all my love,

Granny xxxx

Lydia took a deep breath. Emotions swirled round her head. She forced a smile at Daniel who was looking at her in concern.

"Thanks for this, Dan. And for talking to Dad. I've got some thinking to do. Do you mind leaving me to it?"

He agreed, and slipped unobtrusively away, and Lydia was left alone with thoughts that were suddenly very uncomfortable.

Her grandmother's letter was a wonderful treasure to have, proving how deeply she had been loved, but it had also opened up memories that Lydia usually refused to acknowledge at all.

It *was* easy to blame Delia for everything, and certainly she had got a lot wrong. But it was also apparent from Granny's letter that she and Henry had made mistakes too. That fundamental weakness, that fear of confrontation and desire for an easy life that she knew so well in Dominic was clearly an inherited trait which her grandmother and uncle possessed as well. And then there was her own part in things. Yes, she had been a very young child when she had been taken into the Nicholls family. And in some ways children couldn't be blamed for the situations that their responsible adults put them in. But an innate honesty compelled Lydia to look honestly at her own behaviour to Delia, and she could see that it hadn't always been pretty.

She had realised at a very early age that her friendship with the twins and their conspiratorial closeness needled Delia, and she had done everything she could to foster that closeness, and subtly belittle their mother whenever she could. It wasn't difficult. Delia could be fussy, and old-fashioned and was nowhere near as sharp-witted as Lydia.

She recalled a family holiday to Cornwall when they were all in their mid-teens when she had successfully undermined Delia's plans for wholesome National Trust excursions and family days at the beach and had instead lured the twins off to the nearby resort where the local and holiday-making teens hung out on the seafront, swigging illicit cider and smoking even more illicit spliffs. Delia had actually put up with their behaviour with far better grace than they probably deserved, masking her disappointment at another family day missed as she fried up bacon for their hangover-beating butties the next morning. Deep down Lydia had known it was more than a desire to hang out and have fun that motivated her, it was a sense of triumph that she could get one over on Delia, but she had ignored this knowledge for years.

She could also recall times when Delia had made overtures of conciliation, and she had brutally rejected her every time. When she was about eleven or twelve, for example, and Delia had tried to talk to her about periods. Lydia was already pretty confident of her facts from a combination of Just Seventeen magazine, chat with her friends and school biology lessons, and she had just laughed at Delia's carefully composed little speech.

"I'm not a baby! And you're not my mother!' she had spat as she left the room.

Later she had found on her bed a box which Delia had clearly intended to give her during their orchestrated talk, with 'Lydia's Survival Kit' stencilled on the lid. It contained a pretty wash bag with a selection of different sanitary towels inside, an Usborne book on puberty, a giant family-sized bar of Dairy Milk, a fluffy hot-water bottle and a packet of paracetamol. She had eaten the Dairy Milk, and dumped the rest back on Delia's bed. It had never been referred to again, but Lydia winced now at the memory of how carelessly cruel she had been, and how her behaviour would have contributed to the hurt and resentment Delia felt.

34

Lois felt as light and energised as she could ever remember. Horatio had wrapped himself round her neck, purring ecstatically, and she reached up one hand to caress him, whilst pressing 'send' on the adoption registration form at the same time.

A smile split her face ear to ear, and she couldn't help but contrast this feeling of lightness and rightness with the heavy sense of foreboding which had accompanied her foray into the world of IVF. The registration process should take about two months, and after that, there would be a four-month stage of more in-depth assessment of her, her home, her potential as an adoptive parent, before her case would go before an adoption panel for approval. Emilia, the ultra-helpful and friendly social worker who had been supporting her through the initial stages had been extremely reassuring about her chances. And once she was approved, the fact that she was hoping to adopt a school-age child, meant that it was likely she wouldn't have to wait long before being matched. Coincidentally or not, the whole process looked like it would take about the same length of time as a pregnancy.

The only shadow on the horizon was Michael. He had been customarily polite, friendly, courteous when she told him of her decision to abandon their IVF journey and look to adopt by herself, but she hadn't heard from him since. She felt that she'd treated him very badly, but couldn't for the life of her work out what she could or should do to make amends. Even if by some miracle it proved to be medically possible, she couldn't go through IVF and pregnancy and actually having the baby now she had decided it wasn't the right thing for her. And the social worker advising her had been pretty unequivocal that adopting on your own was fine, adopting as a couple, whether gay or straight, married or unmarried, was fine, but two single and unrelated people adopting together would not be considered a viable option. She had racked her brains to think of any of her lesbian friends who might want children and therefore a sperm donor, but the problem was, the likely contenders were both couples, and *all* they would want would be a sperm donor, not a father for the baby.

In the uncanny way that sometimes happens, just as Lois turned the issue over in her mind for the thousandth time, her phone pinged with a new text message. It was Michael.

Hi Lois, sorry I've not been in touch. Had a lot of thinking to do. Would you mind meeting for a coffee? I've had an idea and I'd really appreciate talking it over with you. Cheers, M x

Lois' light heart turned leaden and plummeted. It sounded horribly like he was going to make an attempt to continue Project Baby with him, and the flat refusal she felt she had no choice but to make was going to hurt him horribly. Still, at the very least she owed him the courtesy of meeting up to discuss it.

Hi Michael, of course, happy to meet up. You free this morning, by any chance? L x

Lois was a firm believer in getting unpleasant tasks over and done with as quickly as possible. Their meeting was arranged, and an hour later they were sitting across the table from one another in the London Review of Books café by the British Museum.

Michael certainly didn't *look* despairing. In fact he looked distinctly bright-eyed and bushy tailed, and had a cardboard wallet full of papers which he laid down on the table.

Lois eyed the folder with misgiving, took a large swig of her flat white, and wished she'd suggested meeting for a drink instead.

They exchanged polite chit chat for a few moments, and despite herself Lois began to relax. There was something so calmly reassuring about Michael that it was hard to remain stressed in his presence for long.

"So, what was it you wanted to talk about?" she enquired at last.

Michael grinned boyishly.

"This!"

He pulled one of the leaflets out of his folder, and waved it at her triumphantly.

'Do <u>you</u> have what it takes to foster in Hackney?'

screamed the heading, and underneath was a picture of a woman with her arms round a little girl.

The penny dropped, and relief surged through Lois.

"Wow! You're thinking about becoming a foster parent?"

He nodded vehemently.

"Yes! It's the perfect thing for me. I don't know why I didn't think of it before." He paused, and frowned. "Well, actually, to tell the truth, I did think of it before, but I didn't have enough confidence in myself to pursue it."

He smiled shyly at Lois.

"Meeting you has done me so much good. You're so confident, so courageous, and I think your example has made me braver too."

Lois laughed.

"Wow, I've certainly never considered myself to be particularly courageous!"

"But you *are*. If you want to make a change you just jump right in and do it, regardless of convention. I mean, come on, advertising for a baby father online isn't exactly the act of a shrinking violet!"

Lois blushed a little.

"No, well. If I am brave, it is thanks to Janey. She was so brave through her illness, so selfless too. And I suppose having faced the worst thing in the world and somehow survived, I didn't see what there was to be scared of in trying to find a little happiness. We know better than most that life is short."

He was nodding again.

"Yes, we do. But that knowledge had the opposite effect on me. I saw the world as a scary place full of people and things that could hurt me, and I didn't think I could stand any more hurt, so I just retreated into my shell. I would never have replied to your advert if my brother hadn't forced me, but once I had, and met you…well, it's given me the impetus I needed to break out of my rut."

Lois laid a gentle hand on his arm.

"I'm sorry. About having crappy old eggs, and reneging on our IVF plan. The downside of being an activist and getting on and doing things is that it can be all too easy to get on and do the wrong thing. And I was making the mistake of trying to do what Janey and I had planned by myself, whereas what I needed was a new plan that's right for the life I've ended up with."

Michael covered her hand with his own and squeezed it.

"Don't be sorry. I knew that day in Harley Street it wasn't going to work, for lots of reasons. It's funny, I'm normally a ridiculously practical and sober person, but I allowed myself to get swept along…anyway. I have been looking into fostering, and I honestly think that will suit me so much better than a new baby would! There are so many children in heart-breaking circumstances – well, you know that from your work – and I have love and time and energy to give. I own my own flat outright, I don't need much money to live on, and you get a generous foster-carers' allowance, so I wouldn't need to work, I could just focus on the children. And, one thing I discovered when my wife was ill, is that I'm actually pretty good at looking after people. So I would be happy to have children with long-term health conditions, who apparently can be very hard to place."

He paused for a second, more because he had run out of breath than because he had run out of things to say.

Lois smiled broadly at him.

"Oh, Michael, I am so glad! You will be an amazing foster father. And it is an incredible thing to do. If I've taught you anything I'm glad, because your love and patience and calm has taught me so much. Not sure how good I am at implementing it yet, but it's always good to have goals!"

She took a forkful of coffee and walnut cake, and paused to analyse the feeling washing over her. A feeling she hadn't experienced for a long time, and had imagined was lost to her forever. Content. She was content. Suddenly, she didn't regret her impulsive decision to get pregnant, or the headlong way she had met Michael and rushed into IVF. Sure, they hadn't been the right decisions in one sense, but they were decisions which meant she had made what she instinctively knew to be a lifelong friendship, and had brought them to where they both were now. Which was exactly the place they needed to be in.

35

Lydia heaved such a heavy sigh that it drew Dominic's attention from *The Guardian* and onto her.

"You okay?"

Another deep sigh.

"Yes. I'm fine. It's just that…Dom, it's only a week until the wedding!"

A smile of pure joy and excitement spread across his face.

"I know! God, Lyddy, I am so excited. I wish it was tomorrow."

She wrinkled her nose, stood up, and began pacing the room, straightening knick-knacks that didn't need straightening, and pausing, as she always did, to look at the photos of her baby self with her mother.

"I know, babe. I'm so excited too. But I'm not *ready*."

Now she had his full attention.

"What do you mean, not ready?" he ticked off on his fingers. "We've done all the paperwork at the Registry Office. You've got your dress, and Juliet's little flower girl dress. I'm wearing a suit, and I've got a nice new tie. We've booked Eat 17 for a meal afterwards. You've ordered flowers, and we've bought the rings – and I haven't lost them, yet. Everything is well in hand for Australia; tickets booked, packing started – and we've got a whole week after the wedding to sort all the last minute things for that. I thought the whole point of having a last-minute, simple, pared down wedding was that there wasn't that much *to* get ready."

She was nodding uneasily.

"Oh yeah. All the practical stuff is sorted. But the elephant in the room, or rather not in the room, is your parents. What do we do about them? Do we invite them to the wedding? Do we talk to them beforehand? Your dad…made it clear to Daniel that the ball was in our court, and that they wanted to make amends but didn't want to harass us. But I don't know what I want to do, what to do for the best."

It was just over a fortnight since Daniel had given her Granny Nicholls' letter, and Lydia still felt she was reeling from it. It put a whole new perspective on the situation, and had to some extent enabled her to see the protagonists as people in their own rights, rather than simply their roles in relation to her.

She had always adored the twins' grandmother, and this love was only strengthened by the knowledge that she had actually been her grandmother too, and the evidence of how much her grandmother had loved her. But equally, she couldn't help feeling frustrated impatience towards the dead woman, that she had not played a more proactive role in helping Lydia to discover the truth about her identity.

Rather to her surprise, she also did feel more sympathy towards Delia than she would ever have believed possible. She hadn't handled things well, emotionally, but equally Lydia *had* grown up in a secure home with plenty of love and affection from those around her. If Delia had point blank refused to have her, things could have been very different. And she could see that if you are already responsible for toddler twins, then taking on another toddler who is no relation of yours, is no laughing matter. Henry hadn't behaved well in this respect, and Dominic and Lydia both remembered from their childhoods that he had left most of the hands-on aspects of parenting to their mother. One of the more uncomfortable things about growing up, she reflected, was the realisation that things are rarely as black and white as they seem when you are younger. People are rarely saints or villains, and everyone makes mistakes but then redeem themselves in other ways.

She knew that the decision was really hers. Dominic and Daniel would unquestionably be loyal to her, but she knew that deep down they did love their parents, and would be happy and relieved if she agreed to receive their apologies and they could begin to paper over the cracks of their shattered family. Could she do that? Could she put aside years of coldness and deceit, the lies which had nearly driven her and Dominic apart?

She dropped down next to Dominic on the sofa, and snuggled her head into his arm.

"It's up to you, lovely girl." He echoed her own thoughts. "Dan and I will support you whatever you decide, but it's only you who can make the decision."

Lydia considered. She had been orphaned as a tiny child, grown up criticised and unloved by her guardian, failed to establish a proper career because she didn't have the confidence to do so, and she and Dom had spent weeks in in mental torment because they were scared they had inadvertently ended up sleeping with their sibling. None of that could be forgotten, but could it be forgiven? Because, also, Granny was right. She *was* strong. None of those things had broken her. And she now had so much – the most wonderful, loving, supportive relationship anyone could ever hope for, an amazing cousin/brother-in-law and his delightful girlfriend and stepdaughter, not to mention two new babies on the way who would be her nieces/nephews. A lovely home, and the chance to make an extended trip to the country she loved with the man she adored and discover her roots. With all that, surely she could be the bigger person?

She nodded, decisively.

"Right, I'm going to do it. I'm going to text Dan and ask him to let them know I'm happy for them to contact me. And then that puts the ball back in their court. If we get a proper apology, if it really seems as though they want to make amends and have a good relationship with us, then we will. We'll let bygones be bygones and invite them to the wedding. But if not…" her voice trailed off.

Dominic kissed her on the mouth.

"You are truly amazing. For what it's worth, I think that's the right thing to do.'

Daniel also breathed a sigh of relief when he got Lydia's text. Always inclined to see the best in people, he had read his grandmother's letter and ended up feeling deeply sorry for everyone involved, and desperately hoping for some kind of reconciliation. He was also adamant that he wouldn't go back on his promise to Lydia not to speak to Delia until she had apologised, but he was finding it harder than he had imagined not to be able to share the news of Claudia's pregnancy with her. Her excitement and joy at another set of twins in the family would be enormous. Lydia was doing the right thing by opening up to them, and now he just desperately hoped that his father would bring his mother up to the mark with a proper apology.

Claudia's pregnancy, not to mention her five-year old daughter, had catapulted her and Daniel into a state of cosy coupledom faster than he would have imagined possible. The demands of his career, along with the classic 'not having met the right girl' yet meant that for most of his twenties he had been single, interspersed with relationships of two or three months, which never really got beyond the initial dating stage before the girl in question got bored of being the one making all the effort, called him a workaholic and dumped him. Perhaps the reason things were working so well with Claudia was that he had met the right woman at last – it certainly felt like it. Or perhaps it was because he met her when he was taking a career break and so had the emotional energy for a relationship. Or perhaps it was because he impregnated her on their first night together, and a difficult pregnancy combined with a five-year old meant that instead of being out at the theatre, the cinema, in trendy restaurants or cool nightclubs, they spent their evenings curled up together on the sofa while he massaged her feet and they talked about anything and everything.

Imperceptibly, there had been a shift, and although there would always be an unbreakable bond between him and his twin, Dominic was no longer the person he was closest to. No longer the first person he texted with a funny story, or wanted to talk to about something which was worrying him. The day Claudia told him she was pregnant he had been experiencing feelings of devastation, almost bereavement, at the thought of not seeing his brother for a year, and at the possibility of Dominic and Lydia deciding to make a new life for themselves in Australia. Now this no longer seemed such a big deal. He would miss them, would miss being able to see them for a quick drink whenever he wanted, but equally he and Claudia would maybe be able to go and see them, and no doubt they would travel back to the UK regularly. Instead of stretching emptily before him, this was going to be the biggest and best year of his life.

The nagging worry about his career, and how he and Claudia could cope with three children and two full-time careers had also been resolved, thanks to a suggestion from his dad. The more he thought about it, the less Daniel could see himself going back to hospital medicine, and the more content he was in his personal life the less he wanted to. Equally, he was pretty sure that giving up medicine when he had worked so hard to become a doctor, and when it gave him so much satisfaction, wasn't the right thing to do either. His dad had suggested that he should consider re-training as a GP, and the more he thought about it, the more it seemed like the right thing to do.

He was going to begin the re-training part-time, starting that autumn. That would still give him time to help look after Juliet, and support Claudia through her pregnancy, and be around for a good proportion of the time when the twins were born. Eventually, by the time he was a qualified GP, he would be able to get a job in a practice, either part-time or full-time, depending on how old the twins were by then, and what they felt like would work for their family. But either way there would be no working every weekend, or night-shifts or weeks of fourteen hour shifts with no break. Some people, like Lois, seemed to be able to cope with that pace, even thrive on it, he now knew that he wasn't one of them. And he knew that, important though his work was to him, it was actually personal ties that made him truly content.

Claudia was lying full length along the sofa now, with her head in his lap, stroking her now softly rounded stomach absent-mindedly.

"Lydia has just texted to ask me to tell Dad he can contact her if he wants. Hopefully they can apologise now, and we can all move on."

"Oh that's great! She's very brave, isn't she? I'm so pleased though, because you really want to be able to share all the baby stuff with your mum, don't you?"

This ability of Claudia to echo his own, sometimes barely acknowledged, thoughts was uncanny.

"You're right. I really do. She's going to be so excited. And it's nice that we've now got some really positive news to share."

Claudia was now three months pregnant, and they had been for another scan the day before. Both babies looked strong and healthy and the right size for their dates, and they had been told that although there were no guarantees, and twin pregnancies were always slightly higher risk, it was all looking more than encouraging, and he and Claudia had given each other permission to start getting excited and to start planning. They had also told Juliet, and her delighted excitement about becoming a big sister was off the scale.

"I wonder if we'll have two boys, or two girls, or one of each?"

Juliet had been adamant that at least one of the babies had to be a girl.

"I want a sister like Samira has. Can you make one

of the babies be a girl, please, Mummy?"

Claudia had explained that, no, she couldn't really do much about it, but this explanation had been received with sceptical dissatisfaction, so she was now finding herself hoping that she would have at least one girl.

Daniel shrugged.

"No idea! Do you want to find out, at the 20 week scan?"

She nodded vehemently.

"Yes! I really do. I think it will be much easier to prepare Juliet if we know, and also we've got to be really organised having twins, and I just feel the more information the better. What do you think?"

"Yes, I'm happy to. I quite like the idea of a surprise, but I think it probably makes more sense to find out. If I had to bet, I'd say two girls. I have a feeling I'm about to be hopelessly outnumbered!"

36

Dominic had got up early to go for a run, come home and taken a shower. Lydia had spent the time lounging in bed with the pretty notebook that was her bible for organising a wedding, house swap, and year's vacation. Lists were the only thing that would get them through, and, as always she knew that with Dominic's "Chill, babe, it'll sort itself out" attitude, if it was all going to work out, she needed to be the driving force. He was calling out from the bathroom, teasing her, trying to persuade her to join him in the shower, when the doorbell rang.

"Leave it – it'll just be the postman wanting to be let in. Someone else will do it."

"No, it's Sunday! No postman!"

"Well, ignore it anyway! No-one we want to see is going to come round on a Sunday morning at 9.30am!"

But Lydia was already on her feet, pulling her white waffle robe over her shoulders as she did so.

"No, some couriers deliver on a Sunday, and I'm waiting for bits, I'm going to get it."

Dominic heaved a sigh of disappointment, and resumed his solo shower.

Lydia picked up the intercom receiver.

"Hello?"

There was a pause, and she was about to hang up, thinking that, now she was out of bed, a shower with Dominic seemed quite enticing after all, when a voice said tentatively

"Is that Lydia?"

"Yes. Who's that?" She knew, though. Her stomach flipped over, and she started shaking slightly.

"It's me. Delia."

"Oh."

"Can I come up?"

"Umm, yes. Sure."

She pressed the buzzer to open the door, and pulled her gown more closely round her. She glanced round the living room to check its tidiness, and then berated herself for doing so – after everything that had happened, she was still acting as though she was desperate for this woman's approval. Approval which nearly decades years of experience had told her would always be withheld.

It *was* reasonably tidy. Suddenly panicked at the idea of her safe space, her haven being the venue for a hideously difficult meeting, she called urgently

"Dominic! Dom!"

He came out, pulling a towel round himself.

"Hey! What is it? You ok, you've gone very pale."

"Mum's here!" she hissed desperately.

He looked round the living room.

"Well, not *here* here, but in the building. She's coming upstairs now. What do I do? Help!"

The doorbell rang.

"Oh shit!"

Dominic knotted the towel firmly round his waist, and Lydia forced her unwilling and wobbly legs across the room, into the hall to open the door.

She opened the door, and stood looking at the woman she had lived with her entire childhood as though seeing her for the first time. The carefully highlighted, carefully blow-dried hair. The make-up, always slightly too heavy, but expensive brands carefully applied. Today she was wearing white linen trousers, tan wedge sandals and a floaty navy top, with a chunky gold necklace. Not an outfit Lydia would choose, but she looked calm and put together, and, unlike anyone else on the planet, she could wear white linen trousers without becoming a stained and crumpled mess.

Lydia felt a flash of resentment. How had she been put in the position of having this discussion with make-up free face, and bedhead, in her dressing gown, while Delia was in a perfectly co-ordinated outfit with expertly coiffed hair and a full face of make-up, apparently without a care in the world, even though she was supposed to be the one on the back foot. Typical. Then she revised her view. Delia was twisting her wedding ring round and round her finger; a gesture which always betrayed her nerves.

"Come in."

Lydia stood back to allow Delia to pass through the tiny hall into the living room.

"Do sit down. Would you like a tea or coffee?"

Lydia could hear herself sounding as though she was hosting a Women's Institute tea party, hoping that the cloak of formal good manners would protect her from...from what, exactly? She wasn't sure, she just knew she felt desperately uncomfortable and ill at ease. At that moment, Dominic emerged from the bedroom. His hair was still damp, and he was barefoot, but he'd pulled on shorts and a t-shirt.

He crossed the room, and kissed the top of Lydia's head.

"Don't worry, sweetheart. I'll make Mum a cup of coffee – I need one myself anyway – you go and get dressed if you want."

Breathing a huge sigh of relief, and filled with gratitude to Dominic for seeing what she needed and making sure she got it, Lydia retreated to the sanctuary of the bathroom. This was what she needed, a little time and space to calm herself down, and prepare mentally and physically.

She splashed her face with cold water, washed it with her zingy grapefruit cleanser, and smoothed on moisturiser. Tugged a brush through her long dark hair until it was smooth and silky. She didn't have time for much make up, but she quickly applied a coat of mascara, and swept blusher across her cheekbones, and a slick of lip balm on her suddenly dry lips. She darted into the bedroom, resisting the temptation to listen and see if she could discover what (if anything) Dominic and Delia were discussing. In the bedroom she grabbed clean pants and bra from her drawer, and then, resisting the temptation to dress up, she pulled on navy yoga pants and a simple white vest top. This was what she would wear, if she was wearing anything, for a normal Sunday morning at home, and she was *not* going to dress for approval. She fastened the silver Tiffany necklace Dominic had given her for her birthday round her neck, and did a little comfort twist of her own beautiful vintage white gold, emerald and diamond engagement ring. The memory of a sunny Saturday in The Laines in Brighton choosing it reminded her that, no matter the outcome of this morning, no-one could now take her happiness with Dom away from her.

She went through into the living room, to be greeted by the smell of fresh coffee, and a plate of warm croissants and pains aux chocolats on the table. Her eyes widened in disbelief – where had they come from? And then she realised that Dominic must have popped into the bakery as he jogged home, and bought these for their breakfast. Suppressing a pang at the thought of that lazy, relaxed crummy breakfast in bed, which would now not happen, she poured herself a cup of coffee, grabbed a pastry, and sat down in the armchair, opposite Delia on the sofa. Dominic pulled one of the dining chairs up and joined them.

Sun was streaming in through the window, and Delia's glance around was reluctantly approving as she took in the charming, cosy room.

"Well, it's obvious you've worked hard at this, Lydia. I can't imagine Dominic making such a lovely home for himself."

Reeling slightly at unsolicited praise, Lydia smiled.

"Well, yes, a lot of it was me. Dom provided the muscle when it came to hulking furniture around!"

An awkward silence.

Then Delia broke it.

"Lydia. I came to apologise. I realise that I said some pretty unforgiveable things to you a few weeks ago, but I am hoping you will be generous enough to make allowances for the stress and shock of the moment, and forgive me anyway." She held up a hand as Lydia opened her mouth to speak.

"Wait a moment, I haven't finished. I also owe you an apology for not being the mother-figure you needed over the years. I know you will find this difficult to believe, but I genuinely did do my best for you, or the best I was capable of. But I felt a lot of resentment – mainly at your father for pushing me into a scenario I had never imagined and never wanted – but instead of sorting it out with him I suppressed it, and took my frustration out on you instead. That wasn't fair, because you were totally innocent. But at first I resented the extra work another child made, and later I was jealous of your bond with the twins. I knew I wasn't behaving well, and then the guilt at that made me resent you even more. I am more sorry than you could know."

Lydia and Dominic were both silent. In thirty years neither could remember hearing this confident, bossy, dominant woman admit that she was wrong, let alone apologise.

Lydia took a deep breath.

"I do forgive you. I won't lie, I did struggle at times, desperately wanting your approval, and never being able to get it. But equally, I didn't have an unhappy childhood. I had Daniel and Dominic, and – thanks to you – I always had physical security. I always had a warm home, a comfortable bed, nice clothes, plenty of good food, books and toys – and compared to many children that makes me very privileged. It makes me privileged compared to what my life would have been if you had refused to take me in, and I'd ended up in a children's home."

Were they tears gleaming in Delia's eyes?

"Thank you. I think that's more than I deserve. I realise that we're never going to have the mother daughter relationship we maybe could have done, and that is entirely my fault. But, do you think we could make a fresh start as mother-in-law and daughter-in-law?"

Lydia nodded, suddenly a little choked with tears herself. She had been so in the habit of demonising Delia, but suddenly she remembered that those hands, now nervously twisting, were the ones which held her hair back from her face when she was sick at 3am, that made freshly squeezed lemonade when she had tonsillitis and it was the only thing she could swallow, which had helped with endless Brownie badge projects involving glue, paint and papier-mache, and which had baked her favourite chocolate fudge cake for her birthday every year. She gave a convulsive sob, and suddenly lunged across the room, and buried her face in Delia's lap.

She felt the suddenly gentle hands awkwardly stroking her hair, and through her tears she heard Dominic's voice.

"Thanks, Mum. And given what you've said about a fresh start as you become Lyddy's mother-in-law – well, would you like to be there at the very beginning of that new relationship? Will you and Dad come to our wedding next Saturday?"

37

"I'm getting married in the morning, ding dong the bells are gonna chime…" Lydia was singing loudly and slightly out of tune as she danced round the kitchen getting plates and glasses out. Dominic picked her up and swung her round, then grabbed the bottle of champagne out of the fridge "Pull out the stopper, and let's have a whopper, but get me to the chu—uurrch onnn ti-iii-me." They both joined in triumphantly with the last line, and smiled giddily at each other. Dominic popped the cork and poured two glasses.

"Cheers. Here's to the best day of our lives tomorrow."

Lydia clinked his glass, and then they curled up one at either end of the sofa with an extra-large takeaway pizza between them, and the rest of the champagne sitting on the coffee table. There were no pre-wedding nerves here, no bridezilla moments, and they were flying in face of tradition by spending their last night before they became husband and wife exactly where they both wanted to be – in each other's arms. Takeaway pizza and champagne seemed like the perfect wedding eve feast, and everything was in train and organised, so there was nothing left to do but enjoy it, and grin inanely at each other.

In one respect they were following tradition – Dominic had not seen Lydia's dress. This was hanging safely in Claudia's house – where Lydia would be going to get ready the next day. Lydia had a clear image in her mind of the dress she wanted, and after extensive searching, she had found it in a little vintage shop on a backstreet of Stoke Newington. It was midi-length, in cream silk. A fitted bodice, not too low-cut but showing a hint of cleavage, and covered with delicate silver beading and embroidery, then a full, swishy skirt that finished mid-calf. Lydia was going to wear it with silver Saltwater sandals ("they'll be useful for Oz afterwards!), and a simple bouquet of cream roses and green leaves. Her hair would be pinned into a messy up-do, with strands escaping to frame her face, and a couple of cream roses fastened into it. Lydia couldn't wait to see Dominic's face when he saw her in it.

They ate their pizza, chatting in a desultory fashion about this and that, and then Lydia suddenly hugged her knees and squealed excitedly.

"Eeek! Can you believe that just a few months ago we didn't think we could even tell your family we were in love because they would have been so horrified, and yet now here we are, getting married tomorrow!"

Dominic pushed the empty pizza box onto the floor and pulled his bride-to-be into his arms.

"I can't believe it." He muttered into her soft hair. "I can't believe I could be this lucky."

***

The wedding ceremony wasn't until 4pm, so the morning was as relaxed as any other. Dominic got up and went for a run, they had breakfast together on their balcony. At midday they both headed over to Claudia and Daniel's.

The weather was perfect – cloudless blue sky, but a gentle breeze preventing it from being too hot.

Daniel opened the door.

"Hey Dom, hey Lyddy. Can I kiss the bride?" He bent down and kissed her cheek, and then stepped back, surveyed them both and grinned.

"I know this wedding is informal, but please tell me you're getting changed?"

Lydia was wearing cut-off denim shorts, a baggy t-shirt with a surf slogan, and Birkenstocks. Dominic looked very similar.

Dominic punched his brother's arm lightly

"Whereas you look the perfect best man already!" He gestured at Daniel's ripped and faded jeans and oil-splashed t-shirt.

"Oh yeah. I was making salad dressing with Juliet. Turns out asking a five-year old to be responsible for screwing the lid on the jam jar before you start shaking it isn't the best idea. I blame Jamie Oliver."

He shut the door.

"Anyway, come on through. Claudia and Juliet are

down in the kitchen. I've made a salad, and a couple of quiche, and some nibbles, just to keep us going. If I know Dominic, no amount of pre-wedding nerves are going to stop him eating, and now Claudia's morning sickness is better she's developed a ferocious appetite."

They followed him through.

"Is Claudia feeling better, now, then?" asked Lydia as they walked down the stairs to the kitchen.

"Yes. Loads better. It was like she turned twelve weeks and someone flicked a switch which stopped the nausea. She still gets a bit tired, but she's got loads more energy than she had a couple of weeks ago, and she's back at work. The scan yesterday showed everything still looks fine."

The kitchen table was loaded with Daniel's concept of a 'few nibbles'. Golden brown home-made quiche, Greek salad, a pile of roasted Mediterranean vegetables slicked with oil, fresh flat breads and bowls of houmous, tzatziki and taramasalata, a green salad and a bowl of cherry tomatoes.

"Oh Dan!" Lydia was touched. "You've gone to so much trouble. You really shouldn't have."

"Don't be silly, Lyds. It's nothing. Didn't want you fainting walking up the aisle or getting pissed drinking champagne on an empty stomach at the reception! Although, having said that..." he opened the fridge and pointed "I did pop a bottle in so we can have a little glass now, just to get us in the mood!"

Lydia hugged him.

"You are the best brother-in-law I could ever have asked for."

They went out into the garden, where Claudia was reclining on a sun-lounger, and Juliet was on her swing. When she saw who had arrived she came sprinting over as fast as her little legs would carry her.

"Auntie Lydia! Guess what? Did you know? My mummy has TWO babies in her tummy! I'm going to be a big sister. Mummy gets really tired because she has to grow the babies from tiny little seeds to being big enough to be born. But they're not going to be born for ages yet – not until after Christmas!" she paused for breath, and Lydia hugged her.

"It's so exciting! I did know, because Daniel told Uncle Dominic. You are going to make such an awesome big sister, these babies are very lucky."

It was a golden couple of hours, sitting relaxing in the garden, eating the delicious food, drinking champagne (Lydia, Dominic and Daniel) and sparkling apple juice (Claudia and Juliet), and chatting about weddings and babies and Australia.

"When you and Daniel get married, Mummy, can I be your bridesmaid as well? Will it be after the babies come, or before? If it's before I think it should be quite soon, before your tummy gets too big to fit into wedding dresses."

Claudia choked slightly, and snorted Appletize through her nose.

"Well, umm, I don't know sweetheart. Erm, Dan and I haven't really talked about it, and erm, I'm still married to Daddy at the moment, so…"

she trailed off, cursing Juliet's direct and outspoken manner.

Dominic and Lydia exchanged amused glances, and Daniel took over.

"You definitely can be bridesmaid when your mummy and I get married. But it won't be for a while yet – definitely not before the babies come, and not before Auntie Lydia and Uncle Dominic come back from Australia. Maybe the summer after next – then, if you get little sisters, you can all be bridesmaids together."

Juliet pouted slightly.

"The summer after next? That's TWO YEARS. I'll be…" she paused to calculate on her fingers. "Seven! Isn't that getting on a bit to be a bridesmaid?"

Daniel, alone of the adults, kept a totally straight face.

"I think it will be alright. Seven isn't *that* old, you know."

Juliet sighed.

"Oh, ok then. As long as you promise it will be then?"

Daniel glanced over at Claudia and raised an eyebrow; a gesture so attractive it took all her self-restraint not to throw herself on him.

"What do you reckon, Claudia? Can you face the

thought of marrying me in order to give Juliet the chance to be a bridesmaid again?"

Claudia pretended to consider, and then a grin split her face from ear-to-ear, and she nodded vehemently, as her throat was too constricted with tears to reply.

Dominic looked at his watch.

"Listen guys, much as I hate to break the party up, we have a wedding to get ready for. Dan, mate, we'd better get going."

Daniel and Dominic were going back to the flat to dress, while Lydia stayed with Claudia and Juliet.

Daniel kissed Claudia on the lips.

"Ok, I'm ready. I'll just go and grab my suit."

"Don't forget the buttonholes!" Claudia yelled after him.

After the boys departed, Claudia turned to Lydia.

"Right, how do you want to do this?"

Lydia shrugged.

"I don't know, it's all new to me! How about, you go and have a shower and get yourself dressed, while Juliet and I hang out here, and then you can get Juliet ready while I have a shower, and then by that time the hairdresser should be here."

Claudia nodded.

"Sounds good!"

Claudia was at that awkward stage of pregnancy when none of her normal clothes fitted her properly, but she was too small still for maternity wear. Dressing for a wedding at this point was tricky, but she had finally solved the dilemma with an emerald green silk trapeze dress. It showed off her slender arms and lower legs, whilst wafting comfortably and forgivingly over everything in the middle. She wore the vintage diamond chandelier ear-rings her parents had bought her for her own wedding, and sandals with a small wedge heel that gave her the lift a 5ft 3 girl needed when dating a 6ft 4 guy, whilst also being reasonably comfortable.

Lydia's reaction when she brought Juliet in from the garden to get ready was gratifying.

"Wow, Claudia! You look beautiful. Truly beautiful. You've definitely got the pregnancy glow, haven't you? Listen, shall I supervise Juliet in the bath so your dress doesn't get splashed?"

"Oh god, Lydia, don't you need to get ready yourself?"

Lydia shrugged.

"It won't take me that long. I washed my hair yesterday, because it needs to be day-old to stay up properly. Quick shower, and into my dress, and I'm done. I did my nails yesterday –" she wiggled coral coloured finger and toe-nails in Claudia's direction, "and the hairdresser is going to do my make-up."

The two women chatted as they bathed and dressed Juliet. She was wearing a cream dress which was a simplified version of Lydia's own, a pair of miniature matching silver Saltwaters, and a wreath of cream rosebuds in her blonde curls. She looked positively angelic.

"So who else is coming to the wedding?" Claudia asked.

"Well, there's Henry and Delia, and my best friend Angela, who I've known from school, who I wasn't going to ask because I didn't know how to explain about all the family schizz, but in the end I bit the bullet and did, and she was cool about it all, and her husband Mark, and then Dominic has asked Simon who is his best mate from uni, and his girlfriend Lena. Heaven knows what they'll think of it all if Delia goes off on one again." She bit her lip, looking worried.

Claudia placed a reassuring hand on her shoulder.

"Look, you don't need to worry about what other people think. You and Dominic haven't done anything wrong, and have nothing to be ashamed of, and I really don't think Delia is going to make any kind of fuss."

Lydia gave herself a little shake.

"Yeah, I know. Anyway, it's all been arranged so quickly that we are keeping it very small. And, actually, that's how I want it anyway. Just the people who we care about most."

Claudia nodded understandingly.

"That makes sense. And a small wedding certainly seems less stressful! There were over 200 at my wedding, and I can honestly say it was horrific. I was so stressed in the run-up that I dropped a dress size, and had to be pinned into my dress on the day. And all the fuss about seating plans and seat covers and cake toppers! I ended up wishing we'd run off to Vegas! I'm certainly not doing anything like that again! We're going to Eat 17 for dinner afterwards, aren't we?"

Lydia nodded.

"Yes, that's right. With a round table, so there's no need for a seating plan! We're going to Huck's – you know the place right opposite the Registry Office for champagne and cocktails straight afterwards, and then round there for dinner. Is that going to be ok for Juliet?"

Claudia shook her head.

"No, probably not. So I've got my friend Lois – you know, Daniel's old boss – to meet us at the Registry Office after the ceremony and photos, and then you're going off for a sleepover at Auntie Lo's, aren't you poppet? And Dan and I can let our hair down. As much as I can with these two, anyway." She patted her tummy.

In no time at all, Lydia was dressed and made up and coiffed and pronounced utterly beautiful by Claudia and Juliet. Then they made their way to where Claudia's neighbour, who just happened to own a powder blue vintage Triumph, was waiting outside to drive them to the Registry Office.

It was a perfect day. Lying in bed that night, trying to ignore the incipient heartburn, Claudia reflected on the day, and couldn't decide on her favourite moment. Daniel, looking achingly handsome in his pale grey suit, had played his dual role to perfection, giving the bride away, and then stepping to his brother's side as best man. Delia and Henry had not, as she knew Daniel, Dominic and Lydia had all half-feared, spoilt it with glum faces or made any kind of a scene, and in fact had beamed with slightly bewildered pride all day. Claudia herself, as the mother of Delia's unborn grandchildren, was now firmly established in the highest place in her esteem. And, having seen how lovely she was with a slightly bored Juliet during the photos, Claudia could see that Delia was going to be a very valuable ally when it came to looking after baby twins.

Then there had been the heartrending expression of pride and adoration on Dominic's face as Lydia floated down the aisle towards him, looking more Disney princess perfect than ever, but with an equally besotted smile on her beautiful face. Claudia's heart had contracted with pride at Juliet walking in behind, looking so pretty, and so serious as she concentrated on her steps. The sun had stayed out for the photos in the charming garden behind the Registry Office, and then Lois had collected Juliet before the adults adjourned for delicious cocktails and a relaxed and convivial meal.

Daniel had made the only speech, a very brief one.

"I'm playing two roles here today – supporting my brother as his best man, and one of my best friends and new sister-in-law by standing in lieu of her father, who died when she was just a baby. It has been a tumultuous year for Dominic and Lydia, for our whole family, in fact. But I am just so happy and thankful that two people I love so much, and who I know will always love each other, to eternity and beyond, have been able to commit to that publicly and formally today. I am so proud of both of them, and so happy for them. I also have to say that Lydia and Dominic's love story has led indirectly to my own, so I'm deeply grateful to them both for that. As best man I should compliment the bridesmaid, and as stepfather-to-be I am so proud of how beautiful Juliet looks and how beautifully she has carried out her role.

This has been an unconventional wedding, but I know it will be the best of marriages. So, ladies and gentlemen, please join me in raising your glasses to the bride and groom – to Lydia and Dominic.

ACKNOWLEDGMENTS

This book has been a long time in the writing, and as such I have a long list of people who have been involved with it and who I would like to thank.

First of these has to be my husband, Thomas, whose passionate belief in me, and my writing and this book in particular has been unwavering.

Then there are my fabulous agents – Heather Holden-Brown and Elly James of HHB literary agency who took me on and have been a fount of ideas, inspiration and common-sense advice.

At various points Rosalind Taylor-Hook, Rhiannon Looseley-Burnet, Sue Chandler, Sheila Ableman, Margaret Last and Jenny Steward have all read various drafts of this manuscript and been so generous with their time and insight in feeding back to me. And then Celia Hayley did a brilliant job in editing it professionally.

Thanks to Anna McCarthy for making the process of taking my author photo as fun and pain free as possible!

And finally, thank you to my wonderful daughters, Anna and Sophia, who are very proud of their mummy being an author.

Printed in Great Britain
by Amazon